Also by Anna Harrington

LORDS OF THE ARMORY
An Inconvenient Duke
An Unexpected Earl
An Extraordinary Lord
A Relentless Rake

A REMARKABLE ROGUE

ANNA HARRINGTON

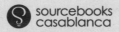

sourcebooks casablanca

Published by Sourcebooks Casablanca, an imprint of Sourcebooks
P.O. Box 4410, Naperville, Illinois 60567-4410
(630) 961-3900
sourcebooks.com

Printed and bound in Canada.
MBP 10 9 8 7 6 5 4 3 2 1

One

LADY ROWLAND.

Captain Nate Reed lifted the glass of cognac to his lips as he watched her from across the crowded club.

Her hand played delicately with a gold locket dangling around her neck as she placed her bet at the faro table. Dressed in the shimmering green satin of a low-cut gown and emerald jewels, whose bright color and cost announced to everyone who saw her that she was happily widowed, Sydney Rowland was certainly striking. Undeniably regal. Graceful. Beautiful.

And most likely a traitor.

Nate took a slow sip of brandy and narrowed his eyes on her. After two days of watching every move she made around London and trailing her from one soiree to the next, he was still no closer to solving the mystery of her connection to Scepter's assassination attempt on the prime minister and prince regent, except that he knew for certain she was involved. What he didn't know was how deeply. Was the baroness one of the masterminds behind the group, or was she merely another pawn in their game?

Tonight, he planned on finding out.

Slowly, he made his way across the room toward her.

Barton's was filled with elegantly dressed ladies in furs and jewels, foppish men adorned just as ostentatiously, and the lot of them drinking far more than they could tolerate, smoking cigars, and flirting shamelessly. A few of them surrendered to the lure of the high-priced prostitutes lurking in the club and retired upstairs for an hour's worth of private amusement. Both gentlemen and ladies enjoyed themselves with all the pleasures offered by the club. It was one of the few places in London that welcomed women through its doors and at its gambling tables, where the uniformed attendants brought glasses of liquor to the ladies as well as the men, and where it was accepted that no one inside need fear for their reputation.

Barton's belonged to the underbelly of London society. It was an exclusive club whose name everyone in the *ton* knew but that no one would ever dare admit to having entered.

Nate was only here himself because of Sinclair. Thanks to his half brother, Alexander Sinclair, Earl of St James, all Nate had to do to gain admittance was dress the part of a society dandy. With the help of the earl's valet, he now wore exquisite evening clothes of black superfine and blue brocade, finished off with a diamond cravat pin that surely cost more than his captain's commission.

No more soldier. Tonight, he wore the borrowed uniform of a gentleman.

When he'd given St James's name to the doorman, the

guard let him enter the club without a second glance. It had been that easy.

Getting close to Lady Rowland, however, was proving much harder.

Normally, she moved in exclusive social circles he couldn't infiltrate, so for the past few days he'd been forced to note from a distance every place she went and every person she spoke with. As a cavalry officer, he was used to reconnaissance, but he preferred rushing into the fray for a quick and decisive ending. His patience had worn thin from waiting. It was time to attack the enemy head-on, no matter that the enemy was draped in soft satin.

Nate approached the faro table, sat down on the chair next to the baroness, and tossed a coin to the dealer. He silently played out two hands, lost both, and slowly finished his cognac as he bided his time.

If Sarah could have seen him tonight, oh how she would have laughed! He was doing his best to fit in with a crowd of people who would never have given him the time of day, yet they'd all expected him to kill—and be killed, if necessary—fighting the French. Tonight, he was among them in an attempt to get closer to one of their own beautiful widows.

Well, perhaps his late wife wouldn't have laughed at *that*.

Sarah had always been a jealous woman although she'd never had any worries in that regard. He'd never betrayed her through the long stretches of separation forced upon them by the war. Not once. Not during the two years of their marriage, and not a day since it ended.

He pulled in a deep breath. He could never make right

what happened to her and not being there when she needed him. But at last he had the opportunity to provide the best future possible for both their mothers with the reward money he'd earn for stopping Scepter.

The woman sitting next to him held the key.

Nate slid a slow, sideways glance in her direction. "Would you like another drink, my lady?"

Her bright green eyes blinked as she acknowledged him for the first time. "Pardon?"

"I asked if you'd like a drink." He signaled to the attendant. "I'm ordering one for myself, and in this crush, it might be a while before you can get another."

She hesitated, then conceded to his generosity. "Yes, thank you."

He held up a second finger and gestured at the baroness. The attendant nodded, then hurried behind the bar to pour their drinks.

Taking the opportunity to start a conversation, Nate murmured, "So you like to gamble."

She returned her emerald gaze to the dealer and corrected, "I like to win."

"So do I."

A quick tension emanated from her as her fingers toyed with the gold locket dangling from a simple chain around her elegant neck, oddly mixed with a necklace of expensive emeralds. "Then I fear faro is not your game." Her eyes remained focused on the cards. "Perhaps you'd find more enjoyment playing at something else."

Had he not just spent the past hour watching her outright

dismiss every attempt by a roomful of men to proposition her, Nate might have thought she was inviting flirtation. But he knew better. What she wanted was for him to leave. "My game is here."

"How unfortunate, then," she commented dryly. "I don't believe you'll end up winning tonight."

"Then I suppose I'll just have to find satisfaction elsewhere."

She froze, and her fingers stilled on her locket. Nate could see that she couldn't tell whether he was propositioning her or rebuffing her. Truthfully, he didn't know himself, although getting her attention was all that mattered, and he'd certainly done that.

Her red lips pursed with irritation. She tossed in a coin for the next hand and ignored him.

"This is my first time at Barton's." He'd force the conversation onto her whether she liked it or not. "Do you often spend evenings here?"

She lifted her chin, and a stray tendril of sable hair tickled against the nape of her neck. "Occasionally."

"Then perhaps you can tell me—"

"No." With a tired sigh, she turned on her chair to face him and unwittingly gave him a full-on view of her low-cut neckline. "I am sorry, sir, but—"

"Captain Nate Reed," he interrupted with a forced introduction.

She caught her breath. "I am sorry, Captain," she began again, her words a well-practiced recitation, "but I am not interested in accompanying you upstairs this evening, nor returning with you to your home, nor even enjoying your company for a few minutes in one of the alcoves along the back hall. So if you don't mind—"

"Good."

She blinked at his unexpected refusal and repeated as if she hadn't heard correctly, "Good?"

"I'm a soldier, my lady, not a rake. I have no intention of inviting you upstairs tonight nor to my home on any night." He turned back to the dealer to signal for cards. "As for a few minutes alone in an alcove, I would never ask a lady to share her pleasures in such a demeaning place." He slid her a sideways glance. "And be assured that your enjoyment would be for much longer than a few minutes."

Her red lips parted delicately, stunned speechless.

He punctuated his refusal by tossing a coin to the attendant as the man set two drinks on the table in front of them. But even as Nate silently reached for his cognac, he could still feel her curious gaze on him, as if she didn't know what to make of him.

Good. That meant he'd captured her attention, and he'd done so by purposefully behaving exactly opposite of every other man in the place who'd approached her.

Fighting Napoleon had taught him the value of taking an opponent by surprise. Tonight, he'd use that to his advantage, even if down deep he was truly no better than the other cads. Even now his cock tingled at the tempting thought of taking her to any place where they could be alone. Including into a cramped alcove.

He would never act on that temptation. He'd never once betrayed Sarah, and he had no intention of doing so tonight, especially with Sydney Rowland, a woman he couldn't trust as far as he could spit. But he was still a man, for God's sake, and he still felt the pull of a beautiful woman.

It had been a long time since he'd been in a woman's bed, that was all. Three years, two months, three weeks...

"My apologies, Captain Reed," she offered quietly. "I didn't mean to offend."

He tossed in a coin for the next round of cards—and another for her, to keep her in the game and in the chair beside him. He wasn't finished with her yet. "No offense taken."

"Usually, when a man sits next to me, he's not interested in playing cards. His intentions lie elsewhere." She grimaced as she dryly added, "In lying elsewhere."

Despite himself, he grinned at her clever turn of phrase. She was sharp. "I'm only interested in conversation, I assure you." He handed her the second glass of cognac. "Now, shall we begin again?"

She hesitated, then took a deep breath. "All right." She accepted the drink. "It's a pleasure to meet you, Captain Reed."

He inclined his head slightly. "Baroness Rowland."

"No."

His brow inched up at that. "No? Am I mistaken that—"

"I'm never addressed as 'baroness' but simply as 'lady,'" she corrected self-consciously, her voice low so she wouldn't embarrass him. "Lady Rowland. I am not a peeress *suo jure*."

"A woman as regal and self-possessed as you? You should be." He boldly met her gaze. "Or perhaps the men of the aristocracy don't wish to be bested." He lifted his glass to her in a toast and purposely misstated, "Baroness."

Her lips curled into a smile with a surprising touch of shyness at the rim of her glass. "Captain."

There. Introductions made, conversation begun. He let out the breath he'd been holding. That hadn't been so difficult...so why was his gut clenched in a knot?

Sydney Rowland was nothing more than a mission asset, after all, just another link in the chain he had to sever before Scepter could kill again. Tonight was simply questions and answers in a polite conversation...or in an interrogation session if she failed to cooperate willingly.

"You've never been here before?" she asked. Now that she knew he wasn't interested in ravishing her, she visibly relaxed into the conversation. Still turned toward him, she draped her arm along the back of her chair and smiled faintly. Her presence was as soft as her lilting voice against the boisterous club around them. "I thought everyone had been to Barton's."

With her full attention on him, she was even more beautiful now than only a few moments ago. Nate realized like a punch why Scepter had chosen her as their liaison for mathematician Henry Everett. A besotted schoolmaster who desperately wanted to be included in society's ranks would never have stood a chance against the baroness's beauty and charms.

But she'd have no such effect on him, no matter that he wondered if her lips tasted of brandy.

He cleared his throat. "A friend recommended this place. Perhaps you know him." He watched her over the rim of his glass as he raised it toward his mouth. "Henry Everett."

Her eyes flashed wide, startled. Yet within a heartbeat, she'd skillfully recovered.

She turned back toward the table. "I've met his sister, Olivia, on a few occasions. She's a wonderful woman, very dedicated to reform." She expertly maneuvered the conversation away from Henry Everett. "We're both interested in children's charities and so had a natural connection. I'm certain I've met her brother, but only in passing."

If she wasn't working for Scepter, Nate mused, then her talents were being greatly wasted. The Home Office could use someone like her, *if* she didn't turn them all double agents first.

Her hand returned to the locket at her neck. "They run a school in Westminster, I believe."

"They used to."

"Oh?" This time, she'd been prepared for his peculiar correction, and there was no widening of eyes, no catching of breath. Nothing except a heartbeat's hesitation. But he noticed.

Of course he noticed. How could any living man not notice every move this woman made, no matter how small?

"Haven't you heard?" He forced himself not to stare at her red lips. "It burned down a few days ago."

Her hand began to tremble. "Burned down?"

He nodded, then told her the same lie the Home Office was reporting to the world: "Henry Everett died in the fire."

The glass slipped from her fingers.

He darted out his hand and caught it but not before the brandy splashed onto her skirt. He set the drink down, but her outstretched fingers remained empty in the air as she stared at him. A stricken expression blanched her face.

Slowly, she lowered her hand and brushed futilely with shaking fingers at the liquor as it seeped into her gown. All of her trembled as harshly as her hands, and she didn't lift her gaze from the stain. "I-I didn't know," she stammered. "I hadn't heard…"

From her stunned reaction, she was telling the truth. For once.

Nate narrowed his eyes on her. Was there more between Henry Everett and Sydney Rowland than he knew? Henry Everett had denied they were lovers when Clayton questioned him after the fire, yet her shock at hearing the news of his death was not the reaction of a passing acquaintance.

Nate knew grief—and guilt—and both flashed across her pale face.

"I'm…so very sorry to hear that." Her voice emerged so softly from her lips that it was almost lost beneath the noise of the club. "I'll have to…send my condolences and…"

Unable to finish, she pressed the back of her hand against her mouth.

Regret pierced him. She was truly distraught. Not even a Covent Garden actress could pretend such distress. But she could never learn the truth—that Henry Everett was alive and on his way to exile in exchange for information about Scepter, that the Home Office faked his death and left another charred body in the school's ruins to take his place. The well-orchestrated ruse meant a few days of grief for the baroness, but the lives of countless others would be saved.

Still, Nate knew the shattering pain of losing a lover, and if she truly hadn't known about Everett until that moment... *Christ.*

"I'm sorry," he murmured sincerely and low enough that no one around them could overhear. "To lose someone you loved that way—"

Her head snapped up, and her glistening eyes flared in the lamplight.

"You are mistaken, Captain. Mr. Everett was nothing more to me than a passing acquaintance. I am grieving for his sister, that is all." She paused, and her hands rested lightly against the table to steady herself as she took a deep breath and began to rise from her chair. "If you'll excuse me, I must see to my dress."

"Stay." He put his hand over her wrist and stopped her, forcing her to remain unless she wanted to cause a scene and draw the attention of everyone in the room.

Stiffly, she eased down onto her seat. "Release me this—"

"Only an acquaintance?"

"Yes."

"Then why did you give him money?" He forced a pleasant smile for anyone who might have been watching them. He wanted to appear to be nothing more than another in the long line of men determined to persuade her to visit his bed tonight.

Everyone would believe it, too, from the way she glared at him. "I did no such thing."

"A great deal of money, in fact. You bought up his gambling debts. Twelve hundred pounds in all."

She stared down at her hand, which now trembled

beneath his, not with anger but fear. Years of watching soldiers march into battle had taught him the difference. But who was she afraid of—him…or Scepter?

"Let go of me, or I'll scream."

"No, you won't." He coolly dismissed her weak threat. "Everett brought attention to himself, and look how that ended. You're far too smart to do the same."

The tops of her breasts rose and fell rapidly over her low neckline as her breath came shallow and quick. She looked up at him in a heated mixture of fear and fury that left no doubt she'd scratch his eyes out if given half a chance.

"You bought up his debts, then asked for immediate repayment even though you knew he couldn't pay. Not a poor schoolmaster." When Nate was convinced she wouldn't flee or cause a scene—or attack him—he slowly released her wrist and leaned back in his chair. His eyes pinned her. "Why?"

She pulled her hand out of his reach, then rubbed at her wrist as if his touch had scalded her. "Who told you that?"

"I have my sources." He had no intention of telling her that those sources came from within her own household or that she should pay her groom a larger salary in order to ensure his loyalty. "You're wealthy already. Why bother with a few hundred pounds from an indebted mathematician?"

Her stormy eyes gleamed as she tried to see through the carefully controlled expression he wore like a mask. "You're not one of the messengers, then?"

"What messengers?"

She started to reply, then snapped her mouth shut. Whatever she was about to say vanished.

Nate turned cold. She knew far more than he and Sinclair suspected.

Without warning, she shot to her feet before he could stop her.

Damnation. His gaze darted to the mountain-sized men standing at the sides of the room who provided security for the club. He'd be tossed into the street on his arse if he made a grab for her now, and all the ground he'd gained tonight would be lost.

"You're not leaving this club," he warned as he rose to his feet, as if he were truly a gentleman instead of the soldier set on arresting her.

She sniffed haughtily. "You spilt brandy on my dress."

He'd done no such thing, although he strongly suspected *she* would have tossed her drink directly into his face if she didn't have to brush past him to reach it.

"I have no intention of leaving before I'm ready," she informed him coldly, then snatched up her reticule from the table. "But even you, Captain, must be enough of a gentleman not to prevent a lady from visiting the retiring room to clean up a spill."

He bit back a curse. She'd cornered him. By standing, she'd shown the front of her dress to the crowd. Anyone watching would think it peculiar if she remained at the table instead of attending to the stain, and she would draw the type of curiosity neither of them wanted.

He had no choice but to let her go.

For now.

"Very well," he conceded. She may think she'd won, but

the battle had just begun. "When you return, we'll continue our conversation."

"Right where we left off?" Her eyebrow rose in mocking challenge. "With you accusing me of extorting money from Henry Everett?"

Oh, this woman was a handful! If she and Everett had truly been lovers, Nate suspected, she would have devoured the scrawny schoolmaster in a single gulp.

"If you'll excuse me, Captain."

She slid past him as she stepped away from the crowded table. The side of her breast brushed against his arm and shot heat straight down to his groin.

He sucked in a mouthful of air through clenched teeth.

With a sashay of her hips, she slipped her way through the crowded club, not toward the retiring room in the rear but straight toward its front doors. By the time she reached the steps, she was running.

Nate blew out a frustrated curse. *Stubborn woman.* Why did she have to make this so damned difficult?

Two

SYDNEY ROWLAND CAST A FRANTIC GLANCE OVER HER shoulder, then hitched up her skirts and ran out of the club, down its stairs, and along the street. Her carriage stood only a few yards away. Without waiting for the tiger to help her, she flung open the door and jumped inside.

"Go—quickly!"

The surprised driver flipped the ribbons, leaving the young tiger scrambling to find his seat.

Only when the vehicle began to roll through the London streets toward the safety of her town house did Sydney let herself surrender to the pulsing terror inside her and release a shuddering cry. She leaned back against the velvet squabs and pressed the heels of her hands against her eyes.

Oh God...Henry Everett was dead!

She'd seen him just a few days ago at Vauxhall, argued with him right there in the shadows next to the stone folly. He'd been furious at her that she was once more pressing him for the remaining debts he owed her, but he'd been alive when he'd stormed away. Now he was dead, and the sickening guilt rising like bile on her tongue told her she was to blame. That was why Captain Reed had come after her tonight—she'd failed to get the money from Mr. Everett as she'd been ordered.

A fresh terror turned her blood to ice. The blackmailers were coming after her now, but they might also make good on their threats to hurt Robert. If anything happened to him, dear God, how would she survive it?

The door yanked open. Before she could scream, Captain Reed swung inside in one fluid motion and shut the door after himself. He nodded calmly as he settled onto the seat across from her. "Baroness."

"You're mad!" she cried out at the speed of the coach he'd just recklessly flung himself into. That same speed prevented him from being seen by her driver and tiger, who were focused on the foggy street in front of them.

"I've been called worse." He leaned forward, elbows on knees, and his eyes glowed intensely even in the shadows of the dim carriage lamps. "Shall we finish our conversation, then? That is, since you don't seem to need the retiring room after all."

She drew further back against the seat to keep out of his reach, even though she knew he could have his hands around her throat in a heartbeat. He might kill her, but she wouldn't die without a fight. *Never* would she allow any man to attack her again without fighting back.

"Captain," she spat out mockingly to distract him as she slipped her hand down beside her on the seat and beneath the cover of her skirt. "More like a murderous merce-nary." Her fingers felt along the edge of the cushion, and she scowled disdainfully to hide a sob of relief when her fingertips touched smooth ivory. "Is this what becomes of His Majesty's officers in peacetime?"

His face darkened. "That's not what—"

"You're not one of the regular messengers, and you haven't uttered a word of blackmail yet like the others did. But I know why you're here. How much are they paying you?" she asked bluntly despite the fear in her trembling voice, which was starkly obvious even to her own ears. Her hand closed around the handle of the knife she kept hidden in the carriage. "I'll double it if you let me go."

"What are you talking about?" He frowned sharply. "You can't buy my loyalty, and I have no intention of letting you—"

She yanked the knife free and lunged across the compartment toward him. The small blade flashed in the lamplight as it slashed through the air toward his shoulder.

He sprang from his seat. With one raised arm deflecting the thrust of the blade, he grabbed her around the waist with the other and propelled her across the compartment and against the hard squabs. His large body crashed into hers with such force that her breath ripped from her lungs. Pinned beneath him, she couldn't move as his hand clamped over her mouth to keep her from screaming and the other squeezed her wrist.

With a muffled cry, Sydney dropped the knife to the floor. She closed her eyes and waited for him to kill her.

"What the *hell* are you doing?" he demanded incredulously. Then, pulling in a deep and calming breath, he eased his grip on her wrist and removed his hand from her mouth. "Any other weapons I should know about, Baroness? Got a pistol tucked up your skirt?"

Her eyes flew open. His face hovered so close to hers that she noticed the sweet scent of brandy on his lips, along with the more masculine scent of leather and horse that surrounded him. "I would use them if I did!"

"Oh, I'm certain of that."

She groaned in agonized frustration, unable to do more than wiggle beneath him. He was too large and heavy for her to shove away, and her teeth clenched as her stomach sickened. Her last revenge might just be casting up her accounts all over his fine satin waistcoat. "Just kill me, then, and be quick."

He blinked at her as if she'd gone mad. "I am *not* going to kill you."

"But that's why you..." When her voice trailed off, he crooked a confused brow at her—not at all the look of an assassin. Her heart thudded so hard with relief that she winced. "You're not?"

"Not unless you truly do have a pistol up your skirt," he muttered.

With a hard look in silent warning to behave, he released his hold on her and sat back on the edge of the opposite bench. Far enough away that she could sit up and rub at her wrist where he'd squeezed the knife from her hand, yet close enough that he could pounce in a heartbeat's notice if she tried to flee.

"Who are you?" she demanded.

"I told you at the club. I'm Captain Nate Reed."

"Of the king's Horse Guards, hero of the battle of Toulouse, and personally awarded a medal by Wellington himself after Waterloo." She shook her head, her eyes never leaving his. "I read the papers and know who you are. I recognized your name as soon as you introduced yourself." She lowered her voice as each word came forced from the fear pulsing behind it. "But who *are* you that you're chasing after me like this? No mere horse guard would do that."

When he clenched his jaw, she knew full well that he understood what she was asking—was he friend or foe? And despite his protests, was he capable of hurting her the way the blackmailers had hurt Henry Everett?

"I'm the man sent to arrest you for treason," he said quietly.

Surely, she couldn't have heard— "*Treason?*"

"Henry Everett was involved in plots to assassinate the prince regent and prime minister." His eyes narrowed darkly on her. "And you were involved with Henry Everett."

She stared at him, frozen, her breath held in her throat. Her swirling mind couldn't fathom it all. First the blackmailers' threats, then Mr. Everett's death, now this. She almost laughed. "You cannot believe—"

"The Home Office has evidence linking you to Everett along with his sworn statement that you threatened to put him into debtor's prison if he didn't repay you. You left him with no choice but to work for Scepter."

"I don't know who that is." She didn't bother denying the threats she'd made toward Henry. She'd had no choice. But she had no idea who had forced her to do so or what they'd wanted from the young mathematician. That had been none of her concern, and she gladly left it be.

"Don't lie to me, Baroness."

"I'm not lying. And I told you, do *not* call me that." She lifted her chin defiantly. "I don't know who Scepter is, and I don't care."

He studied her closely in the shadows. "Scepter is a group of revolutionaries determined to overthrow the British government. They've murdered, blackmailed, and assassinated their way into positions of power. They murdered the Duke of Hampton's sister, breaking her neck during a ride in the park because she'd gotten too close to discovering them. A few months ago, they assassinated half a dozen men so they could place their own men into positions of power. And just days ago, they murdered Henry Everett, nearly killing two dozen innocent girls in the process."

Oh God, she was going to be sick!

"They have agents at all levels of society, in all government offices, and in the military." He paused pointedly. "Including the peerage."

"You think that I would—" Her astonishment turned to anger. "Never." *Never knowingly…*

"You're the link between Everett and Scepter." He leaned forward until his face was level with hers in the shadows. "So you can cooperate and tell me what you know, and I'll leave you right here. If you don't cooperate, I'll turn you over to the Home Office." He slowly shook his head. "You should know that when those agents question you, it won't be in the comfort of your carriage, and they won't let you go once they have their answers."

She felt the blood drain from her face. "Prison?"

"More likely the gallows." He reached to trace his fingers down her throat. Could he feel her pounding heartbeat beneath his warm fingertips? "I would hate for anything to happen to this pretty little neck of yours."

"I'm innocent." She swallowed, hard, and she was certain he felt *that* because his lips pulled into a grim smile.

"Are you?" He dropped his hand away, and the heat of his touch dissipated so rapidly that she shivered. "Tell me the truth, and I'll make certain you're protected. But lie to me, and I'll throw you to the wolves. The choice is yours."

She choked out a laugh. *So naïve!* She'd never had choices. "You cannot protect me." If she told him anything, then she really would be dead, and Robert right along with her. The blackmailers would ensure it.

"I told you earlier that I like to win, and I'll win at that."

Oh, he was wrong! Surely, if the men who'd blackmailed her into threatening Henry Everett could find out about Robert when she'd kept him so carefully hidden, then they could be spying on her even now. They would know she'd been speaking to Captain Reed earlier at the club, would have seen him jump into her carriage, would know that she was now riding through the nighttime streets with him, perhaps confiding in him…

Sydney drew a tremulous breath and tried to settle her roiling stomach. If she didn't cooperate with him, she would hang at the gallows for treason. But if she answered his questions, the blackmailers would kill her. *That* was her only choice.

The heartbeat now pounding frantically through her veins was a lie. She was already as good as dead.

"Henry Everett," he pressed gently, the tone of his deep voice encouraging her to trust him. "Why?"

"I'm not telling you anything, Captain." She sniffed with all the regal haughtiness she could summon, given the throbbing of her pulse and the brandy stain on her skirt. And given how her life was shattering around her. "Your threat to hand me over to the Home Office is an empty one."

His jaw clenched. "I assure you that—"

"If you had any proof of my involvement with Mr. Everett beyond our business arrangement of his gambling debts, then the Home Office itself would have arrested me by now." Fear churned the sickening in her stomach into anger, but she wouldn't let him cow her. "They wouldn't have surprised me at the faro table the way you did. For all I know, you have no connection to them whatsoever."

"Believe me, I am far more connected to them than I want to be." A frustrated breath accompanied that. "But you're right. The Home Office wouldn't have come for you at the club. They would have dragged you kicking and screaming right out of your home, hauled you off to Whitehall, and tortured you to get answers, if necessary." Despite the harshness of his words, his voice was calm and oddly cajoling. "Be grateful it was me who came after you tonight and not them."

She swept her gaze over him. He looked like nothing more than a roguish society gentleman with the shadows falling across his handsome face, with his eyes staring at her so heatedly that her toes curled inside her slippers. This man was a wolfish soldier in sheep's clothing.

Enough. She was tired of being frightened and constantly on edge, tired of being sick with worry about Robert's safety and whether the secret of his existence would be revealed.

Enough of all of this!

She banged her fist hard against the roof. Pain shot up her forearm, but she bit her lip against a wince, determined not to let him see her weakness. She'd never let *any* man see her weaknesses or gain a position of power over her again.

"Jenkins!" Another hard bang on the roof. "Jenkins, stop now—please!"

The driver pulled back the team and brought the carriage to a halt.

"Lady Rowland," Captain Reed forced out between clenched teeth, "if you think—"

"We are done," she said with such resolve that she shook with it. "So either arrest me or leave. You will get nothing else from me, I promise you."

The door opened, and a puzzled tiger appeared in the doorway in the dim light of the lamps. His mouth fell open to find a man sitting inside who had not been there when the carriage rolled away from the club.

"This is not over," Captain Reed warned.

"Yes, it is." Defiantly, she locked eyes with his. "Because I *will* have to be tortured before I share anything with you."

The captain stared at her, unmoving and silent, for a long and uncomfortable moment. His carefully masked face didn't betray any of his thoughts, not even when he finally gave her a polite bow of his head and stepped slowly from the carriage into the dark street.

"Home, please, Jenkins," she called out to the driver as the tiger shut the door and hurried back to his seat.

The driver sent the team forward.

"I can only help you if you put your trust in me," Captain Reed warned quietly through the window as he walked beside the carriage for the first few feet. Thankfully, he made no attempt to climb back inside.

"I don't want your help." *I want to be left alone.*

She turned her face away into the shadows as the carriage picked up speed, and he finally moved away. She couldn't help but look behind, but he'd already disappeared into the darkness.

To be left alone… That was all she wanted, all it seemed she'd ever wanted her entire life—no, just since she was eighteen, since that terrible day when her fiancé Michael died. He'd been taken from her only for so much more to be stolen from her in the aftermath.

She'd wanted nothing more than to control her own life and make her own decisions, to no longer be forced to bend to the will of anyone. Every prayer she'd whispered to God during that horrible time had ended with that plea… *Make them leave me alone!*

Two years ago, her prayers had finally been answered when John Rowland died. She didn't know if God had taken pity upon her or if Lucifer simply needed a willing assistant in the fires of hell, and she didn't care which. The husband she'd never loved—and who certainly had never loved her—lay in the churchyard and could no longer humiliate or demean her, could no longer force her to his will.

Now her newfound freedom was once more being ripped away. What was that old saying, that when God wants to punish people, He answers their prayers? He'd punished her by freeing her from the prison of her marriage, only to plunge her into the fresh hell of blackmail and treason.

Her husband told someone about Robert, she was certain. That was the only way the blackmailers could have known about him. The old bastard had found a way to control her even from beyond the grave.

She screwed her eyes shut against the pain. Dear God, would she never be free?

The only salvation she had was knowing that Robert was still safely hidden away in the countryside. And for the moment, that he was still safe.

Her beautiful baby boy… She smiled wistfully as her fingers reached up to the locket at her neck. He wasn't a baby any longer. Robert was six now, although in her heart, she would always think of him as that pink and wrinkle-faced baby whose tiny hand grasped so tightly around her finger when she held him to her breast, when he slept nestled on her bosom. Even when her parents pulled him from her arms and took him away at just three days old—

She choked back an anguished sob as the memory returned with a vengeance, and she struggled to keep her breath against the desolate pain. He was no longer her baby, and she could never claim him as her child. Doing so would destroy any chance he had at a respectable future as part of society.

But she would *never* let any harm come to him again, not from her parents or society. Not from blackmailers who used the secret of his true identity to manipulate her. Not even from her. And certainly not from a handsome cavalry captain whose very presence was enough to place both their lives in danger.

Whatever she had to do to protect Robert, she *would* do it. He belonged to her now, and she would die before she'd let anyone take him away again.

———————

Nate slowed to a stop in front of the Fleet Street alley as the church bell tolled three times. The appointed hour, the appointed place, and from the size of the shadow standing in the damp darkness, Clayton Elliott had beaten him here. The only places Nate could meet with the Home Office undersecretary and newly commissioned general who was overseeing his mission were in secluded areas around the city like this, where they could be certain not to be overheard.

But something was wrong. Nate sensed it in the way his old friend stared unmoving into the darkness of the alley, in the way his hand rested on the pistol he kept hidden beneath his greatcoat.

He stepped up next to Clayton and followed his gaze. A small candle burned on the cobblestones at the far end of the alley, just bright enough to reveal the dead man who had been pinned to the wooden wall of the warehouse with metal rods driven through all four limbs. A puddle of blood spread out from the man's feet.

Nate swallowed down the bile rising in his throat at the scene in front of him. Scepter had done a lot of evil things in their march toward revolution, but this...

"Who?" Nate asked quietly. The corpse's face was unrecognizable.

Clayton turned and faced the street. "Major Thomas Barnes." He tugged at his leather gloves to hide the shaking in his hands and anticipated Nate's next question. "We didn't serve with him. He was in America in the last dustup there."

Thank God. Nate didn't know how he would have borne it if one of the men from the Armory had been killed. Especially like this.

He joined Clayton on the footpath of the wide street. Both men had seen far worse atrocities during the wars against Napoleon, but to see such brutality here on English soil shocked them to their cores.

"He was Scepter's mole in the Home Office," Clayton muttered, squinting against the cold drizzle as he looked away to scan his gaze down the street.

"Are you certain?"

"He wore this." Clayton opened his palm to reveal a key-shaped pin. It was Scepter's sign, and the same key-shaped symbol had been discovered on all the group's leaders whom the men of the Armory had found and stopped from carrying out plans for revolution.

Now, apparently, they were murdering their own.

"Why kill him like this?" Nate asked beneath his breath.

"Perhaps he'd threatened to reveal their identities to the Home Office if they didn't pay him more or give him more power within their organization."

"What makes you think that?" Nate made a terrible guess. "Is his tongue missing?"

"No. It's not missing." Clayton paused. "It's still in Barnes's throat where the murderers stuffed it after cutting it off."

With one last grim look at the figure in the shadows, the two men walked casually through the drizzling darkness toward the Thames, as if doing nothing more than going from one gambling hell or stew to another. They had no choice but to leave the poor bastard hanging on the wall like that, to let some drunken sailor or whore stumble across him and report his murder to the authorities. Their mission to stop Scepter had to remain secret.

"And Lady Rowland?" Clayton asked, his deep voice as low as the rain drizzling around them. "What did you discover?"

Nothing. Except that she was a beautiful, challenging woman who frustrated the daylights out of him. "The evening was not productive," Nate admitted grudgingly. That was the only answer Clayton would receive. "But I plan to keep pressing her for information."

"You'll tell St James?" Clayton asked, yet it was more of an order than a question.

Nate nodded, clearly not happy to be that messenger. The less he had to do with his half brother, the better. But Clayton had picked Nate and Alexander Sinclair to carry out his mission against Scepter specifically because the two men could be in contact with each other without raising suspicion. He also knew their mutual dislike and distrust of each other would create a competitive streak that would push them toward finishing the mission.

"Continue to follow Lady Rowland and stay as close

to her as you can," Clayton ordered as they reached the embankment and started down the stone steps toward the black Thames below. "Report back if you learn anything. You know how to reach me."

Then he stepped into a waiting wherry and gestured to the boatman, who shoved the long boat away from the steps and out into the river's fast current. Nate did the same with a second boat.

The two men glided into the night in opposite directions, although both their thoughts were on the exact same place they'd been for the past month.

On stopping Scepter.

Three

"GOOD MORNING, MY LADY."

Sydney gave a tired smile to the butler at St James House as Bivvens opened the front door and welcomed her into the foyer with a formal bow.

All of her was tired, in fact, from a tortured night spent tossing and turning over troubled thoughts and through endless sobs about Henry Everett. During those rare moments when exhaustion pulled her into sleep, she suffered grief-stricken dreams of Michael mixed with darker visions of the old baron that made her wake with a shudder.

And then there was Captain Reed. Her unbidden dreams about him—

Well, *those* had left her trembling for completely different reasons.

"I'm here to call on Miss Everett." She pulled off her kid gloves and untied the ribbon of her bonnet. "Can you inquire if she's accepting visitors?"

No funeral wreath decorated the front door of the grand house, which Sydney had learned from her maid now served as the temporary Everett School for the girls who had been displaced by the fire, so she assumed that the house wasn't closed to visitors. That, plus an inability to sleep at all once dawn peeked over the city, had her up and dressed at the earliest polite hour to call.

"My apologies, ma'am," Bivvens answered. His drawn face told her he was just as fatigued as she was. "Miss Everett is residing at Harlow House with the countess."

Her chest fell. "I'd heard she was here."

"The girls from the school are here, ma'am." As if on cue, running footsteps pounded overhead, followed by high-pitched laughter and a slamming door. His haggard face drew into a brief scowl. "Until a new building can be found for them."

"I see." Sydney tried not to flinch as another slam echoed through the stately old town house. "I'm sorry to have bothered you. I'll call on her at Harlow House, then."

More shouts and shrieks of laughter, more footsteps pounding up the stairs to the second and third floors... Goodness! The commotion sounded like a herd of stampeding cattle, and every loud noise jarred the already aggrieved butler, whose nerves were visibly frazzled from having his normally distinguished household set on its ear.

"Unfortunately, Miss Everett is not receiving visitors due to being in mourning for her brother," he informed her in monotone as if reciting a preapproved response should anyone inquire about the schoolmistress, "and due to recovering from the fire."

Recovering? Her throat tightened. If Olivia had been hurt, too, because of what Sydney had done... "What happened?" She swallowed hard. "Was she injured?"

"I am afraid I cannot—"

A scream echoed through the house, and Bivvens jumped with a startled gasp. If he wasn't already bald, the man would certainly have lost all his hair by the time the girls vacated the premises.

"My apologies." He glanced nervously up the stairs. "The house is in a bit of a state."

Sydney ignored a second scream. "It's quite all right. I only wanted to pay my condolences to Miss Everett." And to give Olivia the bank draft she carried in her reticule, one equal to twice the sum of money she'd paid to buy off Henry Everett's gambling debts. Donating money to the school could never make up for the harm she'd done to the woman's family, but it was all she could think to do. Yet now, if Olivia was also hurt in the fire, what could Sydney ever do to make amends?

"The earl is in residence this morning." Bivvens did his best to ignore what sounded like wild animal grunts and growls coming from the floor above, but he was unable to hide an annoyed scowl. "He is attempting to work in his study."

Sydney noted the unintentional emphasis he'd placed on *attempting* as another door slammed overhead and shook the house.

"Perhaps his lordship might have more information about Miss Everett for you if you would care to wait."

"Would you inquire for me, please?" She removed her shawl and bonnet. She was willing to stay here all day if necessary. She certainly wasn't ready to return to her town house and be alone with her guilt and fear. Now that it was nearly noon, she wouldn't even have the pretense of trying to sleep to occupy her worried mind. "I would be most grateful."

"Certainly, ma'am." He gestured toward the drawing room with a sweep of his arm. "If you would wait—"

Another scream came from upstairs, followed by a thudding crash and the shatter of breaking ceramic.

Bivvens groaned and slapped his forehead in defeat. "Not the Grecian urn!"

"Go," Sydney urged and motioned the flustered man toward the stairs. "I know the way. I'll settle myself."

"Thank you, my lady," he called out as he scurried toward the stairs and somehow dropped a shallow bow to her as he ran. Exasperation reddened his round face as he took the stairs two at a time and grumbled something beneath his breath about the Ming vase in the library, schoolgirls, and slow ships to Australia.

Poor Bivvens! Sympathy for the man rose inside her as the sound of high-pitched wailing joined the shrieks and crashes. If St James House survived the girls' sojourn, it would be a miracle.

She walked into the drawing room off the front hall, carefully placed her gloves inside her bonnet, and set it on the side table with her shawl and reticule. No footman appeared to take her things. That absence was a telling sign, indeed, about the household's current state.

Still, St James was generous to open his home to the girls. Uncharacteristically generous, in fact. Had more happened between the earl and Miss Everett the night they waltzed at his mother's ball than anyone had assumed?

Nonsense.

Alexander Sinclair was one shade shy of being a rake,

while Olivia Everett was a virtuous schoolmistress who'd been flustered scarlet from simply dancing with him. The two were as incompatible as oil and water and from completely different worlds. Allowing the girls to stay here was most likely his mother's doing, since Isabel Sinclair graciously served on the boards of many children's charities.

Or due to his aunt Agnes's meddling. She had a reputation of always doing the unexpected, mostly with no other purpose than to boil the gossips into a tizzy. And truly, what could Lady Agnes have done to unleash a greater ripple through the current *on-dit* than to put two dozen girls still in braids into the home of one of society's most notorious bachelors?

Sydney couldn't help but smile at that. Lady Agnes was a force of nature.

As she waited for Bivvens to return, she paced the room, unable to find enough calm inside her to sit. She *had* to keep moving. Her body shook, her nervous heart pounded, and each trip she paced across the room made her feel like a trapped animal stalking in its cage, but she couldn't stay still.

She raised her thumb to her mouth and chewed on the nail as she paused in midpace to stare thoughtfully at the doorway. Bivvens said that St James was in his study attempting to work. The study was undoubtedly on the ground floor and not part of the chaos unfolding on the floors above, or he couldn't even be *attempting*.

Sydney stared at the door, so very tempted to go looking for the earl herself. After all, she and he were friends… of a sort. Surely, he wouldn't be angry if an old friend went looking for him. St James would undoubtedly understand, given the current uproar of his household and her concern for Miss Everett.

She straightened her spine against thoughts that she would be breaking all kinds of unspoken social rules—and polite manners—and stepped into the hall.

Bivvens wouldn't be returning for a good long while, judging from the high-pitched wailing and shrieking still echoing from upstairs that was nearly matched in volume by his frantic pleas for the girls to behave like proper young ladies. Surely, she was saving his sanity by giving him one less task this morning by taking her visit into her own hands... Or at least that was her excuse for wandering through St James House and peeking her head tentatively inside each room.

Hmm. Not a footman in sight. Smart men, those, staying as far away from the girls and their chaos as possible. It was good practice for marriage and—

Sydney stopped. Deep voices argued quietly in the next room.

She held her breath and moved slowly to the doors. Peering into the study through the tiny slit between the pocket doors, she could just make out half of the earl's tall body sitting behind his mahogany desk, his expression grim as he spoke irritably to the man with him. The same man whose handsome face had invaded her dreams last night, whose deep voice even now fell through her like a warm summer rain...

Captain Nate Reed.

He leaned against the wall in the perfectly casual pose of a man who couldn't care less about their argument—or one who wanted to appear that way, anyway. His arms were folded across his broad chest, and his head was bowed with his eyes focused on the floor as if he were bored, yet Sydney suspected he was keenly aware of every word St James was saying. A slant of morning sunshine highlighted the red in his chestnut hair, including the stray lock that fell rakishly across his forehead. Jacketless and scandalously relaxed in his shirtsleeves, he wore a workman's coarse shirt beneath a tan waistcoat and matching breeches. He was dressed for a day of hard work rather than a meeting with an earl, right down to his age-creased, dusty boots. Yet try as he might, nothing could hide his soldier's proud bearing.

Sydney frowned. How could it be possible that in his simple clothes he looked even more handsome than he had in superfine and brocade? The man was an enigma.

Last night, she'd been aware of him the moment he entered Barton's, then pretended not to notice that he'd been watching her. Truly, how could she not have noticed him? His presence was like an oncoming storm, large and powerful, and when she'd glanced up from her faro cards to find him at her side, she'd lost her breath at the instant tightening low in her belly. She hadn't felt such a hot rush of physical longing for a man since Michael, all those years ago.

But for it to be Captain Reed of all men, the one set on arresting her for treason—

Oh, what a blasted fool she was! All the threats and fears of the past few weeks had apparently driven her mad.

"...deep in Spain by the end of the sennight," St James commented.

The captain shook his head. "...a mistake."

"You would disagree with Clayton?"

"...the thick...as we are."

"It's done," St James replied. The note of finality in his voice put an end to the argument.

Grudgingly, Captain Reed nodded and made a quiet comment Sydney couldn't quite make out.

Whatever he'd said, though, it made St James clench his jaw in anger.

Alexander Sinclair, Earl of St James, had always possessed an imperial demeanor, one that had perfectly matched his major's command during the years he'd served in the army. As for Captain Reed, Sydney would have expected the soldier in him to follow whatever orders were given, even from St James.

No. This argument was personal. The tension emanating from them proved it.

Sydney shifted closer to bring her cheek against the doors and give herself an unobstructed view of the man who inexplicably both excited and frightened her.

Why *him*, of all men, to snag her attention? After all, London was filled with dashing army officers freshly returned from the wars.

But none of those men possessed the confidence and strong bearing that radiated from every inch of him, a self-assurance that flirted on the knife-edge of arrogance. For that alone, she knew she should stay away from him. The past seven years had taught her never to trust any man, especially one with the power to hurt her.

Yet she also suspected that in his arms she might find the

peace and security she'd not felt since Michael. *That* was why she couldn't shake the man from her mind.

But she had best find a way to rid herself of him, or his arms wouldn't be the only things around her. The noose would come next.

"Nothing," St James answered a question Captain Reed had asked too quietly for Sydney to hear. "Everett's dead to the world and all the evidence destroyed."

Henry Everett. Her eyes stung with the same grief that had kept her in tears for most of the night.

"...can't be happy...gone."

"She isn't," St James answered. "She'd do anything to bring him back." He paused. "And your lead, Reed?"

He shook his head, his eyes still fixed on the floor. "...refused to answer any questions...left me stranded along Pall Mall at two in the morning."

The little hairs on Sydney's arms prickled. They were talking about *her*. Holding her breath, she strained to catch every word over the deafening rush of blood pounding through her ears.

"...denied any connection to Everett beyond his gambling debts."

"You think she's lying?"

The captain's broad shoulders shrugged. "She mentioned messengers."

"The same as with Olivia and Sir George Pittens, then? Blackmail?"

Captain Reed shook his head. "...one way or another. Whatever her secret, she's keeping silent, even now that she thinks Scepter's coming after her."

Sydney drew a ragged breath and swallowed hard her resolve. She *would* continue to keep that secret, too, until the day she died. Even if that day came far sooner than she'd hoped.

"They'll kill her if they think she knows too much," the captain added grimly.

Sydney's heart lurched into her throat. St James gave a muffled reply that Sydney couldn't hear. She shifted closer to the gap in the door.

"…any more innocents be hurt."

"I won't let that happen," Captain Reed answered decisively. "Not to Lady Rowland."

"You believe she's innocent, then?"

"I think—" He raised his eyes and looked straight at her.

Caught. With a startled gasp, she shoved herself away from the doors and ran.

Four

"Tea, Captain Reed?" Lady Agnes Sinclair lifted the teapot from the tray. Around them, the small sitting room at Harlow House was filled with sunshine nearly as bright as the woman's yellow turban.

"Please." Nate smiled and shifted uncomfortably on the small chair as she poured his cup. In truth, the whole meeting made him uncomfortable.

He stared with incredulity as she pulled a bottle of whiskey from the sideboard behind her and splashed in a generous amount.

"There we are." Dozens of bracelets jangled from her wrists as she handed him the teacup and saucer. "Strong tea for one of His Majesty's strong soldiers."

He blinked. *Whiskey?* "There's really no need to…" He fell silent as he watched her pour even more whiskey into her own cup, take a quick sip, and breathe a soft *ahh* of satisfaction.

Well. The Sinclair family was certainly interesting, although her odd, if endearing, behavior did little to put him at ease.

As Agnes's bastard nephew, he shouldn't be in Harlow House at all. England was filled with the unacknowledged by-blows of peers, so many that no one gave them a second thought...except the families to whom they should have belonged. *Those* people avoided their illegitimate offspring as if they carried the plague.

But not the Sinclairs. There was certainly no love lost between Nate and the old earl's family, but far from pretending he'd never been born, the Sinclairs seemed to be welcoming him into their lives. If tangentially.

He frowned into his cup. Apparently, also with lots of whiskey.

He couldn't fathom their motivations for being so polite to him, nor did he trust them. He'd called today at Harlow House and was subjecting himself to a very uncomfortable tea with the woman who should have been his aunt only to learn more about Sydney Rowland. After all, few women in the *ton* were privy to more gossip than Lady Agnes. He'd been prepared to raise St James's name, if necessary, in order to convince her to speak with him. But to his great surprise, when the butler told her that he was waiting in the entry hall to call on her, she scurried downstairs, gleefully grabbed his arm, and pulled him into the sitting room.

Granted, Nate didn't know them well, but the entire female contingent of the Sinclair family struck him as mad.

Lady Agnes was the most flamboyant woman he'd ever met, currently dressed in a yellow turban and orange day dress with large rings on all her fingers, strings of long pearls encircling her neck, and dozens of bracelets jangling from both wrists. But at least she was pleased to see him, unlike Isabel Sinclair. Whenever he'd accidentally met the Countess of St James during the past few weeks, she'd blanched at the sight of him as if seeing a ghost. But then, wasn't she? While he hadn't yet met his half sister, Elizabeth, he wondered if he needed to come armed for his own protection when he did.

Or, he supposed, he could just use the pistols sitting on Lady Agnes's writing desk. *Good Lord.* A society matron who kept a brace of dueling pistols amid feathered quills, inkwells, and monogrammed stationery.

A *very* interesting family.

"It's so very nice of you to stop by, Captain." Agnes reached for the plate of lemon biscuits and helped herself to one. "We've been hoping that you'd start spending more time at Harlow House."

He frowned at her odd choice of words. More time? He had no reason to spend *any* time here and no reason that his Sinclair relatives should want him to.

"Thank you for speaking with me, my lady." He took a sip of his tea and nearly coughed at the strength of the whiskey. "St James said you might be helpful."

"Anything for family." She offered him the plate of biscuits.

He declined them as he corrected gently, "I'm not part of your family, ma'am."

He wanted firm boundaries drawn between them. He was not a Sinclair and never would be.

She waved away his comment as if it were nothing more than a fleeting observation on the weather. "Nevertheless, we are all so proud of you."

"Pardon?" Proud of a by-blow? He suspiciously eyed her

cup of whiskey-tea. How much of the stuff had she drunk before he'd arrived?

"What you've done in the army, of course, in rising to captain in a field promotion, how well you fought in the battle at Toulouse, the way Arthur recognized you…" With a beaming smile, she lifted her cup in toast to him. "You've done England and yourself proud, my boy."

He was unable to follow that stream of information. "Arthur?"

"Wellesley." She blinked and explained slowly as if he were a bedlamite, "The Duke of Wellington."

"Oh yes. Him." He hid the smile playing at his lips by raising his teacup to his mouth. "*Arthur.*"

"Tell me." She lowered her voice and leaned toward him. "Were the accounts of Waterloo correct? Was the fighting truly as gruesome as the papers reported?"

Nate stared into his cup. He didn't want to remember that day, how charge after charge of men clashed on the field, how the screams of dying men and horses filled the air, how the booming explosions of the artillery reverberated through every inch of his body so fiercely that he felt it for days afterward. In some places on the field, blood ran as deep as a horse's fetlock, and he could still feel the agonizing pain shooting through his right arm in its ceaseless slashing of his saber to kill the enemy before they killed him. When his horse was shot out from beneath him, he'd been forced to go forward on foot through the hell of it, certain he would die. Blood covered his uniform and splattered across his face, ran down his legs into his boots where it squished between his toes.

He took a large swallow of his tea to fortify himself against the memories of that day and answered quietly, "Worse."

"I suspected as much." Lady Agnes gave her head a slow, knowing shake and sat back against the settee. "The newspapermen think women cannot handle information about war without fainting straight away, developing the vapors, or some other such nonsense, and so do not publish all the facts." She shook a ring-laden finger at him, then confided as if sharing a secret, "Mark my words. We women are stronger and more capable than men give us credit for being."

"I have no doubt of that, my lady." Once again, his thoughts strayed unbidden to Sydney Rowland. Exactly how strong and capable would she prove herself to be?

"The Sinclair family is proud of you." Her eyes sparkled. "You showed yourself to be a great hero at Toulouse when you single-handedly captured the enemy's cannon line so our English boys could advance and claim the field."

He grimaced. He didn't want to be the hero everyone proclaimed him to be. Certainly not when so many braver men had died that day. "An exaggeration, I assure you."

She arched a brow. "You captured the commanding officer of the cannon line by yourself, did you not?"

He had done that, in fact, but answered unassumingly, "While other men did the more dangerous work of taking the cannons."

"Which they could not have done without you." She shook another finger at him as if she were scolding her nephew St James. "Do not hide your valor, dear boy."

His gut knotted. It wasn't valor that had propelled him

into the heart of the battle with the mind-numbing ferocity of a madman or kept him advancing even when he could have retreated and regrouped as the other men in the cavalry had done.

He'd simply stopped caring if he lived or died.

Only when he'd rescued a group of two dozen women and children who had become trapped in a barn between the colliding armies at Amiens did he feel that he deserved absolution. That he was worth more alive than dead, that his life might have a greater purpose after all.

"But something tells me that you didn't come here to share war stories." She gave a conspiratorial smile from behind her teacup. "Although *I* have my own war stories I could share with *you*."

War stories? What on earth was she referring to? But Nate didn't feel mad enough to inquire. The woman terrified the daylights out of him. "Perhaps another time, ma'am."

"I look forward to it." She leaned toward him and lowered her voice, teasing him with a snippet as she whispered, "During the troubles on the Peninsula, I was heavily involved with leather, whips, and the First Dragoons!"

Nate froze, his teacup raised halfway to his mouth.

She smiled pleasantly and reached for the whiskey. "More tea, Captain?"

He cleared his throat and held out his cup. "Please."

"So then." She refilled both their teacups and replaced the stopper before setting the bottle back into the cabinet. "To what do I owe the pleasure of this visit?"

His attention shifted back to Sydney Rowland, although

she had never strayed far from it since their meeting last night. Even now, thoughts of her spiked his pulse. If he didn't lose his mind by the end of the mission, it would be a miracle.

He took a deep breath and focused on Agnes and her yellow turban—was that a stuffed parakeet glued to the top of it?—in hopes of tamping down the unwanted tingling in his groin. "I believe you're acquainted with Lady Rowland."

"Oh yes! I've known the girl's family for years—the Rowlands, that is. Her late husband's family." Her mouth pulled down into a thin frown as she studied him over the rim of her cup. "Why would you want to know about her?"

He kept his face carefully even. "I met her last night and found her...intriguing."

She sent him a knowing smile. "So you fell for the baroness's beauty and charms, did you, my boy? Well, you're certainly not the first."

Nate tightened his jaw against her accusation that he was no better than those other dandies who'd endlessly propositioned Sydney at Barton's. She was tempting, he'd admit. But no matter how much his body craved hers, he would never act upon it.

Yet he also had faith that a family that produced a man like Alexander Sinclair would have more than a thread of intelligence running through it, despite the surface appearance of madness. So he confided quietly, "The Home Office is interested in Henry Everett, and Everett knew the baroness." He paused. "So does Miss Olivia Everett."

Lady Agnes's eyes flickered. It was the only outward

sign that she understood his unspoken subtext. At that very moment, Olivia Everett was most likely lying naked in St James's arms, planning out their wedding and life together. Nate knew that Agnes Sinclair would never allow anyone to be in a position to harm the future countess and the love of her nephew's life. Not even the beautiful and charming Lady Rowland.

"I had presumed the baroness and Miss Everett were friends," she said carefully.

"They might very well be enemies for all I know of Lady Rowland," he replied just as carefully. "I was hoping you could enlighten me."

With her eyes never leaving Nate, Agnes called over her shoulder to the footman standing at the door. "Richard, please go downstairs and ask Cook for this evening's dinner menu. There's no reason to hurry."

The footman bowed. "Yes, ma'am."

"And close the door after yourself."

With a nod, he did as requested and left the two of them alone.

"Now then, Captain." She set down her cup and raised her gold-rimmed lorgnette as she boldly sized him up. Apparently finding in him whatever she'd been seeking, she lowered it and left it to dangle around her neck. "What would you like to know?"

"Everything," he answered honestly.

"Well, then, I daresay we shall need stronger tea." She stood and moved to the sideboard behind her to fetch two crystal tumblers. Not bothering with the pretense of tea this time, she splashed a generous pour of cognac into each glass and held one out for him.

He accepted it with murmured thanks.

"Sydney Rowland," she began thoughtfully as if searching the dark corners of her mind for information. "At one point, right after she was widowed, I believe that Alexander's mother had hopes for a match between them, but I'm getting ahead of myself." She dismissed that with a wave of her hand as she sat on the sofa and settled in for a long conversation. "Her family—her blood family, that is, *not* the Rowlands— were socially inconsequential in every way except for their wealth. They'd accumulated a great fortune from trade with the Americans. Her father was a self-made man, as they say." Her face scrunched up in disdain. "But no decent gentleman actually *works* for his money, for goodness' sake! And certainly *not* with Americans."

Nate covered the amused twitching of his lips by raising the glass to his mouth.

"Sydney was their only child, which meant all that American money would be hers someday, and a great sum of it did end up in her dowry. Fifty thousand pounds settled on the marriage, if one can believe the rumors."

He choked on his drink. *Sweet Jesus.* "That must have made the baron a very happy man."

"Oh no, not Rowland." Her mouth pulled down grimly. "Michael Berkley."

He blinked. "Who?"

"Michael Berkley, the fourth son of the Earl of Wyeth," she explained with a touch of sadness. "A second son by a second wife and so set to inherit nothing, not even a living. The young man's only chance at avoiding life as a solicitor or soldier was by marrying an heiress."

"So he found Lady Rowland," Nate murmured. His mind whirled as he tried to make the connections between what Lady Agnes was telling him and what very little he knew about the sharp-minded baroness who refused to cooperate last night and spied on him this morning.

"It would have been a perfect match except…" When she shrugged, the puffed sleeves of the orange dress bunched near her neck, and the stuffed bird on her turban shifted precariously.

He prompted, "Except?"

"Except that he was the fourth son of the Earl of Wyeth by his second wife," she repeated quickly with a long-suffering sigh. "Do try to keep up, my boy."

He nodded obediently. "Yes, ma'am."

She sipped her brandy. "Her parents had money and lots of it. What they lacked was a title, but King George would never have given them one, not with their connections to the colonists. George hates all things American, although I really cannot blame him."

"Of course not," he muttered, doing his best to keep his amusement from his voice. Only Lady Agnes could refer to the monarch by his Christian name and get away with it.

"The only way for them to become part of the aristocracy and be accepted by society was through marriage, and the fourth son of an earl was not at all the kind of match her parents had hoped for her." When she shook her head, the dead bird agreed by bobbing its beak. "Even with all their money, though, her prospects were limited. Few would-be lords wanted their family names entangled with hers."

"The American connection," he guessed.

She nodded, then grumbled into her glass as she took another swallow, "She'd have had better luck if her family had fought for Napoleon."

"But she's a baroness, so they must have found a peer for her in the end."

"John Rowland, a man thirty years her senior who had been granted a barony for his service in India. Unfortunately for her parents, she'd already accepted Michael Berkley's proposal. Word of their engagement appeared in the gossip rags the very morning her father planned on publicly announcing the marriage contract to Rowland. She certainly couldn't wed Rowland if she were already engaged." Agnes chuckled admiringly at Sydney's audacity. "The timing was brilliant, I daresay. Quite a stroke of courage on her part to do something as bold as that." She paused, tilting her head thoughtfully. "She was only eighteen then, you know."

No, he hadn't known. Just as he hadn't known about Michael Berkley. Could Berkley be connected to the secret that Scepter had used to blackmail her? "But she married Rowland anyway. What happened to Berkley?"

"After the engagement was publicly known, her parents couldn't call it off. Too much scandal for a family already clinging to the edge of society by their fingernails as it was. And *his* family certainly wouldn't have ended it, not with that much money headed their way." She leaned forward as if sharing a deep secret. "Michael Berkley didn't give a whit about the money, however. He loved the gel and would have wed her even if her parents had refused to give her a ha'penny, and don't doubt for one moment that they didn't threaten her with exactly that." A wistful smile tugged at her lips. "By all accounts, they were terribly happy and very much in love." She lifted her glass to her lips. "And seven weeks into the engagement, Michael Berkley was dead."

Nate's eyes snapped up to hers. "How?"

"Sudden fever, if I remember correctly. Sydney was distraught, beyond consolation." Her voice lowered to a sad whisper. "At the time, some in the *ton* wondered if she might have even considered taking her own life."

He didn't have to wonder. He knew—of course she'd considered it. Just as he'd considered taking his own life after Sarah died. Then he'd rushed back into battle as soon as he could so that someone else could take it from him when he realized he didn't have the courage to do it himself.

"Her parents must have worried as well," Lady Agnes continued, "because they packed her up immediately and removed her to the north country to take her away from anything that reminded her of him and society's prying eyes. They refused all guests, and she stayed away for her entire mourning period."

His heart ached for her. To go through such grief, so young and alone—well, not quite alone... "She married Rowland."

"A year later to the very day Michael Berkley died, in fact." She raised a finger and tapped it in the air for emphasis. "She traded in her black mourning dress for a yellow wedding gown and became Lady Rowland. Her parents finally secured the title they'd wanted."

He grimaced. "And Rowland received her fortune."

"Not all of it, and only for four years." Agnes lifted her glass in a macabre toast. "Then he, too, went to the grave, along with his title. He had no heirs. Sydney Rowland inherited everything and became even wealthier."

"Then she went back into mourning," he added quietly, swirling the brandy in his glass.

The hell she must have gone through by mourning twice for the two men with whom she'd planned to share the rest of her life. Once had nearly killed Nate; he'd never have survived a second.

He took another swallow of brandy, this time finishing off the glass in a gasping gulp.

Lady Agnes continued. "Lady Rowland went quietly into marriage and just as quietly into widowhood. She mourned alone, but this time she remained in London. Her parents had moved to Boston and didn't return to help her grieve." Her eyes sparkled with this next juicy bit of *on-dit*. "Rumors say she's had no contact whatsoever with them since the morning she married."

Dead fiancé, dead husband, estranged parents, a fortune made through questionable trade… *Good Lord.* Nate blew out a harsh breath. When he'd arrived at Harlow House, he'd had no information that could have led to any hidden secrets

Scepter might have used against her. Now, he was swimming in them.

"That reminds me." She gave a thoughtful tap of her finger to her forehead. "The next time you see Lady Rowland—"

Nate bit back a laugh. As if he were in any position to see Sydney Rowland again, except through prison bars.

"Please tell her that Bivvens found the reticule she accidentally left behind this morning at St James House and the bank draft inside it, made out to the Everett School. Alexander brought it directly over here to Miss Everett."

"Bank draft?"

Agnes nodded. "Lady Rowland's donation toward rebuilding."

He stilled. "Was it for twelve hundred pounds?" The same amount she'd paid for Henry Everett's debts. His chest tightened with both unexpected sympathy and dread at that obvious indicator of guilt.

"Heavens no!"

Relief eased though him, although he didn't know why he should care about the baroness's guilty conscious.

"Twice that amount, actually."

Lady Agnes smiled, blithely unaware of the slice she'd made into his gut. It was blood money after all.

"The baroness is quite generous and gives to many charities across the city, especially those for children," Agnes explained. "We're fortunate to have her interest in the Everett School."

"Very much so," he muttered absently, his mind spinning with all he'd learned about her. Who was the real Sydney

Rowland behind her beautiful but cool façade—the merry widow who haunted gambling hells in her finest silks and jewels or the guilt-stricken woman attempting to make restitution? Was she working willingly with Scepter, or was she just another one of its pawns?

"Well then." Lady Agnes rose to her feet, and Nate politely followed to his. "I hope you learned whatever it was you wanted to discover about Lady Rowland."

More than you could imagine. "You were quite helpful, my lady." He sketched her a bow and added wryly, "And the tea was...uniquely enjoyable."

"Indeed! However, you must call me Aunt Agnes." She reached for his hands and squeezed them tightly. He stiffened. The gesture was far too familiar for his comfort. "That is how Alexander and Elizabeth address me, so you must do the same."

But he wasn't the same as St James and Lady Elizabeth. Nor would he ever be.

"My apologies, ma'am." He genuinely didn't want to hurt her feelings, but he also couldn't allow the eccentric woman to continue with whatever fantasies she had about bringing him into the Sinclair family fold. "But I won't do that."

Her smile faded, and sadness clouded her face. But she studied him closely, not surrendering all hope just yet. "Perhaps with time, then, once you've had a chance to grow used to having us all about."

And once hell froze over.

She released his hands. "You must come back soon for

more tea. I have plenty of war stories of my own to share, you know."

His gaze slide sideways to the bottle of whiskey. Of course she did.

"Next time," she promised with a wink, "I'll tell you how I seduced Bonaparte's brother!"

Five

SYDNEY TURNED HER FACE UP TO THE AFTERNOON SUN and closed her eyes to enjoy the open air of her barouche as it rolled through Hyde Park, grateful she was still alive and not locked away in Newgate.

She'd survived yesterday, and she took hope in that. The Home Office hadn't come pounding at her door as Captain Reed had warned. But then, neither had he. Apparently, he was biding his time, yet her blackmailers wouldn't. If they had seen her speaking with the captain at Barton's and knew he was working to stop them, she'd have been killed by now. Of that she was certain. They'd murdered Henry Everett, harmed his sister, and burned down a school with its innocent girls still inside in their beds. They certainly wouldn't hesitate to kill her.

But with each hour that passed without new threats arriving at her doorstep, she breathed a little easier and relaxed just a bit more. She'd done what the blackmailers had wanted by buying Henry Everett's debts and demanding immediate repayment, and she prayed they had no further use for her. She didn't care what side they were on, if they were revolutionaries or government agents. She wanted nothing to do with any of them.

And *absolutely* nothing to do with Captain Reed.

The man bothered her more than she wanted to admit and stole more of her thoughts than she should have allowed. Not just because of the new threat he posed but because something about him lured her attention despite her need to stay away. A shared sense of secrets, perhaps. Or loneliness, because even in the middle of the crowd at Barton's, he'd seemed alone.

Alone. Exactly how she needed to leave him. He might have been a war hero and so strikingly handsome that he took her breath away, but the man was also trouble. And *troubled*. The last thing she needed was to become embroiled with him.

No. Best to stay to herself until all the threats ended.

Even now, she supposed she put herself at risk by being out in the park, but she couldn't bear the thought of being locked up inside her town house for a moment longer on such a beautiful day. She was going mad with nothing to do but worry and pace, pace and worry... So she'd grabbed her bonnet and headed out for fresh air, sunshine, and perhaps a conversation or two among friends to distract her. She wanted peace and quiet, a chance to—

"Baroness." The deep voice seeped into her with a tingling heat. "What an unexpected pleasure."

She opened her eyes and blinked up into the sunlight at the dark shadow leaning over her from the back of a black horse walking slowly beside her rolling barouche, the sky a brilliant blue behind him. Her mind flashed to those ceiling paintings in Carlton House of the god Apollo driving his team across the sky.

A Greek god?

Good Lord. She truly had lost her mind!

"Captain Reed," she rasped out, unable to find her voice.

"I didn't mean to startle you," he apologized. "But I've been walking beside you for a good twenty yards, and you hadn't noticed." His sensuous lips curled in amusement. "Shall I try again? Good afternoon, my lady."

He tapped the brim of his hat as he inclined his head in as much of a bow as possible from horseback. Then he straightened once more into a commanding pose in the saddle, the same one he'd undoubtedly used when he'd led charges against the French. Every inch of him testified that he was a dragoon of the first order. The bright red uniform simply served as an afterthought.

Yet instead of being flattered at his gentlemanly manners, the show of courtesy grated at Sydney, perhaps because she found herself liking it and certainly not wanting to. Or because her heart leapt at the sight of him, as if she were some smitten cake of a girl instead of a grown woman.

"Not enough to approach me at Barton's, is it, Captain?" If she were rude enough, perhaps he would leave her alone, and then she wouldn't have to worry about her voice turning husky each time she spoke to him or her breath growing shallow with arousal. Or the blackmailers thinking she'd deceived them. "Now you're following me on rides through the park. Does His Majesty know that his Horse Guards spend their time stalking ladies?"

"The regent encourages it."

She narrowed her eyes. "Captain Reed, if you—"

He held up his hands as if in self-defense. "My presence in the park is nothing as sinister as that, I assure you. Lord Liverpool is out driving today, and I was assigned to his guard."

She didn't believe for one moment that coming across her in the park was as simple as that. "And ordered to make certain I remain far away from him, I'm sure."

He gestured in the direction of the winding lake. "Actually, I glimpsed you across the lawn and thought I'd ride over to say hello."

Ride over to say hello...as if they were old friends instead of enemies? Ha! No, he was here in a misguided attempt to protect Lord Liverpool from her, as if she truly did have a pistol up her skirt and would use it to assassinate the man at the first opportunity.

Unexpected disappointment squeezed her heart. He might have been dashing in his red uniform and every inch a selfless hero, but he still believed she was involved with revolutionaries. Worse, by allowing everyone in the park to see them together, he was putting her life in danger.

"Well then. You've said hello, so you have no reason to linger." Her voice dripped with biting sarcasm. It was a tone she'd practiced well during her marriage to keep Rowland away. "Don't let me detain you from your duties."

Instead of being offended as she'd hoped, the blasted man smiled at her with amusement. "Oh, I've plenty of time for conversation with you, Baroness."

"Conversation?" She scoffed at the idea with a haughty sniff and muttered, "Committing a flanking maneuver against the enemy, more like."

She wanted no part of this battle. So she banged her parasol against the side of the barouche to signal to her driver to increase the team's speed and leave the aggravating man behind.

Instead of taking her not so subtle hint and leaving, Captain Reed set his horse into a trot and kept pace.

She rolled her eyes beneath her bonnet. Hopefully, anyone who saw them would think he was simply another admirer...one she wished to avoid because her barouche kept going, as it often did when men boldly approached her during her rides as if she were some kind of courtesan. At least that was what she hoped the people in the park assumed, because speaking to him in broad daylight made her extremely nervous.

Although speaking to him privately in the darkness had made her even more nervous. *That* wasn't because of Scepter.

"You know military strategy," he commented appreciatively. "I'm impressed."

So was she as she watched him control his horse with gentle taps of his heels while his hands barely touched the reins. He was an expert horseman. Seeing him mounted on the large black gelding in his red uniform, even on a slow afternoon ride through the park, she could easily imagine him brandishing a saber and riding into battle at full charge.

She could also easily imagine what he must have looked like *out* of his uniform.

She turned away before he could see her cheeks flush. "I know a little."

A lie. Unfortunately, she knew a great deal, but not because she found warfare the least bit interesting. The old baron loved to expound upon military maneuvers during those incredibly dull dinners he'd forced her to attend with his old army compatriots. Her presence was more a decoration for the table than because Rowland wanted her company. She'd been there only to prove that he owned her and could force her into his bidding.

But he'd never been able to force himself into her bed.

"An understatement, I'm certain, from a woman who keeps knives at her fingertips." He nodded toward the seat. "Do you keep a knife tucked beneath that cushion, too?"

She smiled sweetly. "Come closer, and you can find out."

He laughed, and the rich sound wrapped around her like warm velvet. It was the first unguarded reaction she'd seen from him, and in response, a nervous tingle fluttered low in her belly.

Oh, this man was dangerous. Not just because he thought she was complicit in assassination and sedition, not just because the blackmailers might see them together and know why he was pursuing her. Shamefully, it was arousal for him, pure and simple. Years had passed since she'd last been touched by a man and been held in protecting arms, and the longing that rose inside her for Nate Reed to do exactly that stunned the daylights out of her. Just looking at him, she could tell that surrendering to him would be wonderful.

It would also end her.

"I know why you're bothering with me, Captain, but your concerns are misplaced," she said bluntly. "I am simply taking an afternoon drive. Lord Liverpool has nothing to fear from me unless you think I'm capable of skewering the man with my parasol." To make her point, she banged it again on the side of the barouche to signal to the driver to go even faster. "Good day, Captain. Wouldn't want to delay you!"

Instead of falling back as the barouche rolled away, the well-trained gelding increased its gait without any noticeable command from Captain Reed.

"Not at all, my lady." He tipped his hat with all the grace of a blue-blooded gentleman. "It would be my pleasure to escort you across the park."

Oh, she was certain of that…and right out the other side. Was he mad? To think that a lady in muslin was capable of assassinating the prime minister in broad daylight in the middle of Hyde Park—ludicrous!

"Especially since you're alone," he added, his hazel eyes shining as they studied her. "A beautiful woman like you…"

Her lips parted at the compliment dropped so easily that she wondered if he'd noticed he'd given it at all.

"I would have thought you'd be mobbed by admirers."

He was wrong. No one mobbed after her. The ladies avoided her as competition for the men, and *she* avoided the men, who wanted her only for her money or her body.

The gossips thought her a merry widow, but that was the farthest thing from the truth. She didn't have it in her to take a string of lovers or spend time engaged in scandalous acts of any kind. In the seven years since Michael died, she'd been intimate with only one man, only once, and had regretted it since the night it happened. Oh, he had been sweet and kind, yet the protection and solace she sought in his arms eluded her, and she left his bed feeling just as lonely as when she'd arrived. She hadn't had the heart to give herself to another man since, although none had really captured her attention.

Until him, the strikingly handsome captain keeping pace with her.

"I don't need admirers, Captain. I have you," she teased wryly. Then lowered her voice so her driver and groom couldn't overhear. "My own personal guard who follows me everywhere I go."

"Not everywhere," he returned in a deep rumble nearly as soft as the crunch of gravel beneath the carriage's wheels. "I didn't have to follow you to St James House. You went there on your own to spy on me."

"I wasn't *spying* on you," she countered, although that was exactly what she'd ended up doing. "I needed to speak to St James, so I sought him out in his study and peered into the room to see if he was alone before I entered. You happened to be there. I was impatient to speak with him, that's all. You think impatience proves guilt?"

"You know what they say. A bird in the hand"—his hazel eyes flickered hungrily as they moved tantalizingly over her as if he were imagining her naked body beneath her dress, and God help her, her skin tingled everywhere he looked— "gets outflanked by the enemy."

Blast you! She'd had enough of his torment. It was time to put an end to his intrusion into her life and to the confusion he brought her. If she didn't stop this madness now, in only a few minutes her hands would be on him, although whether to throttle his neck or to rip off his clothes she couldn't have said.

She reached forward and thumped her parasol against the back of the driver's seat. "Jenkins, please stop!"

"Aye, m'lady."

Her driver pulled up the team, and the barouche slowed to a stop. Angrily, she turned toward Captain Reed so quickly that her hand went to the top of her bonnet to keep it in place as she glared at him.

His black gelding stopped immediately beside her. Well, that figured. Even the horse was against her.

"Walk with me, Captain." She rose from her seat. "I believe we have things to discuss." Her eyes darted toward her driver and groom. "Privately."

He dropped to the ground in a fluid motion. "I would be honored, Baroness."

He ignored the glare she gave him, opened the little carriage door, and held out his hand to her. Giving up on any chance of convincing him to properly address her, she grudgingly placed her gloved hand in his.

As soon as her shoes touched the gravel, she popped open her parasol and nearly took off his ear if not for his well-timed duck.

She spun on her heel and headed toward the path meandering alongside the water. Nate fell into step beside her, his long strides slowing to match her shorter ones, and he took her elbow in his hand as if he were a proper gentleman accompanying her on a walk instead of the man who believed her capable of treason.

His horse followed obediently along behind them.

She darted a glance over her shoulder. "You should have left that beast with my groom," she grumbled although she reached behind to affectionately run her hand gently down the animal's broad forehead.

"A dragoon never separates himself from his horse."

The big gelding's eyes drooped sleepily as she scratched beneath its forelock. At least her charms worked on one of them. "Because he needs you to take care of him?"

"Because a cavalryman on foot is a dead man," he answered quietly.

She dropped her hand away from the horse with a shudder and turned back toward the path. "I think I prefer my explanation."

"So do I," he agreed earnestly. "But I don't think you invited me to walk with you to discuss warfare." He slid her a sideways glance. "Are you ready to tell me the truth about your involvement with Henry Everett?"

"I have told you the truth." As much of it as she would ever tell him, that is.

He said nothing for a long while, and his silence shouted that he didn't believe her. Yet instead of pressing the issue, he commented, "You said you were blackmailed."

"Yes."

"By whom?"

"I don't know."

"With what secret?"

Her heart lurched painfully. She would never reveal Robert and endanger him. She might not be part of his life, but she would always keep him safe. "I can't tell you."

"Then what proof do you have of your innocence?"

"None," she answered truthfully.

He blew out a hard breath, now as frustrated as she was. "I can't help you if you aren't honest with me."

"Is that what you're doing—helping me?" Ha! He'd help her right into Newgate if she wasn't careful. "And here I thought you were ordered to guard me in case my afternoon outing was actually a diabolical ruse to kill Lord Liverpool."

"I can do both." He winked at her. "I'm multitalented."

The man was infuriating! Her hand tightened around the parasol handle. Just one good whack of it over his head, and—

"I *can* help you if you'd let me." He stopped and gazed somberly down at her. "But you're not letting me. You have to trust me."

She bit her bottom lip. She couldn't do that…could she?

They'd stopped at the edge of the winding lake, and she glanced at the path. Should they go north or south?

No, holding her ground was best. So she stayed right where she was and tilted the parasol to shield her eyes as she fixed her gaze on him with far more bravery than she felt. He claimed he wanted to help her, so… "Why were you talking to St James about me?"

"We're working together to catch the men who killed Henry Everett." His gloved hand tightened almost imperceptibly on her elbow, but she noticed. "I was briefing him on our conversation at Barton's."

Her breath lodged in her throat. "Should you be telling me this? I *am* your enemy, or so you think."

"I don't know what to think about you," he admitted quietly, squinting against the sun as he glanced casually at the stretch of park around them. "Except that you know more than you're telling." His gaze returned to her, and the unsettling look he gave her tingled through her right down to her toes. "So tell me the truth, Baroness, and prove your innocence."

"You told St James that you think I might be killed." She pulled her arm away from him because the protective feel of his hand on her elbow was nice. Far too nice for comfort. She couldn't let him continue to touch her like that, or else she'd very much want to continue to be touched... Good Lord, did a person know when she'd gone completely mad? "Hearing that doesn't make me want to place my trust in you, Captain."

He tucked beneath her bonnet a stray curl that had come loose and stirred against her cheek in the gentle breeze. He murmured, "Sinclair and I are the only ones you can trust."

"*You* are putting me in danger, don't you realize that?" Although they were alone, she lowered her voice to barely above a breathless whisper. "I'm being watched, and if they see me talking to you, spending time with you like this—if they know you and St James are trying to stop them—" She shivered despite the warmth of the day and begged, "Leave me alone, please."

His expression sobered. "I can't do that."

Desperation pulsed through her. "I've told you everything I can."

"You've told me practically nothing."

"That's all I can!"

He shook his head. "Scepter will come after you, whether to silence you as they did Henry Everett or to use you again in their plots." When his hazel gaze flickered over her face, the sunlight caught the golden flecks deep in his eyes. "I will be there when they do."

She pressed her hand against her belly as fear sickened her. "So I'm bait for your trap?"

"You won't be harmed, I promise you." He brushed his hand up her arm to comfort her, heedless of the people around them in the park who might see. "As long as you cooperate."

She pulled in a deep breath to force down her frustration and fear. "If you have any mercy inside you at all, you will—"

The sound of a gunshot boomed across the park.

Nate grabbed her around the waist and pulled her to the ground. She landed on her back with a jarring thud that knocked the air out of her.

Two more shots rang out in rapid succession.

"Stay down!" he ordered and pinned her to the ground beneath him.

But she was too terrified to do anything except cling to him as she gasped for breath. His large body covered hers, and his shoulder shielded her head as he tucked her beneath him.

"They're shooting at us!" she cried.

"Not at us." He lifted his head and scanned his gaze across the park. "They would have hit us or the ground next to us. No bullets came this way."

But his words didn't comfort her, and she shuddered violently in his arms. Dear God, she'd thought she was going to die! All the fear and worry of the past few weeks overwhelmed her, and a hard sob escaped her.

"It's all right," he assured her, his voice compassionate and soft.

He rolled off her and sat up, then pulled her into his arms. She clung to him, unwilling to let go and plunge back into the terror alone.

Slowly, he unwrapped her arms from around his shoulders and shifted away only far enough to palm her cheek and raise her head until she opened her eyes. The look of concern on his face nearly undid her.

"Baroness, are you all right?"

Clenching the front of his uniform in her fists, she shook her head, unable to speak around the knot in her throat. No, she *wasn't* all right. Nothing was all right! Most likely it never would be again.

"No one aimed at us." He cupped her face between his gloved hands. The leather felt cool and smooth against her cheeks. Just as smooth and cool as his voice as he assured her, "No one tried to hurt you."

She pulled in a jerking breath and nodded, yet she wasn't at all convinced.

He rose to his feet and gently lifted her to hers, then took her arm to lead her as quickly back to the barouche as her wobbly legs allowed. "Let's get you—"

Shouts went up across the wide lawn, followed by the screams of women.

A flash of movement caught Sydney's attention, and she glanced over Nate's shoulder. A gasp tore from her lips.

On the far end of the lawn, a landau careened out of control. It bounced wildly across the grass as it headed straight for the trees at the far end of the lake. Its driver pulled frantically at a single ribbon, the other one having fallen from his grasp and dangling on the ground, but the team tossed their heads in fear and ran on. In the back, holding on desperately to the carriage as it rose and fell beneath him like a bucking horse—

Lord Liverpool.

"Stay here!" Nate ordered.

He leapt onto his horse. The gelding started forward into a canter before Nate's feet found the stirrups. Pressed low over the animal's back, he raced across the park at a thundering gallop.

Ignoring his order, Sydney hitched up her skirts and chased after him.

The black horse ate up the ground to the runaway landau in only a few long strides. Nate drew alongside the team as the driver and prime minister held tightly for dear life. They were bounced wildly about on their seats and flew up from the cushions at each jarring rut and bump that passed beneath the spinning wheels, yet the carriage traveled too fast for them to leap to safety.

The right wheel hit a bump and sent the entire rig high into the air. When it landed with a wood-cracking jolt, the last ribbon snapped from the driver's hand. The driver was unable to do anything more than cling to the bench as the team raced on fully unchecked.

Nate gave his horse free rein, but the well-trained animal kept on a parallel path with the racing carriage and an even pace with the lead horse. Nate leaned far out of the saddle toward the team. The entire weight of his body hung dangerously off his right stirrup as he made a frantic grab for the rein at the runaway horse's head—

And missed.

Sydney cried out in fear for him as she chased them through the grass. In front of her, the uncontrolled team ran on, heading straight toward the trees.

Nate lined up for another grab at the ribbons as the trees rushed toward them. His hand swooped down and caught the rein at the lead horse's head.

With a straining groan Sydney could hear across the park, he held on and pulled back with all his might. The team began to swing in a circle toward his horse, and the landau's wheel spun toward the gelding's front legs.

The black horse darted out of the way as Nate still hung off its side in midair between the saddle and the team. All his weight balanced precariously on a single stirrup. If the leather broke, if the saddle girth came loose, if his horse misstepped just once—

Sydney pressed her hand over her mouth to keep back a terrified scream.

His gloved hand fisted like an unbreakable manacle around the rein. He pulled back again to slow the speeding team, and his own horse reduced its strides to match until the horses all slowed together to a trot, then to a walk. Finally, he stopped them completely. Angling his horse in front of them as a barrier, he swung down to the ground and grabbed both horses' heads to hold them still.

The trees were less than fifty feet ahead.

Nate glanced grimly over the horses' flickering ears as

Sydney approached. He fought to catch his own breath, just as the three horses heaved for air beside him. She slowed to a walk as she came closer so she wouldn't frighten the already nervous team or the two occupants of the landau who had somehow managed to remain onboard.

His hazel eyes pinned hers in silent warning, and she halted in midstep several yards away. The message was clear—

Stay back.

The sound of pounding hooves rushed upon them from around the park as half a dozen Horse Guards galloped past Sydney and surrounded the landau. They swarmed like scarlet-coated bees who'd been agitated by the excitement of the runaway team and by curious onlookers who had come running, most likely to see the carnage of the wreck rather than to help. They expertly moved their horses between the carriage and the gathering crowd to keep everyone at a distance.

Sydney stepped to the side of the lawn, well out of the guards' way, and watched one of the soldiers help Lord Liverpool and his driver to the ground. Their faces were white, and their legs shook so violently they could barely stand, but they had survived and were already giving their grateful thanks to Nate.

He accepted it with a simple nod.

"Hold the horses," he ordered the young guard to his left.

"Yes, Captain." The guard took hold of the team, who now hung their heavy heads in exhaustion.

Nate moved forward to check the horses' legs for any cuts or injuries. He ran his hands slowly over each horse, softly talking to each one to keep them calm, and the team responded with attentive flicks of their ears as if they understood what he was telling them. Then he turned his attention to the harness and ran his hands over each length of leather and brass. He held up one of the ends of the torn ribbons and laid it over the back of the lead horse.

Finished with his examination, Nate stepped away from the rig and ordered two other guards to unhitch the team. Even Sydney could see that the landau was in no state to be pulled anywhere, and its team was still too agitated to be controlled even if it had been.

Then Nate strode directly toward her. Without a word, he took her arm to lead her along with him as he stalked away from the prime minister.

Sydney had to nearly run to match his long strides as he hurried her across the grass toward her waiting barouche, with his horse trotting easily along behind. The battle-conditioned gelding was barely breathing hard now, but the man leading him radiated tension.

"What you did back there—that was—" she huffed out as she struggled to keep up with him. "I can't believe you did that."

He was simply amazing. She'd read about his heroics on the battlefield, but it was one thing to read about him in the papers; it was another completely to watch with her own eyes as he risked his life. This selflessly reckless side of him excited and terrified her until she wasn't certain which emotion had her heart pounding except that Nate had sent it somersaulting.

She shook her head. "You could have—"

He bit out a fierce curse and halted in his steps so suddenly she nearly ran into his side and the horse into his back. "I can't help people who won't help themselves."

He didn't mean the runaway landau. "I don't—"

He jabbed a finger behind them at the broken rig. "Scepter just tried to kill the prime minister."

Her stomach lurched. "That was an accident." Sickened at the possibility, she pressed her hand to her belly to keep down both her accounts and her fear. "The horses heard gunfire and panicked."

"Someone purposefully fired those pistols to startle the team so they would pull hard on the reins. I examined the harness. The ribbons had been cut. All it took was one strong pull by the horses, and they snapped." The harshness of his expression sent an icy chill crawling down her spine. "The only thing keeping you from being arrested right now is that you haven't been out of my sight all day."

Her lips parted wordlessly in stunned horror. Scepter, the Home Office, the Guards—the threats were coming at her from all sides now.

"Tell me the truth now," he demanded, lowering his voice as her barouche rolled toward them to collect her. "What do you know about the men who have been blackmailing you?"

"Nothing," she whispered. That was the God's truth. "They sent boys to deliver messages to me. I don't know who or why."

"What did they use to threaten you?"

She refused to answer.

He clenched his jaw so hard that the sinews pulsed in his neck. He let go of her arm and stepped back as the barouche stopped in front of them.

"When you decide the time's finally come to trust me," he warned as he moved to his horse's side, "it might just be too late."

He mounted his horse. The black gelding pranced uneasily beneath him, sensing Nate's agitation. He pulled the horse into a tight circle to bring him under control.

"I can't help you if you won't let me." Nate leaned down until his face was even with hers. "I don't know what secret Scepter has over you, but it can't be worth being killed for."

Oh, he was wrong. Her secret was worth *exactly* that. Because if anything happened to Robert, she might as well be dead.

"I don't need your help, Captain," she rasped out, her voice shaking. "I need you to leave me alone."

"Until you tell me what you know about Scepter," he assured her in a tone that brooked no argument, "I have no intention of doing that."

He touched his heels to the horse's sides. The gelding lunged forward to canter away from her and back toward Lord Liverpool, who waited amid the circle of guards.

She watched him go, unable to bring herself to call him back. Despite her pounding heart and racing blood, both at the words of his cold warning and at the heat of its delivery, she still couldn't bring herself to confess.

"My lady?" Jenkins called out to her with concern from the barouche. "Are you all right?"

Sydney nodded, yet Jenkins and her groom must think her mad. Running toward her carriage two nights ago to fling herself inside, a strange man appearing mysteriously inside the compartment with her, then fleeing from St James House yesterday morning as if being chased—and now, after sprinting across Hyde Park like a bedlamite, she stared after the captain like some besotted schoolgirl.

Perhaps she *was* mad. Captain Reed was certainly driving her out of her mind.

"I'm fine." She pulled in a deep breath and forced a smile, half to reassure her driver and half to convince herself. The groom opened the little carriage door and took her arm to help her into the barouche. She stepped up with relief. "Home, please, Jenkins, and—"

She turned for her seat and froze.

On the cushion waiting for her lay a small wooden soldier, a child's toy painted in bright red and white.

Its head had been snapped off.

Six

SYDNEY LEANED AGAINST THE OPEN STALL DOOR IN THE Horse Guards stables and lost her breath.

In the soft glow of the oil lamp hanging on a post over the stall, Nate Reed groomed his black horse with a brush in his right hand and a soft cloth in his left until the gelding's coat shined like obsidian. He spoke softly to the horse, his deep voice so low that Sydney couldn't make out the words, but the horse's velvet ears flicked back and forth to catch each soothing sound. His hands slid over the smooth muscles, and each stroke of the brush and cloth was a gentle caress.

She shouldn't be here, and certainly not staring like this. But she couldn't look away, neither from the large hands moving over the horse's velvet coat nor from the man himself who stood there wearing only his stone-colored riding breeches and black boots. His shirt had been peeled off and tossed over the stall wall, and his braces dangled around his thighs. He was bare from the waist up.

Her fingers longed to caress his flesh the same way his hands brushed over the horse. His skin would feel just as warm and smooth, his muscles just as hard…

Inwardly, she groaned.

Why him? Of all the men she knew in the *ton*, all the men

she'd encountered in London, why did the one man since Michael who both stirred fires low in her belly and had her longing to be held protected in his arms have to be him, the same man who thought she was a traitor?

Yet she wanted him. Just the sight of him had her craving to run the tip of her tongue over his collarbone and taste the beads of salty sweat clinging to his skin.

But more than just physical attraction drew her. She'd never known a more heroic man, more selfless, and so full of determination and dedication. He exuded a natural ease that captivated her, and although she wasn't willing to let herself contemplate it, she also sensed a deep grief inside him. The same depth of grief she carried inside herself.

She chewed her bottom lip. She was a widow, free to spend her time with whomever she wanted as long as she was discreet. Would it be so wrong to seek solace in his arms?

Nate could give her that, she knew. Just as she held no delusions that whatever happened between them could never be anything more than temporary. She would never give any man a position of power over her. Her late husband had controlled her life and Michael her heart. One man had loved her and one had hated her, yet they'd both taught her well—to never again surrender to a man.

The next time, she might not survive it.

The brush stilled against the horse's side. Slowly, Nate lifted his head, and his hazel eyes locked with hers long enough for her heart to stop with a painful thud. Then he lowered his gaze to deliberately take her in.

She stood perfectly still beneath his scrutiny and shamelessly let him look.

If he was surprised to see her standing in the stables wearing boys' clothes, complete with a cap large enough to hide her hair, the emotion never registered on his face. He did nothing, in fact, but toss the brush into the corner and turn back to the horse to finish wiping the cloth across its black satiny coat.

Yet Sydney sensed a change in him…a tensing of his muscles, a quickening of his breath. She trembled.

"You're a long way from Barton's tonight, Baroness," he said quietly and discarded the cloth after the brush.

"I'm a bit underdressed for the club, don't you think?"

His lips twitched, but he made no comment as he reached for the water bucket at his feet. The rippling muscles in his arms and shoulders captured her attention as he lifted the bucket into the air and poured it over his head. The cold water splashed down his tall body and washed away the bits of hay clinging to his bare skin.

He dropped the bucket to the floor, then slicked back his wet hair with both hands. Droplets of water clung to his chest and ran in rivulets over the hard ridges of his abdomen and down to the waistband of his breeches. She sucked in a breath through clenched teeth. *Goodness.*

"Did anyone see you come in?" He stepped slowly toward her.

She swallowed. Hard. "No."

"Good. Because no one who sees you will believe for one moment that you're not a woman." He looked over her shoulder into the aisle behind her to make certain no one else was there, then slanted a narrowed look at her. "Where did you get those clothes?"

She reached up to make certain the tweed cap was still in place and hiding her hair. "From my stable boy." She'd had to disguise herself to escape her own home without being followed and slip into the Horse Guards without being noticed. "Why? What's wrong with them?"

He trailed his gaze over her again and gave a faint shake of his head. "Next time, steal from the groom. A pair of trousers that don't cling to your hips like that." His gaze heated everywhere he looked. "A greatcoat to hide the fullness of your bosom." He leaned over slightly to level his eyes with hers. "And rough up those pretty cheeks of yours with some dirt. You want to pretend you're a boy? Boys aren't clean."

"Thank you, Captain." She flashed him a mockingly bright smile. "Tomorrow, I'll instruct *you* on how to wear a dress."

He chuckled. Even from a foot away, the low rumble of it cascaded through her and curled her toes in the ill-fitting boots. The mocking humor drained out of her, replaced by something hot and aching.

"Why are you here?" He folded his arms across his chest, and a pang of disappointment pierced her that he'd covered himself from her eyes. "I thought you only haunted the hallways of St James House with your spying."

A blush flamed from the back of her neck in her embarrassment at being caught. Or perhaps it was because he stood so close now that she could caress his bare chest by simply lifting her hand.

She tucked both hands behind her back to keep from reaching for him. "I need to speak with you, and you live here in the barracks."

"Surprised by that?"

"Not at all. You have the soul of a soldier. I have the feeling that if a new war began tomorrow and Wellington called for fighters, you'd be the first to volunteer." It was her turn to study him now, and she eyed him closely. "Is that why you're coming after me? Something to fill your time until the next war begins, when you can lose yourself once more on the battlefield?"

He leaned in closer, and the two of them now stood nearly nose to nose. "I'm coming after you, Baroness, because I've pledged to stop Scepter."

"Then you're looking in the wrong place." She warned somberly, "And if you don't stop looking, you'll get us all killed."

She reached up to unfasten the top two buttons of her boys' waistcoat. His eyes followed, watching her chest as a haunted expression darkened his face.

Her fingers trembled beneath the heat of his stare. If he were any other man, she would have said he wanted her. But not him. She doubted that an uncontrolled bone existed anywhere in his highly regimented body that would have broken under a desire to reach for her, no matter how much she wanted him to do just that.

She withdrew the decapitated toy soldier she'd tucked into her short stays.

He frowned at the mutilated toy. "What's that?"

"A warning to stay away from you." She held it out to him. "It was left in my barouche in the park this afternoon after we'd taken our walk together. They're coming after me now." She pulled in a trembling breath. "They'll come after you, too, if you don't leave me alone."

He closed his hand around the toy and stepped closer, blatantly ignoring her warning to keep away. *Keep away?* If he were any closer, she'd be pressed against his bare chest... although she suspected that wouldn't have been so terrible.

His eyes lingered on her mouth. "You're frightened."

She wished she could stop the shaking in her hands and the prickling at the backs of her knees, wished the sensation wasn't as much from him as it was from fear. But her indignant response emerged as barely more than a breathless whisper. "Of course I'm frightened."

"Then tell me what you know," he murmured, "and I'll protect you."

"Please, Captain Reed, for both our sakes, stop—"

Without warning, he grabbed her arm with one hand and clamped the other over her mouth as she began to cry out in surprise. He pulled her inside the stall, then closed the door silently behind them with a tap of his boot and pressed her against the side wall.

"Shh," he whispered, his lips close to her ear. The heat of his breath fanned over her cheek and sent her belly fluttering with longing. She was certain he was going to kiss her, thoroughly and properly, until he warned, "Someone's coming."

She strained to listen through the silence of the stable for any sound, but she heard only the restless moving of horses, a dog barking outside...Nate's steady and deep breathing.

Then she heard it—

Footsteps crunched on the gravel.

The quiet sound echoed down the stable aisle as the person moved slowly toward them. A watchman?

Dread squeezed her stomach. If she was found here— Good Lord, if they were found together looking like *this!*— she could be arrested for trespassing, Nate could be put into the stocks if not court-martialed, both of their reputations would be ruined, and all of it would be her fault for coming here in the first place.

Sydney trembled. "Captain—"

"Hush," he silently breathed out. He pressed his fingers to her lips and leaned even closer until his hips shifted against hers and held her pinned against the wall where they couldn't be seen through the narrow rectangle of bars in the stall door.

The watchman paused just outside the stall.

She clutched at Nate's bare shoulders to hold herself steady. His large body was folded around hers, she knew, in his attempt to protect her. But her heart pounded so hard that her chest ached from the panic-filled tattoo of it. So hard she knew he could feel it.

Footsteps shifted in the gravel as the guard turned toward the stall.

She clamped her eyes shut, held her breath, and waited for the watchman to yank open the stall door and find them, for her life to come crashing down around her—

The guard moved on down the aisle. The crunch of footsteps grew fainter and farther away as he walked to the end of the stable aisle. The reverberating clank of metal on wood signaled that he'd slid open the rear stable door, then slammed it shut with a clang against the latch a moment later.

The stables fell silent except for the soft movement of horses shifting quietly in their hay-strewn stalls and the roar of her pulse in her ears.

With a tremulous shudder, she eased her desperate hold on Nate only enough to sag against the wall behind her, but her hands still rested on his hard shoulders. She wasn't ready to release him completely.

"Thank God that watchman didn't find us." She gave him an unsteady smile.

No relief registered on his somber face. "That wasn't a watchman."

The little hairs on her arms prickled, and she dreaded his answer even as she asked, "How do you know?"

"Because I'm the stable guard on duty tonight."

Icy fear spiraled down her spine, and she forced herself to take a calming breath to keep from casting up her accounts all over his boots. "Then who was he?"

Nate placed his hands on the wall on either side of her shoulders, trapping her between his arms and broad chest. "You tell me."

He was so close she could feel his body heat warming into her skin even through her clothes, and the delicious scent of soap and leather, musk and man filled her senses. The combination made her head swim. "I don't know."

"Oh, I think you do," he murmured and lowered his head

until his mouth lingered above hers, almost touching but achingly still so far away.

When she began to protest her innocence, he put a finger to her lips and silenced her.

"I've been watching you. Apparently, so has the man who just walked past. Most likely he followed you all the way from your house." His brows pulled into a small frown as he stared at her mouth. "But you were out of his sight too long, so he came to check on you to make certain you were still here."

Her mouth fell open, half from surprise at his audacity and half from the way his fingertip began to rub her bottom lip. "How do you know that?"

"Because I would have done the same."

That didn't put her at ease. "If Scepter knows I'm with you, if they believe I've confided in you," she said so softly the whispered confession was barely audible, "they'll kill both of us."

"No," he assured her quietly, but his troubled frown deepened. "They want you alive. For now."

His hand slid down her neck to stroke across her shoulder and along her arm in long, slow caresses of his palm.

Heavens, he was trying to calm her the same way he'd soothed his horse! She should have laughed. It was absurd...

Except that it was working. His touch soothed the fear from her, eased the shaking in her knees, untangled the knot in the pit of her stomach...as long as she ignored the heat in his eyes, that is. There was nothing calming in those hazel depths.

"Tell me the truth now, Baroness," he cajoled. "You said you'd received messages of blackmail. What messages?"

Silk. Sweet heavens, his voice was *silk*, and she felt the sudden desire to wrap herself in it. And in him.

She pressed her fingers into the muscles of his bare arms to draw from his resilience, but she also knew she was putting her life in danger even as she confessed, "A messenger was sent to my house about six weeks ago."

"A boy," he guessed. "A street urchin."

"How did you—" Then she closed her gaping mouth with a grimace. Of course he knew. He seemed to know almost everything about her. But how would he react if he knew she wanted to be in his arms, kissing him and welcoming his touch? "Yes. I'd never seen him before. Neither had any of my servants."

The gold flecks in his eyes shined in the lamplight. "What was the message?"

"I was ordered to buy up Henry Everett's gambling debts."

He stroked his hand slowly up and down her arm. Goose bumps formed deliciously in his wake. "Why?"

"I don't know. But I did as I was told. I was too frightened not to. They knew..." *They knew about Robert.* She paused to consider her words. "They knew things about my past."

His hand slipped beneath her arm to trail down her side and rest against the curve of her hip. "They threatened you if you didn't do as they asked."

"Yes," she breathed, although her voice emerged far raspier than she intended.

"With what secret?"

"I questioned the boy," she dodged, "tried to bribe him for information, but he didn't know the name of the man who'd sent him. He described him as a finely dressed gentleman with brown hair, brown eyes…" She shook her head with frustration. "He could have been anyone. So I followed the boy when he left."

"Because the man promised to pay him a second coin once the message was delivered?"

She nodded. "But the man never appeared. Eventually, the boy left, and I went home."

"Following him was brave of you." His fingers curled into the spot where her hip sloped into her waist.

"It wasn't bravery." Her chest heated at the notion that she might have impressed him, but her actions were desperate, not heroic. The threat had been clear. Do as the blackmailers wanted, or they would kill Robert. "I had no choice, so I bought up his debts. One week later, a second boy arrived with another message."

"To demand repayment from Everett," he guessed correctly. He lowered his other hand from the wall and caressed down her left side until both hands rested on her hips. "Why?"

When he shifted closer, a long-repressed ache flared between her legs and distracted her so much that she could barely concentrate on what he was asking.

"I don't know. They never told me what to do with the money if Mr. Everett ever found a way to pay it." She kept her gaze trained to his bare chest, unable to bring herself to look into his knowing eyes. She was afraid of the accusation and contempt she might see in him and of the shameless desire he might see in her. "I did as I was told."

"But Everett didn't have the money to repay you."

"No." She'd known it, too, and fresh guilt bubbled inside her. "He was a schoolteacher. He barely had enough money to buy new shoes."

"It had to be his money?" His hands tightened almost imperceptibly on her hips, but she felt the change, just as she felt every move he made when he was with her, no matter how small. "You couldn't hand over your own and claim you'd received it from him, just to make Scepter go away?"

She'd considered doing just that, but... "I was being watched. They told me when to meet with him and where, to keep pressuring him to repay, to threaten to send him to debtor's prison if he didn't. The last time I spoke to him was at Vauxhall about a fortnight ago. I asked again for the money. He didn't have it, and we argued." She squeezed her eyes shut and choked out past the knot in her throat, "That night at Barton's when you told me he was dead, I thought that you were another messenger and that he had been killed because of me."

"Shh." His hand slid behind to the small of her back and gently shifted her toward him until she rested against his front, safe and secure. He whispered into her hair, "That man's death isn't on your head."

She wanted so desperately to believe him, to trust him to protect her and keep Robert safe. But she'd been lied to by men too many times before to blindly put her trust in another, even in one so heroic. "How do you know that when I don't even know for certain?"

He began to answer, then asked instead, "That's all Everett was to you? Someone whose gambling debts you were forced to buy?" He brushed his hand slowly up and down her spine. The slow caresses spiked her pulse, and she was certain he could feel it beneath his fingertips. "Nothing more?"

"Nothing more." Although at that moment, she certainly wanted more. From Nate.

"Not lovers, then?"

She and Henry! She laughed at the notion.

"You have a lover, though, surely, a beautiful woman like you." His mouth hovered just above hers, close enough that every word teased at her lips. He tensed as if restraining himself from simply lowering his head and claiming the kiss she so desperately wanted him to take. One that would leave her breathless and free of the fear she'd experienced during the past few weeks. "Someone who knows all your secrets."

He touched her throat. As his fingertips trailed over the curve in her neck, she tilted her head to the side to give him both access and permission to keep touching her. *More.* She wanted more.

She admitted breathlessly, "There's no one." *But there could be…*

His fingertips stilled. "Not since your husband died?"

She gazed up at him. Did her own eyes appear just as heated, just as dark and confused as his? "Only one man," she confessed. "But he would never have been able to blackmail me."

"Why?"

Because it was only one night, only a desperate attempt for solace… "Because I never told him my secrets." In fact, she'd told no one. Not even Robert himself. Not even the woman now responsible for raising and caring for Robert, a woman who was proving to be a better mother to him than Sydney most likely would ever have been.

"No." His fingers strayed lower toward the unbuttoned gap in her waistcoat. "I meant…why take a lover?"

Their conversation had gone astray. She suspected they were now discussing two very different topics, only to not care about the conversation at all when he slowly unfastened another button between her breasts.

She forced out from trembling lips, "The same reasons anyone takes a lover." Another button, and she shivered with longing. Only a few inches from his fingers, her nipples hardened and ached to be touched. "I was lonely. I wanted pleasure."

His forefinger swiped under the waistcoat and caught the wide collar of her shirt to tug it out of the way and caress against the bare skin beneath. She sighed. *What a wonderful tease…* But she wasn't in the mood for play.

She said huskily, "The same reasons you take lovers, I'm sure." *The same reasons I want you to take me.*

Not answering, he fixed his gaze on her mouth as if he knew how much she wanted him to kiss her but torturously refused to grant her what she craved. She groaned inwardly. His refusal only made her desire him more.

He took another teasing caress over the bare skin beneath her shirt. "Didn't it feel as if you were betraying your husband?"

"No." Not him. *Never* him. "Doesn't everyone have needs?"

"Not me. Not anymore."

His denial came so low that she could barely hear it, and she suspected he spoke more to convince himself than her. "I don't believe you." Especially as he drew slow circles with his fingertip against the warm flesh of her chest just above her right breast. He shifted his hips away from her, most likely to hide any evidence of the very need he denied possessing. "You're a man."

He drawled with amusement, "Therefore I tup every woman who comes along?"

"Of course not. I meant," she tried again, although at that moment he made thinking quite challenging, "that every man has need of a woman's pleasures." And every woman need of a man's. Certainly she did. "Even you."

His lips curled upward in the faintest of smiles. "You don't know me, Baroness."

"I know enough. For instance—" She pulled in a breath to summon her courage. "I know you want me."

He stilled at her unexpected boldness, his fingertips lingering against her bare skin, and evaded, "Lots of men want you."

Triumph surged through her that he hadn't denied it. "Perhaps." The tip of her tongue darted out to wet her suddenly dry lips. "But *I* don't want most men." The words were soft as a breath as she confessed, "I want you."

"Sydney." Her name was an aching protest, yet he didn't move away from her, as if he couldn't find the will.

She arched herself against him in invitation. Even if he gave her only one night in his arms, she would gladly take it. In the morning, she would worry about what came next, what new threats Scepter would make against them, and what charges the Home Office would accuse her of committing.

Tonight, she only wanted to think about Nate.

With a groan of frustration and need, she rose onto her tiptoes and snaked her arms around his neck to draw herself against him. He wanted her, she knew it. Sweet heavens, pressed up against him like this, she could *feel* it.

Yet even now he resisted encircling her in his arms. He inhaled sharply, and his tense body shook as if her touch burned him.

Then with a faint groan, he softened in surrender and lowered his head to slide his mouth against the corner of hers, to finally take the small taste of her that he'd been denying himself. Yet this kiss wasn't quite a kiss, and beneath her fingertips, she felt his muscles trembling with restraint.

"Nate," she begged and turned her mouth fully into his. "Please."

At her soft plea, his restraint snapped, and his mouth captured hers so greedily that he stole her breath away and left her gasping even as his lips fed hungrily on hers. His tongue teased at her lips, and when she parted them, he stroked inside her mouth.

Sydney lost herself against the ferocity of his spicy sweetness, just as she'd longed to do from the moment she walked into the stables and saw him—no, since long before that. Since she saw him at Barton's when he made her laugh and momentarily forget the fear and suffering inside her. All of it was cemented by his promise to protect her. Her body ached in turns between the acute arousal he flamed inside her and her own emotions.

She brushed her hands over the hard planes of his bare chest. Was all of him this smooth and warm, this hard beneath? And would he let her find out?

She tore her mouth away from his to place a delicate kiss to his bare chest, right over his pounding heart. "Come home with me," she tempted, and this time, instead of a simple kiss, she caressed her lips across his skin in an openmouthed kiss. It was a promise of what would happen if only he gave her the chance. "Let me have you tonight."

She pressed her hips against his and thrilled at the hard ridge in his breeches that pressed back.

He groaned. "Sydney—"

"Come home with me," she repeated, willing her voice not to tremble as fiercely as the rest of her.

He rested his forehead against hers and squeezed his eyes shut. "I can't."

Her mind churned in confusion. He wanted her. He was shaking with it, for heaven's sake! "Yes, you can."

"No," he insisted, his voice a barely controlled rasp. "I can't do that."

She slipped her arms from around him and let them fall to her sides. "I'm sorry." She breathed hard as she tried to sort through the desire-fogged turmoil in her mind, to keep the stinging rejection at bay. "I thought—I thought you wanted me."

"Of course I want you." He blew out a harsh breath and admitted, "You have no idea how much. But I can't... *I won't.*"

He stepped back and stared at her as if she were some

sort of siren come to take his soul. Yet she could still see the desire in him, and the confusion it spawned shook the ground beneath her.

"Go home, Baroness," he said quietly, "before that man comes looking for you again."

"I don't understand." Leaving was the last thing she wanted to do. She wanted to remain right here with this enthralling and challenging man who bothered her body and bewitched her mind. "Why are you—"

She choked off as the dreadful realization seeped over her like ice water.

"Who is she?" she asked quietly but with absolute certainty. "The woman you think you'll be betraying by being with me?"

Darkness shadowed his face and proved her right. This wasn't about her.

Another woman stood between them.

"Go home," he repeated. "You'll be safe there."

"You don't know that." The only place she would feel safe tonight was in his arms, but he'd denied her that solace. Her chest panged, already dreading the rest of the wretched, lonely night ahead and the nightmares that came nearly every time she closed her eyes.

"But I do know," he assured her, "because I will protect you."

He meant outside, watching her house. Yes, he'd protect her, but not the way she wanted.

"Besides, Scepter doesn't want you dead." He tucked the toy soldier back inside her stays, then buttoned her waistcoat over it. "Or they'd have killed you by now."

A shiver of fear came over her like a winter's freeze, all the way down to her bones, and extinguished the last heat of arousal in her belly. "Then what do they want from me?"

"I don't know." Her cap had been knocked loose during their kisses. He put it in place over her hair and tucked a stray strand behind her ear. "But I plan to find out."

Seven

HAVING GIVEN UP ON ANY CHANCE HE'D BE ABLE TO sleep any longer, Nate headed on foot through the pre-dawn streets of London toward Mayfair. The faint blues and pinks of the coming sunrise were just beginning to lighten the horizon beyond the Thames. Around him, the city still slept, its streets silent and tranquil.

He hunched his shoulders against the cold and cursed himself.

He'd had that dream again. The one that had plagued him since Sarah's death.

As always in his dream, a faceless woman in a white dress had come unbidden to him from the darkness. Amid a tangle of red satin sheets, he'd peeled away the white silk clinging to her smooth skin and trailed his mouth after, dragging his lips across every inch of warm flesh he revealed until she lay completely naked beneath him. Soft hair cascaded in a dark curtain around her shoulders and over her firm, bare breasts. Her nipples hardened deliciously against his tongue when he lowered his mouth to suckle them. Smooth thighs parted invitingly as he settled between them. She welcomed him eagerly inside her warmth and moaned her delight, and he took his pleasure in her, without guilt or regret. The woman's face remained hidden. No matter how much he struggled to see her, she always turned away.

Until last night when she shifted just far enough for him to glimpse the smooth plane of her cheek and the elegant arch of her neck, when she turned in his arms and revealed herself...

Sydney Rowland.

He'd awoken with a startled gasp. The dream had been so vivid, her body so real and warm to him that he'd searched the blankets to make certain he hadn't ejaculated in his sleep.

His body wanted her, even if his heart was too dead to admit it.

He reached the alley behind her town house and glanced up at the rear façade. No light glowed from any of the rooms. The household still slept, with Sydney most likely in a warm bed of feather down and satin.

Damn that woman for getting under his skin!

No. He blew out a shamefaced sigh, his breath clouding on the cold air in the blue-gray light. Damn himself for letting her.

Her refusal to tell the truth about Henry Everett had him shaking with anger, and the nearness of her last night, so close he could smell her heady scent of oranges and spices, had him shaking for an entirely different reason. Of all the frustrating situations to be thrown into—*this*. With her, of all women. The most impossible, obstinate, challenging, and alluring woman he'd ever met.

One who had to remain untouched.

Yet he had no choice but to stay close to her. The desperate if poorly executed attack on the prime minister in the park meant Scepter was ramping up their plot, and their need to frighten Sydney into submission meant they planned on using her again. And soon.

He searched for the young sergeant who had been guarding her house through the night. Even though Sydney still kept secrets from him, Nate was determined to protect her as best he could and had given strict orders to his man to immediately report anything suspicious and not let anyone inside who didn't go through the front door at the invitation of the butler.

"Sir?" A quiet voice broke the early morning silence of the rear garden.

"Sergeant Baker." Nate tugged his gloves into place and nodded at the man, not bothering with the formality of returning the sergeant's startled salute. "I'm here to replace you."

"But—but you're early."

Nate ignored that. He had no intention of explaining the reason for his appearance two hours earlier than scheduled. "Anything to report?"

"I didn't expect you so soon, sir." The young soldier glanced over his shoulder at the house. "You don't have to be here, Captain. You can trust me to finish my shift."

Nate smiled at the young soldier's nervousness. Had he ever been that earnest, that eager to please his commanding officers?

"It's all right, Baker. I needed some fresh air." Along with a cold, cold morning to settle his blood and force Sydney Rowland from his head.

Baker insisted, "I can finish my duties, sir."

"I'm certain you can." But his sudden nervousness raised Nate's suspicions. "Is something wrong, Sergeant?"

"No…" Baker glanced around at the dark shadows of the alley and those clinging to the house. "The baroness returned from an outing last night around midnight."

An outing to see me. Nate kept his expression carefully guarded despite the skip of his heart. How much did Baker know? "You followed her?"

"No, sir." Guilt flickered shamefully across his face. "The lady sneaked away somehow. I didn't see her leave. I didn't know she was even gone until she returned."

"It's all right." Relief coursed through him. The last thing he needed was for the Horse Guards to know that Lady Rowland had dressed in boys' clothes to sneak into their own stables last night to find him. "I know where she went."

But his assurance didn't seem to put the sergeant at ease.

Nate frowned. Baker was one of the young men who had joined the Guards since the end of the war. A slew of slots had opened to men who would never have been considered when Wellington was still fighting Bonaparte. But the lad was ambitious, followed orders, and still naïvely believed that war and armies actually brought peace. He was also irritatingly young, not more than nineteen or twenty, while at twenty-seven Nate was now one of the oldest captains in the barracks. It was time he, too, moved on and left the Guards to the younger men like Baker.

As soon as this mission was over and the Home Office paid him his reward, he would do just that. Then he'd never have to worry over—or dream about—Sydney Rowland again.

"Head back to the barracks and get some rest," Nate

ordered and gave the sergeant an appreciative slap on the back. "Send Reynolds to relieve me in eight hours."

Baker tugged at his hat in an abbreviated salute, then hesitated. "Captain, we haven't been told anything about this assignment. Why are we watching the baroness?"

"Penance," Nate muttered grimly.

Baker blinked. "Sir?"

"Never mind. Go get some sleep."

"Yes, sir." The young man glanced over his shoulder one last time, then quickly headed down the alley, around the corner, and out of sight.

With a heaving sigh that fogged the cold air, Nate stared up at the town house. Sydney was in there somewhere, and if he possessed one grain less of resolve, he would have been inside with her.

Last night, when he'd looked up from his horse and found her standing in the stables, he'd thought he was hallucinating. The baroness in boys' clothing, alone with him in a horse stall, for God's sake... *Of course* he thought he'd been hallucinating, the same way he'd seen Sarah's ghost everywhere he looked for the first few months after her death, the way he thought he heard a baby crying even in the middle of battle.

But Sydney wasn't a ghost, even if the frustrating woman was haunting him. She was flesh and blood, warm and real, and it had taken a bucket of cold water over his head to make him believe it.

Unfortunately, there wasn't enough cold water in the Thames to make him stop wanting her. He'd called upon every ounce of restraint he possessed not to rip those ridiculous boys' clothes from her body and take her right there against the stable wall. And when she'd invited him home... *Sweet Lucifer*.

Worse, she tempted him with more than those red lips, full curves, and stormy green eyes. She'd done what he hadn't yet had the courage to do—she'd taken a lover after her husband's death. She'd found a way to quench the need for arousal and release, a way to fend off the lonely nights.

But Nate wasn't selfish enough to bed her. How would he ever be able to lose himself in another woman without feeling the guilt of betraying Sarah, especially when he'd disappointed her in so many other ways for which he could never forgive himself?

A movement caught the corner of his eye, and he froze. A dark form slid through the shadows of the side garden toward the rear of the house.

Crouching low, Nate moved silently across the service yard toward the garden. He slipped through the shadows still clinging to the base of the tall stone wall and was helped by the thick bushes and bowers decorating the walk that curved around the house toward the front portico.

He stopped at the back corner of the town house, then reached his right hand into his left sleeve for the knife he kept sheathed there. He held his breath and waited.

A large man slinked past in the shadows. Nate freed his knife and lunged.

He shoved the trespasser against the stone wall and pinned him there with his left forearm across the man's upper chest. The knife blade lay against the thug's throat.

"Who are you?" Nate demanded through clenched teeth. When the brute hesitated to answer, he pressed the knife just far enough into his throat to cause pain but not enough to cut the skin. A warning.

The intruder's eyes bulged, but he knew enough not to move. Nowhere near the age of the boy messengers whom Scepter had sent before, he was gray at his temples with leathery skin wrinkled from years of hard work in the sun and large biceps beneath a frayed coat. He reeked of fish, sewage, cheap ale—a dock worker hired from one of the seedy pubs lining the Thames, not a professional killer.

Nate pressed the knife deeper into the man's throat and repeated, "Who are you?"

"William Murker," the man gurgled with spittle running down his chin. From the way he shook and stared with fear-filled eyes, he was very surprised to find Nate here. Clearly, he hadn't expected the house to be guarded.

"Why are you here?"

Murker's gaze darted toward the rear of the house as if searching for someone. A partner? Yet Nate kept his eyes fixed on the attacker. He had a knife, but this thug dominated him in physical size.

"I—I was sent after the lady who lives here."

"*My* lady," Nate corrected through clenched teeth. "She's under my protection." Fury pulsated through his limbs to find this brute so close to Sydney while she slept helplessly in her bed. "Who hired you? Tell me." Nate moved the knife in silent threat across Murker's throat. "Or I'll slit you from ear to ear like a pig."

"I don't know!" Panic widened his eyes. "A man came into th' tavern—"

"A finely dressed gentleman with brown hair and eyes." Nate's guess wasn't a question.

"Yes! Yes—that's him."

"What else about him?"

"Nothin'! He didn't give no name."

With the tip of the knife, he pricked Murker's skin beneath his ear. A trickle of blood ran down his neck and dripped onto his dirty collar. "What did he hire you to do?"

"To come 'ere this mornin' an' give her a message. Fright'n her good wit' it."

Nate slid the knife down Murker's throat until the point poised at the pulsing heartbeat at the base of his neck. Nate could kill him with one soft push. Frighten her good— *bastards.* Hadn't they terrified her enough already? "What was the message?"

Murker recited carefully, "Keep yer silence, or we'll kill Robert."

Who the hell was Robert? Nate's blood turned cold as he realized... Sydney's lover. "And the baroness? Were you supposed to hurt her?"

"No! Just scare her." The man swallowed, his Adam's apple undulating against the knife's edge. "But make her believe it."

"Why?" Nate demanded. "What do they want from her?"

"I don't know! I was only hired for this, I swear!"

With a ferocious growl, Nate released him and stepped back until he was out of Murker's reach. He held the knife ready should the thug attack, but Murker remained at the wall, too afraid to flee. His only movement was to reach up to rub at the tiny cut beneath his ear, and his face blanched when sticky blood smeared his fingertips.

His eyes widened as he glanced from the blood to Nate. "The man who hired me—if he finds out I talked to you, he'll kill me!"

"Then leave London on the next ship," Nate ordered. "And if I ever see you anywhere around Lady Rowland again, I'll kill you myself."

Murker clamped his hand over his throat, turned, and ran. His boots scraped against the brick path as he fled toward the street as fast as his bowed legs could scramble.

Nate bit out a harsh curse and sheathed the knife. The danger for Sydney was escalating. They knew she'd been speaking with him; the toy soldier had been proof of that. It was their first warning. This thug was the second.

Nate feared there wouldn't be a third.

He circled the house to check the perimeter and resume his post in the rear. He glanced up one last time at the brick town house and froze.

Sydney stood at her bedroom window and stared down at him through the light of the brightening dawn. In a white night rail framed by the darkness of the room behind, her sable hair hanging loose around her shoulders, she appeared as if she'd materialized from his dream…the woman in white who stepped from the darkness to drape herself across the red satin sheets and tangle her body with his.

He could go to her. Right now. Just scale the side of the

brick house and climb through the window into her room, take her into his arms, and carry her to the bed. She wouldn't refuse him. For God's sake, she'd invited him and would welcome him with open arms, delicious kisses, and wanton touches.

But at what cost? Unfaithfulness to Sarah and an affront to all they'd wanted for their future? The destruction of his mission to stop Scepter?

Oh, the intimacy would be exquisite, certainly. But the price he'd have to pay would be far too dear.

Sucking a harsh breath through clenched teeth, he summoned what was left of his thin thread of restraint, turned his back to her, and walked away.

Eight

"LADY ROWLAND?"

Sydney frowned into her teacup, oblivious to the people around her in the drawing room of St James House. The tea had grown cold while her thoughts had once again strayed to Nate Reed.

He said he'd been guarding her, and she'd witnessed it herself this morning in her garden. Surely, he'd been watching her home for days and following her everywhere she went, and not just to Barton's but to every social call she'd made, every soiree she'd attended. Was he here at St James House, too, watching over her even now?

"My lady?"

While there was no doubt in her mind why Nate tempted her so, the man himself was a mystery. He was heralded as the hero of Toulouse, yet he did his best to avoid drawing attention to himself. He lived in a barracks when he could have had the luxury of well-appointed rooms. When she'd been in his arms, practically begging to share a perfectly good, large, and soft bed with him, he'd sent her away and chose instead his hard, narrow—and lonely—bunk.

His rejection came from more than just duty. Something deeper tortured him, and she easily recognized it. After all, she knew torment better than anyone. Not just the loss of Michael and Robert either, but the four long years of her marriage that followed. John Rowland was a cruel son of a bitch who wanted to bend her to his will almost as much as he'd wanted her money. Yet he'd never once attempted to claim his marriage right. *Thank God.* He'd held her in too much contempt to place himself where Michael Berkley had planted his seed. Besides, she would have killed him if he'd ever tried to force himself on her.

When he died in a drunken fall from his horse, Sydney had dutifully donned black and gone to the funeral, not to mourn but to make certain he was truly dead and buried and could never hurt her again.

"Lady Rowland."

Startled, she glanced up to find seven pairs of eyes focused on her. "Pardon?"

With a smile, Lady Agnes Sinclair reached to pat her knee. "You are a thousand miles away this afternoon, my dear."

"My apologies." She covered the embarrassed blush threatening at her cheeks by taking a sip of cold tea and doing her best not to make a face at the taste. "I'm just a little distracted."

Olivia Everett's eyes narrowed on her. So did Alexander Sinclair's as the earl sat close beside Miss Everett on the sofa and gazed at Sydney with a stone-hard expression. Nate said she could trust him, but could she trust anyone now, including Nate himself?

Lady Agnes, however, appeared oddly thrilled by the admission. But then, Agnes Sinclair had always been eccentric. Today she was no less interesting than usual, having donned a gauzy white frock with crinoline ruffles and a large red hat with ostrich feathers stretching nearly two feet above her head. The entirety made her resemble a gigantic chicken.

Still, Sydney liked the woman very much. She wished she possessed just half of Agnes's exuberance.

"Lord and Lady Gantry were commenting upon the most urgent measures to be taken for the school," Miss Everett repeated, not just for Sydney's sake but the room at large. "That *is* why we're all here today after all. To discuss the future of the Everett School."

Lady Gantry nodded enthusiastically, while Lord Gantry appeared bored out of his mind. As the school's two most important patrons, their opinions would be eagerly sought out and listened to, then most likely ignored, as was usual with every charity on which Sydney served with them.

Lord Hawking, the newest member to the school's board, sat on the other side of the room next to Lord Gantry. Sydney knew the marquess well from years of serving with him on various charity boards, including the Foundling Hospital and the Orphan Working School. At social events, he'd been gentlemanly enough to rescue her from cads and dandies who pressed their attentions too far and to defend her to gossipy old hens. He'd always been kind and concerned about her welfare even when her own husband hadn't, and she'd come to trust him even more since Rowland's death, often asking him for advice. He'd never steered her wrong.

Alexander Sinclair, Earl of St James, was substituting at this meeting for his mother, who had agreed to help with the school's construction. But the countess had other commitments that prevented her from attending.

Why Sydney had been invited, though, she had no idea. The invitation arrived just that morning. Yet she'd eagerly accepted in hopes of a chance to speak with Miss Everett about her brother. Guilt over Henry's death knotted her belly.

"As you all know," Miss Everett continued, "Lady Rowland made a very generous donation toward our rebuilding fund, and she serves on the board of many charities. We would be very fortunate to have her experience guiding us as we open the new Everett School."

Sydney forced a smile. If they knew the real reason why she gave so generously to orphanages, schools, and children's charities, she would be blacklisted from Mayfair, and no one in the room would ever speak to her again.

But she had no intention of unleashing the scandal of Robert's true identity. Keeping him safe meant never acknowledging she was his mother. Not even to him.

"So the first action we would like to take," Miss Everett announced, "is to officially invite Lady Rowland to join the board."

Sydney froze, the teacup poised at her lips. *What* did she just say?

Pleased smiles beamed from Lady Gantry and Lady Agnes at the idea, while Lord Gantry and Lord Hawking seemed simply amused by the proceedings and would gladly have left the whole ordeal up to the ladies if they could have found a way to excuse themselves to the billiards room. St James's hard gaze never wavered from her.

Olivia Everett frowned, seemingly unhappy about the invitation she'd just extended. But then, could she have been happy about anything today? That the young schoolmistress even had the strength to hold this meeting in the midst of her grief testified to her love for the girls who attended the school, many of whom had no other home.

They were all staring at Sydney, all waiting for an answer. She drew a deep breath and smiled. "I would be honored."

"Wonderful." Yet the smile Miss Everett returned felt just as strained as her own. "Lord St James has been very generous to offer his home for the school's use, but as you can imagine, the board is eager to find another property and to return to him his quiet solitude."

"As am I," he muttered beneath his breath.

As if on cue, a loud crash reverberated from the floor above, followed by stomping feet and angry shouts. St James sighed and slid a patient sideways glance at Miss Everett, who uncomfortably bit her bottom lip and wisely continued to stare straight ahead.

"Now," Miss Everett continued, "if we can discuss our options…"

As the conversation wore on, Sydney's attention wandered again, back to the same place it had strayed since she'd glimpsed Nate walking into Barton's. She fought back a smile at the memory. In spite of his brocade and superfine, the young captain had been a fish out of water among the members of the *ton*, paradoxically just as much as he'd been perfectly at home last night in the stables when he'd worn practically nothing at all.

Sydney set her cup aside and reached for her fan. The tea may have been cold, but she suddenly felt rather warm.

So did Olivia Everett, apparently, based on the way she flushed every time St James cast glances in her direction. *Interesting.* The rake and the schoolmistress…whoever would have thought?

It was a devilish pairing. Perhaps one as mad as a baroness and an army captain.

"Lady Rowland?" Charles Langley, Marquess of Hawking, stood next to her chair and frowned down at her. Then quietly, in a concerned voice, he asked, "Sydney, my dear, are you unwell?"

She blinked. She'd been so distracted that she hadn't noticed the meeting breaking up around her and the others rising to move about the room to make their goodbyes. Including St James, who excused himself with an explanation about being needed by his mother at Harlow House.

With a touch of embarrassment, she gave Lord Hawking a smile as she rose to her feet. "I'm fine. Just a bit distracted." A bit? *Ha!* If she were any more distracted, she'd forget her own name.

He kept his voice low. "I worry about you."

"I'm fine, Charles, truly." She reassured him by giving his arm a quick squeeze. "But I am grateful as always for your concern."

"It's more than just concern." His eyes moved around the room to make certain no one paid them undue attention. "You know I care about you."

She did. That was one of the most endearing aspects of their friendship and one she dearly appreciated. "You've always been a great support whenever I've needed one."

"That's why it frets me that you spend so many evenings alone and so much time at Barton's." Concern shone in his eyes…along with something brighter. "If you're in need of company or help, I am always available to you."

Her heart skipped. She'd been propositioned by enough men to know one when she heard it, no matter how gentle-manly delivered.

Oh, she liked Charles. He'd always been kind to her, and she'd always had the utmost respect for him. But sharing his bed was an invitation she would never accept. They would never be that kind of friends, and she needed to remind him of that.

So she gave him an overly bright smile and gently patted his arm. "You are such a dear *friend*."

Hawking took her hand and raised it to his lips, the gesture oddly rakish for a man in his late forties who had become a fix-ture in Parliament in recent years and a patron of such stodgy organizations as the Royal Society. "I think you realize," he murmured, "that I consider you more than simply a friend."

There was certainly no confusion what he meant by *that*.

It was time to put an end to this.

"I'm sorry, Charles." She chose her words carefully, want-ing to discourage him but not embarrass him. He *was* a dear friend, and she wanted to keep him that way. "But I don't think it's wise for us to be anything more."

The warmth vanished from his eyes. "Are you saying it's a mistake to deepen our feelings for each other?"

Oh no... "Please understand. I'm very grateful that you are here for me whenever I need you." She gave him a softened look of feigned regret. "But what a shame it would be to ruin such a wonderful friendship by doing anything that might cause you to think less of me."

"Ah, you misunderstand. I'm not proposing you become my mistress." He chuckled lightly at the idea. "Nothing of the sort!"

Wasn't he? Heavens! Apparently this whole business with Nate Reed had confused her to the point where she couldn't read men at all anymore. She felt like such a goose! She sighed with chagrin. "Well, that's—"

"I want you to become my marchioness." Earnestness filled his voice. "We're both alone now in our lives, and as you said, we're dear friends. We'd make a good marriage, and I wouldn't worry so much about you if you were at my side."

He was...*proposing*? Her mouth fell open. She had no idea what to say except, "I-I couldn't possibly...ruin our friendship with marriage." She had no intention of ever marrying again, not even to a man as fine and dear to her as Lord Hawking. "Besides, I need good friends now more than I need a husband. I hope you can understand."

A strained smile pulled at his lips. "I hope you will reconsider and give me the chance to win you over."

She said as gently as possible, her heart breaking for him, "I won't."

"Very well." He released her hand with a grimace of regret. "Still, you cannot fault a man for trying."

"Not at all."

His smile remained in place, but she knew the exchange had cost him a great deal of pride. With a nodded goodbye to the room in general, he sauntered into the hall toward the front door to take his leave.

Sydney drew a deep breath of relief. She didn't realize until that moment that her hands were shaking.

He was only being kind, she knew, as the dear friend he'd always been. Most men of his social standing believed all women needed husbands to protect them and complete them.

Yet she wanted nothing of the kind, and she certainly didn't want Charles Langley.

No, the man she wanted made her tremble in arousal with only a heated glance, had her longing to trail her lips across every inch of his muscular body, had her aching for the pleasure he could give. Being in his bed wouldn't be simply chasing away a night of loneliness. It would be a meeting of bodies and spirits, urgent and fierce, unlike anything she'd ever experienced be—

"Captain Reed."

With a gasp, she spun around and came face-to-face with Agnes Sinclair. Sydney's cheeks pulsed hot with an instant blush. Good heavens! Had she accidentally uttered her wanton desires aloud?

But the plump older woman only beamed brightly at her from beneath her gigantic feathered bonnet. "Captain Reed," she repeated and looped her arm through Sydney's to lead her for a turn about the room, "recently paid me an afternoon visit. Lovely man, the captain. Knows how to hold his tea."

Sydney opened her mouth, then closed it. What on earth was she supposed to say to that?

Lady Agnes's lips twisted into a smile of private amusement like a cat who'd found the cream. "Such a dashing young man, don't you agree?"

Very much. "Well, I cannot say."

"But you've met him, of course. What do you think of him?"

Sydney caught the curious glance Agnes slid her way, as if the question were some kind of a test. *Odd.* Why should she care what Sydney thought of the captain? "I'm afraid we've only spoken briefly." *And kissed for not long enough at all.*

"Yes, my dear." Agnes patted her arm, then demanded, "But what do you *think* of him?"

What she thought was that Nate Reed was capable of both boiling her blood and soothing her racing heart the way no other man ever had. Not even Michael. It was as if he personally knew the pain of what she'd been through, as if he knew her own heartache.

She certainly wasn't going to share any of that! But with Lady Agnes doggedly awaiting a response, she had to say something. "I think...the captain is quite heroic."

"Ah, you mean Toulouse!" A touch of pride sounded in the older woman's voice.

Sydney frowned. Pride for Captain Reed? How peculiar. How did Lady Agnes even know Nate?

The older woman's eyes shone brightly. "But do you also know about Amiens?"

Sydney's heart lodged in her throat. "He was nearly killed in another battle?"

"Many, many battles, according to what Arthur has told me." Agnes gently squeezed Sydney's arm to reassure her. "But Captain Reed didn't fight at Amiens. There he was too busy rescuing two dozen women and children who had gotten trapped in artillery crossfire and leading them to safety."

Sydney blinked. Nate rescued women and children in the war?

"That was why Arthur truly gave him that medal and promotion, you know. Not because of Toulouse or even Waterloo but Amiens." Agnes tugged Sydney forward on their turn about the room. "He found them huddled together in an abandoned farmhouse and led them away to safety before the two armies could advance." She lowered her voice. "They were French, you know, but he saved them just the same. Show me any other man among the British ranks that day who would have risked his life for French women and children, I ask you."

Sydney couldn't. Nor could she wrap her mind around this new bit of information. Nate had never mentioned Amiens or what he'd done in the war. The mystery of him deepened with each new bit of information she unraveled, like pulling a loose end of yarn from a piece of knitting.

The two women reached the end of the room near the doorway. Bivvens dutifully appeared, silently holding both the shawl and reticule she'd brought today and the one she'd left the other morning in her flight from the house.

She smiled gratefully at the butler's thoughtfulness.

"Captain Reed asked me about you," Lady Agnes commented casually.

Sydney froze, her hand in midair as she reached for her shawl. "Oh?"

Agnes nodded, sending her ostrich feathers bobbing, and a conspiratorial gleam lit her eyes. "I do believe the dashing captain is smitten with you!"

Sydney swallowed. Hard. He wasn't smitten. The dashing captain wanted to arrest her for treason, while she simply wanted...

Him.

Nine

THE HORSE'S HOOVES RANG OUT ON THE COBBLESTONES as Nate trotted through the open iron gates and up the short drive to Harlow House.

He reined his horse to a stop and dismounted, then turned to gaze up at the town house. Although it was less than half the size of St James House, the dowager house was still impressive; its white stone façade demanded appreciation of its elegance and commanded attention from the wide street fronting it.

Isabel Sinclair, Countess of St James, had requested his presence at afternoon tea in an invitation delivered to him at the barracks by a uniformed footman. Not a summons exactly, but as an officer, he couldn't refuse an invitation from a family who were close acquaintances with Lord Liverpool and the War Secretary—not if he valued his military career. He was certain both the earl and Lady St James realized that, too. Judging from how the groom hustled to take his horse and the butler waited at the front door to greet him, she'd informed her household staff to expect him.

He grimaced. This was far different from dropping by for tea with Lady Agnes. Being formally asked here unnerved him. Why on earth had the countess invited him, when he'd made clear that he wanted nothing to do with the Sinclairs?

"This way, sir." The butler bowed and gestured for Nate to follow him through the house to the rear gardens. Lady St James and Alexander Sinclair waited on the terrace, where a small table was elegantly set for tea.

"Captain Reed, you've arrived." Isabel Sinclair came forward to greet him. At her overly bright smile, Nate suspected she was just as uneasy as he was. "How wonderful you've come."

"Countess." Nate bowed politely, not bothering to hide his grim expression. Then he shot an equally somber glance at Alec. "Sinclair."

Alec nodded. "Reed."

Nate and his half brother had worked well together since Clayton Elliott and the Home Office assigned them the mission to stop Scepter. Nate couldn't deny that. Yet their interaction was still contentious.

Certainly Sinclair must have found it trying to have his bastard half brother thrust into his life like this. True, Nate had known for the past decade that Alexander Sinclair was his brother, and he hadn't cared one whit that he was. But Sinclair had known for less than two years, and to him, Nate was a living reminder of the old earl's depraved life.

"Thank you for coming." The countess took Nate's arm and led him forward to the table as if she were afraid he might bolt. The idea was damnably appealing.

Rose-patterned china and silverware immaculately decorated the round table, complete with rosebuds floating in a bowl for the centerpiece and lace-edged napkins gracing each plate. It was more formality and elegance than he was used to as a soldier, and far more than he wanted.

Yet to prove he could behave like a gentleman, he assisted the countess with her chair. Then he took the place she indicated to her right as St James dropped into the chair opposite him.

She signaled to the butler to begin the tea service.

Nate shifted uncomfortably on his chair. The meeting was all oh-so quaint and friendly, as if they did this sort of thing together every afternoon. As if he wasn't the bastard son of her debauched late husband. That was the elephant in the room.

Elephant? Hell, it was the whole damned Tower menagerie.

"To what do I owe this invitation, ma'am?" His question was polite but to the point and exactly how he planned on conducting the rest of their conversation until they finished their tea and this awkward afternoon ended.

"I've been remiss in inviting you to Harlow House since you arrived in London." Her beaming smile remained glued in place despite the nervous trembling of her hands as she unfolded her napkin and placed it on her lap. "I wanted to make amends by inviting you this afternoon. I thought we might enjoy tea in the garden since the flowers are blooming so beautifully...and perhaps chat a little...to come to know each other better."

He leaned back in the chair and ignored the butler and footman as they poured his tea and placed tiny cakes and sandwiches onto his plate. He had no intention of tasting any of it. Nor sniffing any flowers. "That isn't necessary."

Her smile wavered only a moment at his response. She was trying hard. *Very* hard. Even St James was behaving extremely well despite not saying much. Or perhaps because of it.

Why they were both working so hard to put him at ease, though, he had no idea, but the attempt was making him damnably uncomfortable.

"Well," she agreed, "perhaps not necessary, but hopefully enjoyable." Her smile grew impossibly brighter. "Can't we all share a pleasant afternoon tea?"

Nate leveled his gaze on her. "No."

Isabel Sinclair's smile vanished. Lowering her gaze to the napkin on her lap, she said nothing while the footman finished the service.

If what she was hoping for was an erasure of the family's guilt, Nate could tell her right now that he didn't plan to grant absolution. Some battles couldn't be won. He would tolerate this farce of a friendly tea for his mother's sake, but he wouldn't make this easy for any of the Sinclairs.

When the footman finished pouring the cups and retreated to the edge of the terrace, she exhaled a long sigh of acquiescence. "Very well." She reached for her teacup. "If you wish to proceed right to the matter, we can."

He pushed his own cup away, not wanting either of them to wrongly believe he brooked society pretense. Or thought he truly belonged at an afternoon tea with a countess and an earl. "I think that best."

She frowned, her drawn brows marring her forehead with a faint wrinkle.

Isabel Sinclair was a striking woman for her age, Nate reflected as he watched her struggle with where to begin the explanation of why he was here. The reminder of how wealth could maintain beauty was clear. His mother was the same age as the countess, yet her hands were gnarled and arthritic from working in kitchens, scrubbing pots and pans with harsh soaps, and wringing out laundry. The dark circles beneath his mother's eyes gave an appearance of constant fatigue and continuous strain that made her look two decades older.

In his earliest memories, when his mother was still young, she'd been just as beautiful as the countess. If not more. Undoubtedly, that same beauty had caught the attention of Rupert Sinclair, late Earl of St James, who forced himself on her and got her with child.

With him.

"I've been wanting to speak with you for several months." The countess folded her hands delicately in her lap. For a moment, she reminded him of Sydney Rowland, so elegant and feminine on the surface, so resilient and determined beneath. "But the time wasn't right until now."

A warning chilled down Nate's spine. "Speak to me in regard to what?"

"I don't know exactly how to begin." She lost the battle to remain still, and her fingers played nervously with her teacup on its saucer. As if realizing she was fidgeting, she dropped her hands to her lap and forced another overly bright smile. "I think perhaps... Well, I'm not certain..."

St James rested his hand reassuringly on her arm. "Just begin, Mother." His eyes darted back to Nate. They were the same hazel color as his. The same eyes, Nate had been told, as their father. "There's no way to make this easier for any of us."

Nate steeled himself as she nodded once, decisively, and rushed out, "We want to recognize you as a son of St James and welcome you into the family."

His heart stopped. In that terrible moment, he could do nothing more in his shock than stare at her while the soft whisper of her voice echoed like a pistol shot inside his head.

Recognized? Now, after all these years... No.

Hell no.

"We are *not* family." Each harsh word tore from Nate through clenched teeth. He shoved back from the table and stood. Tea was over before it had begun. "And you have no right to—"

"Captain Reed—Nate." With a pained expression, she slipped to her feet and placed her hand on his arm. "Please hear us out."

"Us?" Nate's eyes narrowed at Sinclair as the man rose from his chair. A stab of betrayal pierced him. "*You've* played a role in this?"

"Mother is hoping for better relations between you and our family," Sinclair admitted. "She's hoping you and I can make amends." He paused. "I'm hoping for it as well."

Nate clenched his hands into fists. When his mother found herself with child, she had no choice but to flee. Only the lie of being a widow and the kindness of distant relatives had saved them. Even then, their existence had been hand-to-mouth on a maid's salary that was barely enough to put food in their bellies and clothes on their backs.

And now the Sinclairs wanted to *make amends*?

"It's too late for that," he bit out. Twenty-seven years too late.

"No," she corrected quickly, almost desperately. "I don't believe that. I've—I've been trying for seven years." Her voice grew so soft that he could barely hear her. "You just didn't know..."

Seven years? Nate had known about the Sinclairs for over a decade. At fifteen, he'd accidentally discovered that his real father was the Earl of St James. That fact had made no difference to him then, and it made no difference to him now. But how could the countess have been trying for seven years? Seven years ago, he'd just entered the army and was happily headed to... *Christ.*

The world shifted beneath his feet, and Nate held his breath, waiting for the earth to crack open and plunge him into the fires of hell.

Except that he was already there.

"When the earl died, I was able to give money to your mother," the countess admitted, her voice trembling. She reached out with far too much familiarity to touch the red sleeve of his uniform, and it was all he could do not to yank his arm away. "She used it to buy your commission, and Lady Agnes called on her acquaintances in the War Office to have you become part of the First Dragoons." She guiltily dropped her gaze to the table, where none of the food or tea had been touched. "It wasn't much, but it was all we could do at the time," she explained quickly as if desperate to soften the blow of the news. "Now, we can do more, if you'll let us. All it takes is a first step." She gestured at the table in futile hope of convincing him to rejoin her and finish the tea.

But Nate was done here. For good.

When he didn't return to his chair, she admitted softly, "I cannot make up for all the years that you and your mother were wronged by what my husband did, but I'd hoped—"

"Is that what you think happened to us?" Nate let out a bitter laugh. "We were wronged?"

She flinched at the venom in his voice, but he didn't care any longer if he upset her. *Wronged* didn't begin to describe the hell his mother had gone through.

Isabel Sinclair bravely answered his accusation. "In terrible ways that I cannot even begin to imagine or deign to think that I could ever put right. Yet I want to try, if you'll let me."

Never. He threw his napkin onto the table and spun on his heel to leave. "Good day, Countess."

"You had tea with Agnes yesterday," she called out quickly. "That's what gave me the idea to invite you this afternoon. I only wanted to try to..." When he walked on, she blurted out, "I was jealous of Agnes."

Nate stopped in his tracks. Jealous? She couldn't be serious!

"She said she had a marvelous time in your company."

It wasn't his company; it was the whiskey. Still... He faced her. "Lady Agnes is a good woman," he admitted grudgingly.

"I think—" She drew a tremulous breath and tried again. "I think you'll find we're all good people if you give us the chance to prove ourselves." She took a hesitant step toward him. "That's all I ask. If we could make an effort to be friendly to each other. Then maybe someday you'll let us officially welcome you as part of the Sinclair family."

"No," he firmly refused. Did they think him mad? Or so easily won over by the potential trappings of being part of a society family? He wanted none of it.

Tears of grief and pain formed at her lashes. "My husband was a terrible man, and what he did to your mother…" Her voice choked. She shook her head, for a moment unable to speak before continuing. "I cannot change the past, but we *can* change the future." She took another step forward, and then another, and she slowly closed the gap between them. "I'd like to try, at least, if you can find it in your heart to stop hating us."

"I don't hate you." In fact, in his whole life, he'd given the Sinclairs as little thought as possible. "I simply want nothing to do with you." He gazed over her shoulder at Sinclair to make certain he understood as well. "I don't need your name, your money, or your influence." His eyes dropped back to the countess. "I don't want any of it."

"Then you want no sister as well?"

He whirled at the sound of the soft voice behind him.

Lady Elizabeth Sinclair stood by the terrace steps from where she'd been listening to their argument. A look of grief darkened her face that he simply couldn't fathom.

A sister. He couldn't answer, not with so much anger

coursing through him. Lady Elizabeth was an innocent in this mess, just as he was, and she didn't deserve to be hurt. Yet she was still a Sinclair.

Without another word, he walked from the garden toward the front of the house and called out for the groom to bring his horse. He was leaving. Now.

"Wait!" Footsteps ran after him on the gravel. "Captain Reed!"

Drawing a ragged breath of long-suffering patience, he braced himself as he faced Lady Elizabeth.

The troublesome gel ran straight for him, flung herself against him, and wrapped both arms around his neck in a tight hug.

Nate froze, his arms sticking out straight from his sides. *Good Lord*, were all the women in this family as mad as hatters?

"Lady Elizabeth, I simply want to—"

"Beth," she insisted. "My family calls me Beth, and like it or not, Nate, you are family."

Was he supposed to take that as a compliment or a warning? Yet he raised his hand briefly to her back to return the unexpected embrace before setting her away.

"I'd love to have another brother. Frankly, I'm tired of the one I already have," she teased, but he knew her joking was to cover her nervousness. None of the Sinclairs were comfortable around him, and he sure as hell wasn't at ease around them. But it was hard to be angry when she smiled at him with such clear longing for acceptance. "It would be nice to have someone on my side in family arguments for a change."

When he didn't immediately respond, she threw her arms around him to hug him again.

Then, she rose up onto tiptoes and whispered into his ear, "Please reconsider your feelings for us. It isn't any of our faults that our father was a monster. He took away so much from so many people... Don't let him take you away from us, too."

She placed an impetuous kiss to his cheek and dashed away, back to the garden where her real family waited.

Ten

NATE STOPPED IN FRONT OF THE MOUNTAINOUS MAN guarding the front door of Viscount Chilton's Piccadilly town house. Music and laughter poured out into the night from the party already underway inside. With a frown beneath the papier-mâché demi mask that covered the upper half of his face, he handed over the white card bearing only tonight's date. The viscount's personal insignia embossed the corner.

"I'm a guest of Lady Flame," he told the footman and failed to keep the wry sarcasm from his voice.

The man examined the card carefully, then handed it back and stepped aside to let Nate pass. "Enjoy your evening, Lord Panther."

Nate gritted his teeth at that bit of nonsense and entered the house.

He followed the strains of music as he moved through the house toward the ballroom and the heart of the salacious gathering, letting the sounds and sights of the very private party engulf him. Like him, everyone inside the house wore masks and costumes to hide their identities. One glance at the ballroom explained why.

Masked men danced front against front with women in tightly fitted dresses whose necklines plunged so low they almost revealed their nipples. Both men and women held glasses of whiskey, brandy, and champagne that were constantly being refilled by a small army of footmen circulating through the room. Musicians played from the minstrels' balcony, but no one seemed to notice the music as each couple moved to their own scandalous rhythms. As one couple circled past, the man's hand slipped down his partner's back to cup her buttock.

Three sets of French doors stood open wide to the gardens beyond the ballroom. Dark beneath the moonless night, the pathways wound through the bushes and trees, and couples moved unhindered between the house and the gardens. The night breeze gave respite from the smoke of the dim chandeliers and the heat of the bodies crowding into the house and stirred the curtains of a series of alcoves lining the far end of the room. One curtain billowed open and gave a fleeting glimpse of a finely dressed man leaning against the wall and a woman disguised as a butterfly kneeling in front of him. Her antennae fluttered with each bob of her head at his crotch.

The room was a sea of jewels and satins, glitter and sequins, and long stretches of bare flesh, all shining and shimmering in the lamplight. A masquerade of costumes of all kinds and shapes paraded past, and both men and women exploited the secrecy to engage in pleasures they'd never dare attempt at a proper society ball.

Not at all happy to be here, Nate walked into the ballroom and snagged a glass of cognac from the tray of a passing footman. He lifted it to his lips and ignored the lascivious stares of a group of women standing near the stairs as he circled the room.

A ginger-haired siren placed her thumb in her mouth and

sucked suggestively as he passed. When he only politely bowed his head at her without stopping, she drunkenly giggled and teetered on her slippers.

Blowing out an irritated breath, he scanned the room. Somewhere in this debauchery was Sydney Rowland. The sooner he found her, the sooner he could leave.

A small box had arrived for him that morning at the barracks, delivered by Sydney's stable boy. Nate had recognized the lad only because he wore the same clothes she'd donned for her midnight visit three nights ago, and the preposterous yet wholly luscious way she'd looked in those clothes had been seared into his mind. No note accompanied the box, only a strange invitation with the words *Guest of Lady Flame* scribbled across the bottom and the panther mask he now wore. A private message, certainly.

But he had no idea why she'd sent it and certainly no idea why she'd picked this place to bring him to. If she were playing games with him—

He froze. *Sydney.*

The baroness stood by the open French doors. The soft night air stirred around her long legs the flowing skirt of a red satin dress, one cut daringly low across her full breasts, which were thrust high by the tight Spanish-style bodice. Long gloves in the same red satin commanded his gaze up her arms to the smooth skin of her shoulders, bare except for two thin straps of ribbon. Her sable hair was swept up high to show off her elegant neck, and her sensuous lips were painted nearly as red as her dress. Like all the other women, she wore a mask to hide her identity.

Yet even with that mask, he recognized her. Only Sydney Rowland possessed the confidence to wear such a daringly risqué dress and the beauty to shine so brilliantly in it.

But it was how she shimmered in the candlelight that captured his imagination and had him staring shamelessly. How the rubies at her throat and earlobes resembled smoldering coals. How the traces of gold dust brushed across stretches of bare skin appeared as if flames were flaring up from her flesh and down into the valley between her breasts.

Lady Flame...a siren of fire and brimstone. In all his life, he'd never seen another woman like her.

As he approached, she smiled and held out her gloved hand. He lifted it to his lips, unable to resist placing a delicate kiss in her palm. "Lady Flame."

"My Lord Panther," she returned on a throaty breath, and the husky purr of her voice heated through him.

For a moment, he could do nothing more than stare, mesmerized. She was a female devil in red satin come to take his soul, and God help him, he nearly handed it right over in exchange for possessing her for the night. Her fire would consume him, but the burn would be exquisite.

Her lips curled into a tight smile, and she placed her hand on his arm. "Shall we dance, my lord?"

"It would be my pleasure." And sheer torment.

She led him toward the dance floor. He went willingly under her siren's song, and each movement of her hips beneath the shimmering light of the chandeliers seemed to spark a fire in her wake.

He took her into position and held her much closer than he

should have, but compared to the other couples on the dance floor, no one would have noticed. Her gloved fingers folded warmly over his left hand, and his right pressed at the small of her back as he stepped her into the wanton waltz swirling around them. They danced very differently from the balls he'd been forced to attend over the years, when his presence had been required to partner with prim generals' daughters whom he'd held at arm's length. In this dance, propriety mattered nothing, and Sydney's breasts brushed tantalizingly against his chest each time he turned her through their steps. He breathed in the scent of her, an exotic perfume of orange and spice that filled his senses, and an ache of longing shot through him down to the tip of his cock.

God help him, he wanted her, and if she wasn't careful with the sway of her hips against his, she'd soon discover exactly how much.

"I wasn't certain if you would understand my message to come here tonight," she told him, barely louder than the soft strains of the violins and cellos so she wouldn't be overhead. "But I'm very glad you're here."

"Are you?" He shifted away from her to put more distance between them before he forgot himself and pulled her into an alcove. That dress, her scent, the heat of her body seeping through the satin material—everything about her made him long to lift her skirt and pin her against the wall, to have her thighs spread wide and shaking around him as he stroked into her. He knew she'd take away the loneliness and longing that plagued him.

But she would never be able to dissolve the guilt that

would follow. That alone fueled his resolve to resist, no matter how much he wanted to succumb.

"I know when to resign the offensive and call in reinforcements," she commented.

"Which am I—the offensive or the reinforcements?"

"That depends." She slid him a testing glance from behind her mask. "Am I still the enemy or an ally?" She turned her face away and murmured, "And know that I've already accepted that we'll never be comrades in arms."

His mouth tightened with chagrin. Only the baroness could frame his rejection of her as a military strategy. "Sydney—"

"Lady Flame." She stepped forward and gave him no choice but to increase his close hold of her. "And tonight, you're Lord Panther." They continued their scandalous waltz with his arm wrapped around her waist and her fingers teasing at his collar. Each brush of her fingers through his hair sent an electric spark twirling down his spine. "Real names are never used here. Too many scandalous activities will happen here tonight. Revealing yourself to the wrong person could very well ruin your life."

He glanced over her shoulder at the other couples dancing around them and those sitting at the tables edging the room. Their interactions grew increasingly bolder as the evening went on, with more of them wandering off into the gardens, up the stairs to rooms on the upper floors, or into the alcoves. The ginger-haired woman who'd giggled at him now stood with a man in a lion's mask whose hand openly caressed her breast as they talked in the dimly lit corner.

Nate frowned at Sydney. Her oval face was upturned toward his, beautiful even with the mask hiding nearly everything but those gleaming green eyes and her full red lips. "What kind of party is this?"

"One of Viscount Chilton's private ones. Right now, it's a masquerade." She reached up to run a fingertip along his temple and down to the black whiskers curling out from beside the triangular-shaped nose of his panther mask. The casual touch wasn't meant for him, he knew, but for anyone who might be watching. "By dawn, it will be an orgy."

He halted, and the other couples danced on around them. Was this the kind of place Sydney frequented? "You've been to one of these before, then."

"No." She dropped her hand to his shoulder and turned her face away. "But my late husband was a frequent guest. Rowland enjoyed trying to shock me with stories of what he did here."

Good Lord...what kind of marriage had she had?

"Dance with me," she cajoled and swayed her hips against his. "People are watching, and we need to blend in."

Nate had no intention of blending into this crowd. For God's sake, a man at the rear table was stroking his hand beneath a woman's skirt as she perched on his lap.

But he did as Sydney instructed and once again pulled her close, once again leading her through the scandalous waltz. In truth, he was a terrible dancer, but he no longer cared if he bungled his steps, not with the way she pressed herself against him. One slender arm wrapped around his neck to hold her close, and the closeness gave him lovely views down her dress—views any other man would have shamelessly taken.

He fixed his eyes on her emerald-green ones to keep his gaze from straying lower. "I don't think you're blending in, Lady Flame."

She could have worn a burlap sack and she still would have been the most beautiful woman in the room. But in that tight red satin, shimmering like the flames of a wildfire…

He grimaced. "You're simply stunning."

"Such a pained compliment." She gave a soft laugh, which only grew his consternation. "You sound downright aggrieved about my appearance."

He was. The fact that she was so damned alluring wasn't helping him keep his focus on his mission or his thoughts on anything but ravishing her.

She gave him a flirtatious smile that only added to his frustration. "Next time, I'll dress as a washerwoman in rags if that makes you more comfortable, my lord."

"I am not your lord." He wasn't anyone's lord and never would be. Bastard sons weren't let into the club of the aristocracy.

"Tonight, you are." In gentle correction, she outlined his frown with her fingertip, as if attempting to ease his irritation and help him to relax in this den of wolves. Despite being nothing more than pretense, her touch was electric. "As far as everyone here is concerned, you're just another aristocrat attending a private party, one whom I find attractive enough to dance with."

He dropped a slow glance down her front. "That's why you wore this costume, then, because you wanted to blend in?"

She smiled at his sarcasm. "With all these people here, I had to make certain you noticed me."

"Oh, I noticed," he murmured. When he'd walked into the ballroom and saw her, a bolt of lightning had slammed through the back of his skull.

"Good, because it wouldn't have done to have you mistakenly dance with another woman tonight." She rested her hand on his chest. "Or me with another man."

His arms tightened around her. Wild horses couldn't have ripped her away to put her into the arms of another, not with the warmth of her body heating into him. Not with her fingers curling possessively into his chest as if she, too, didn't want to let go tonight. Eventually, he would have to release her, but for now, he could enjoy having her close.

He asked, "Why am I here?"

"Because I need you."

Obviously, she didn't mean that as it sounded. Yet the temptation of her soft words spun inside his head and tormented him as much as her body as she swayed in his arms in half time to the music. He forced himself to concentrate on something other than the soft press of her breasts against his chest and the brush of her thighs against his. The curtained alcoves and the privacy they promised were too damned close.

He wanted her with a primal need he'd never felt for another woman. Not even Sarah. It wasn't love; he held no delusions that what he felt for Sydney was anything more than lust. Yet the hot longing in his gut left him craving to taste her spicy sweetness, to sink into her softness, and to feel her shudder around him in release.

But to cast aside his vows to Sarah... How would he live with himself?

She rested her cheek against his to bring her lips close to his ear. Her ripe body electrified his flesh everywhere it touched along the front of his. "Tell me...did you really save all those women and children at Amiens?"

His heart skipped. How the hell did she know about that? Only a handful of men knew what happened that day, most of them lost in other battles, and only he knew the truth. He hadn't found those women and children because he'd been searching for innocents in that farmhouse. He'd stumbled across them while racing toward the enemy artillery with the reckless disregard for his own life that he'd possessed since Sarah died.

"Nate?" She brushed her lips along his jaw. "Did you?"

"Yes." But in truth, they'd saved him because that was the day he'd started living again, redeeming himself with every woman and child he rescued. He could never absolve himself completely for failing Sarah, he knew that. But each woman who kissed his cheeks and thanked him for saving her life eased the guilt a little more and made him realize that life went on even after horrible death and loss, even if the pain would always remain.

"Then I know you'll save me, too," she whispered. "I need your protection tonight. A great deal."

When she pulled back from him, her lips fluttered lightly over his. His heart skipped, not at the fleeting kiss but at the fear in her eyes. "What's happened?"

"The blackmailers have given me another chore."

Another chore...and another attempt for him to find the men who were using her as their pawn. "What is it?"

She shook her head as the music ended and the dancing stopped.

"Perhaps we can continue this conversation upstairs," she offered loudly so that the couples around them overheard. Another part of the pretense, as if he'd propositioned her and she was consenting. "In private."

Stepping out of his arms, she raised his hand to her lips and kissed his fingers, then placed his hand over her breast.

He inhaled sharply. Her gesture was nothing more than show to anyone who might be watching, a touch that paled in comparison to what others were doing around them, yet the feel of her still burned him. God help him, he didn't pull away.

Sydney leaned up to touch her lips to his. "Upstairs, first floor, last room on the left," she murmured. "Follow me."

With one last caress of her fingers across his cheek, she slipped away and left him standing there. She glided up the marble stairs. When she reached the first-floor landing, she paused to glance over her shoulder invitingly at him before disappearing down the hall.

Nate stared after her and did his best to control his spiking pulse and the hot hum of his blood surging through his body. *Dear Lord.* If that encounter had been only for show, God help him if she ever decided to truly seduce him.

He dragged in a deep, jerking breath and followed.

Eleven

SYDNEY NERVOUSLY CAUGHT HER BREATH AS THE DOOR opened and Nate stepped into the dimly lit sitting room.

"What trouble are you stirring up tonight, Baroness?" He closed the door and threw the lock, which spiked her nervousness even higher. Then he stalked toward her, and each step reminded her of the lithe, dangerous panther his mask portrayed.

Fitting, then, because Sydney suddenly felt like prey. "None of my own making, I assure you."

"Explain yourself." He stopped in front of her.

She trembled with equal parts arousal and wariness. "Another messenger came by the house this morning. I've been ordered to deliver a message at tonight's party."

He removed his mask and revealed his handsome face, the strong cheekbones she'd come to know well, and the troubled frown of his brow she'd come to know *too* well. "Another boy?"

She nodded. "He had a memorized message for me and no idea of the name of the man who'd paid him to deliver it, just as before."

Nate gave a disbelieving shake of his head. "Impossible. I had a guard watching your house this morning. He reported nothing to me about another messenger."

"Then you need to find a new guard." Whoever watched over her was either incompetent or could no longer be trusted, and Sydney feared she knew which. From the way Nate stiffened, so did he. "The boy handed me an invitation to tonight's party and a message to deliver to General James Braxton." She hated showing any weakness, yet she admitted, "I had no choice but to come tonight, and I wanted you here with me."

"To protect you."

"Yes." She lowered her voice to a whisper although no one could overhear. "This chore frightens me."

His hard expression softened with concern. "What's the message?"

She placed her foot on the seat of a nearby chair and slowly lifted her skirt to bare her left thigh. The heat of his gaze raked across her flesh, and she did her best to ignore it even if she couldn't stop the soft tremble that rippled through her in its wake.

"This." She nodded at the folded piece of paper she'd tucked beneath the garter of her red stocking.

He slowly reached for it. Her breath hitched when his fingers brushed against her thigh as he pulled it free.

"When I deliver it, I'm to tell the general…Bois Saint-Louis." She dropped her skirt back into place. "What is that note? What does it all mean?"

He unfolded the message and scanned it. "A quartermaster's request," he murmured, "for explosives to be delivered to a warehouse in St Giles at dawn. *Lots* of explosives. Enough to blow up a building."

Fear curled down her spine, and she reached for the

back of the chair to steady herself. "And the other part of the message—Bois Saint-Louis? Was it a battle in France?"

"Not that I know of. But there were hundreds of skirmishes across the continent. It could refer to anything." His eyes raised slowly to hers. "Whatever it means, though, it's the next piece of blackmail."

Confusion mixed with her fear. "Pardon?"

"Braxton would face court-martial if he were caught providing these supplies to known revolutionaries. He'd only cooperate if he had no choice, if the secret he's keeping is so ruinous that he'd rather risk the gallows than have it discovered." He refolded the note. "How well do you know the general?"

She shook her head. "Only in passing."

"Yet Scepter knew he'd be here tonight."

Taking extreme liberties, Nate knelt in front of her and slid her skirt up to midthigh. A sharp inhalation crossed her trembling lips when his fingers brushed against her bare leg as he returned the folded paper to her garter.

When Nate withdrew his hand, his fingers caressed along her thigh before he dropped her skirt and stood. She fought to keep herself from shamelessly begging Nate to put his hand back on her thigh.

She cleared her throat in order to continue as evenly as possible. "Braxton has a certain reputation for being a libertine. The anonymity of a masquerade would appeal to him, especially one like this. If Scepter suspected his name would be on the guest list, it would be easy to confirm."

"How will you find him if he's in costume?"

"The general sports a very rotund figure." A sly smile

teased at her lips. "I spotted him earlier with a woman dressed as Lady Swan to his Lord Peacock."

"Thank you."

Warmth blossomed inside her. "For finally trusting you?"

He quirked a brow. "For not dressing me as a peacock."

She laughed, and her shoulders relaxed as her fear eased. The notion was absurd. How could Nate be anything but the dark panther she imagined him to be?

Thank God he was here. She didn't know how she would have survived the night without him. An increasingly warm, tingling part of her hoped he would be with her until dawn.

"Happy to oblige." She added with a wink from behind her mask, "My Lord Panther."

She turned toward the door. Without warning, he swept her up in his arms. He dropped into the chair and brought her down with him across his lap.

She gasped in surprise, then struggled to catch her breath against the thumping of her heart.

"What would make *me* happy, Baroness, is to be told the truth." He untied her mask and let it fall to her lap. "Now."

The sudden arousal that had sped through her only heartbeats before vanished. Suddenly, she felt trapped. "I told you everything." She struggled to push herself away, but her feet couldn't find purchase against the floor. The toes of her slippers barely touched the rug, and she could do nothing more than wiggle futilely on his lap. "A boy came to the house—"

"No." His arm went around her waist to hold her in place. "The secret you're keeping. What is Scepter using to make you risk your life like this?"

"Let me up, please." He wanted to know about Robert, and from the resolute expression on his face, he wasn't letting her go until she told him. But she would *never* share that secret.

"Not until you tell me."

"Then I'll scream."

"Go ahead." He shrugged. "Anyone who hears will just think we're enjoying ourselves."

Gaping at his audacity, she shoved at him, and he grabbed her hand. He leaned over her, putting her further off-balance until she had no choice but to wrap her free arm around his neck to keep from tumbling backward onto the floor. "Let me go, Captain!"

"Lord Panther," he corrected, deadpan.

Anger flared inside her, flamed by her desperation to keep Robert safe. "Why, you arrogant, pompous—"

"Tell me your secret, Baroness." He trailed his fingers down her neck to her low-cut neckline, which rose and fell rapidly with her quickening breaths. "What are they using to blackmail you?"

He drew slow circles through the gold dust she'd powdered at her cleavage to make her skin shimmer like fire in the candlelight. It had been the last touch to her costume, one she'd applied in hopes of gaining his attention. Now she certainly had it, but for all the wrong reasons.

The man was infuriating, maddening, exasperating to the last thread of her patience—

His finger stroked down into the valley between her breasts, and her breath choked. Immediately, she stopped her struggling and stilled in his arms as a familiar longing tightened between her thighs.

"I can't help you unless you confide in me," he cajoled as gently as his fingertips caressed the swells of her breasts.

"I won't tell you." But her husky whisper undercut all resolve in her answer.

"I think you're afraid to tell me," he murmured and traced a circle in the gold dust, "because it might be your secret you're keeping, but it isn't yourself you're protecting, is it?"

Her heart pounded so fiercely that she was certain he could feel it racing beneath his fingertips. "I don't know what you mean."

With a wry smile at her blatant lie, he pushed the satin ribbon strap off her shoulder and down her upper arm, baring her right shoulder.

"At first, I thought your secret involved Michael Berkley." His voice grew hoarse as he drew over her shoulder with his fingertip and left a trail of gold across her skin in its wake. "But you were engaged to him publicly, and his death wasn't suspicious. No secrets there."

None that Nate would ever discover. "Michael died a long time ago."

"I know," he said quietly. His compassion for her was evident in his gentle caress of her shoulder.

Her arm tightened around his neck as her body arched traitorously toward him. She should run away from him as fast as her slippered feet would take her, yet she couldn't find the willpower. Not when goose bumps sprang up across her skin beneath his tantalizing caresses. Not when he stared down at her cleavage with the haunted look of a starving man.

Shamelessly, she wanted to let him devour her.

"Then I thought it was something about your late husband," he mused. "But you never loved him, did you?"

When he pushed the ribbon off her other shoulder, his palm brushed lightly down her arm, and a shiver followed after. He was undressing her, one tiny piece at a time, and she wanted him to keep going until she was naked in his arms.

"If not enough to properly mourn his death"—his hand returned to the valley between her breasts and drew a rasping inhalation from her—"then certainly not enough to keep secret anything that might endanger his reputation, even in the grave."

"No," she admitted. "I hated that man, and he hated me."

He stilled at her confession, but except for a flick of his eyes up to hers, he registered no surprise at her brutal honesty. For a moment, she thought he wanted further explanation about Rowland and their farce of a marriage. Instead, he leaned forward and placed a soft kiss on her shoulder.

Somehow both arousing and unexpectedly soothing, his kiss stirred an aching warmth inside her that she couldn't deny and that she didn't want to stop. She closed her eyes beneath the lingering caress of his mouth as it swept back and forth across her bare shoulder. The delicious sensation of this featherlight tease sparked through her and made her tremble.

Yet even now she felt the distance between them and recognized the fine line he trod between wanting her and keeping his desire in check. He was caressing her because it was only a fleeting touch, she knew, and kissing her because it was only a taste of the feast he wouldn't let himself enjoy. Joining his body with hers was a far cry from this.

Frustration burned through her. She didn't want him to hold back. She wanted his hands to caress her entire body and his mouth to lick over every inch of her. Sweet heavens, she wanted him to pull down her bodice and kiss her breasts the same way he was kissing her shoulder.

"But there was another man," he murmured against her skin. When he lifted his head, she whimpered at the loss of his mouth, unable to suppress the sound of her desire for him. "The lover you took after your husband died."

Her eyes flew open in sudden bewilderment, and she blinked at his dark expression as he waited for her to confirm his suspicions. Her...*lover?*

"Is he the one you're protecting?"

"He wasn't my lover." *Lover* implied a relationship, ongoing meetings, and happy times shared. He'd been nothing like that. "He was..."

A mistake.

At that moment, she couldn't remember a second of being in that other man's arms. All she knew was Nate, the wonderful feel of his mouth against her and the undeniable feeling of being protected and safe.

She gave an awkward laugh and caressed her hand against his cheek to encourage him to keep kissing her. And to stop interrogating her. "He wasn't what you think."

"What I think, Baroness, is that Scepter is using that man to manipulate you." He took her hand and lowered it.

"The thug at your house was there to warn you to keep your silence or Scepter would harm Robert."

Robert. Her body flashed numb, and she would have fallen off his lap if not for the tightening of his arm against the small of her back to hold her in place.

"That's why you're helping them, isn't it?" he pressed. "That's the leverage they're holding over your head. They've threatened your lover."

Oh, he was wrong! So very, very wrong… But Sydney couldn't correct him, because as long as Nate believed that, then her secret was still hers. Everything she did now was to keep Robert safe. Her own life mattered nothing.

She dodged in a breathless whisper, "They've threatened Robert's life in all the messages they've sent." Guilt stabbed her for her lie of omission to Nate, yet she had no choice. "I will do whatever I have to in order to protect him, including delivering that message to General Braxton."

"No, you won't." He shifted away from her, and his back drew up ramrod straight. A coldness settled over him as he carefully pulled the satin ribbons back into place over her shoulders and signaled an end to his kisses. "I won't let you put yourself at risk."

Disappointment panged inside her. Well, wasn't that just like the Nate Reed she'd come to know—still protecting her even as he pushed her away?

She did her best to keep the frustration of this new rejection from registering on her face. "If you are correct that it's Scepter who's been blackmailing me, then its men are waiting for me to deliver that message. If I don't approach the general tonight, they'll know something's wrong. They'll think I've betrayed them."

"I'll protect you."

A tormented laugh tore from her. "You can't! They've already warned me to keep away from you. If they discover that I told you about this, that you didn't let me deliver the message—" She forced out past the knot of fear choking her throat, "They'll kill you, too."

With a reassuring smile that did little to put her at ease, he lifted her hand to his lips and placed a kiss on her palm. "I won't let them." Then he set her onto her feet and stood. "I want you to go home where you'll be safe. I'll have my men waiting in St Giles to arrest Scepter when they come to collect the explosives from Braxton. There's no need for you to speak to the general."

Her fingers closed around her gold locket, and she drew from it the strength to defy him. "Have your men waiting, but I *will* deliver that message to Braxton tonight. If I don't, Scepter will kill Robert just as they killed Henry Everett. I will never put him at risk."

With shaking fingers, she picked up his discarded mask and handed it to him.

"As soon as I deliver this last message, then I'll be useless to them." *And to you...* "They'll have no reason to involve me again, and General Braxton will provide your next link in finding their leaders." Her voice trembled even as she assured him, "After tonight, you won't have to worry about me again."

Twelve

SYDNEY WAITED IN THE DARKNESS AT THE REAR OF THE gardens and did her best to ignore the dome-shaped rose bower at the end of the path under which General Braxton had disappeared about twenty minutes ago. Its wooden frame and thick growth that cascaded to the ground shook violently, yet the rustling leaves weren't loud enough to drown out the grunts and groans of sex coming from beneath its innocent flowers.

Thank God Nate wasn't here to overhear this. She couldn't have survived the embarrassment.

No, he was waiting in the ballroom where she'd left him. He would be less conspicuous there while she slipped into the garden to find the general and deliver the message. But the women there leered at him as if hunting season were underway and he was their game.

Sydney twisted her mouth with a grimace and tapped her foot in impatient irritation, both at the shaking bower and at Nate. Certainly, a man that handsome would catch the attention of women, but she hadn't expected the way he'd turned so many female heads throughout the ballroom. Or the jealousy that pricked her when he nodded toward a foxed ginger-haired woman as if they were old friends.

She'd have to be a crazy goose to be jealous over Nate Reed, but she was exactly that.

She knew he wasn't hers. He'd only entered her life because he was determined to stop Scepter, and when that danger ended and his mission finished, he would leave her life just as easily as he'd entered it. Yet she found herself not wanting him to go.

A sharp, masculine curse of triumph bellowed from the bower. The branches and leaves shook violently, then suddenly fell still.

Two minutes later, a woman dressed as a swan emerged from beneath the bower. She paused to straighten her feathered bodice and beaked mask, then swept her hands over her mussed white gown. With a sashay in her step, she walked toward the house and the amusements inside. Her playtime in the garden was over.

Sydney's heart thudded as she waited unseen in the shadows for General Braxton's distinctly robust figure to duck out from beneath the cover of the bower. Wrinkles marred his bright blue-and-green waistcoat, his cravat hung loose around his neck, and the orange beak on his mask was askew. But he had more immediate concerns on his hands as he fumbled at his groin to fasten up the fall of his green trousers.

She pulled in a deep breath. The time to deliver her message had arrived. *Finally.* She stepped into the path and blocked Braxton's way.

The general halted. A quick curse crossed his lips before he glanced up and saw her. Then his mouth pulled into a lecherous grin as his eyes dropped blatantly to her breasts.

Sydney felt soiled from that look.

"My lady, good evening." He cast a glance up the path behind her into the darkness. "A beautiful woman shouldn't wander through this garden by herself. Good thing you found me to protect you." He licked his lips. "Or to entertain you in other ways."

Soiled…and sickened. She ignored the chill that shuddered down her spine and clung to her resolve to get through this as quickly as possible and to flee back to the ballroom and Nate's protection.

"I came looking for you, General."

"Lord Peacock," he corrected, his voice a low warning to keep his identity secret even though everyone knew exactly who he was.

"My lord." She gave a shallow curtsy of apology and loathed that she had to show him this undeserved deference. "Forgive my thoughtlessness."

He sniffed at her apology and stepped toward her to close the shadowy distance between them. "So you were searching for me, were you? And what service can I provide to you tonight, pretty?" He sent her a wide, greasy smile. "I am at your pleasure."

She would *never* be at his. "I have a note for you."

His eyes followed as she reached beneath her skirt to remove the folded paper and handed it to him. She was careful not to let his fingers brush against hers.

He frowned at the note.

"And a message to accompany it." Her heart pounded furiously as she whispered, "Bois Saint-Louis."

His eyes snapped up to hers. They were suddenly enraged

and glowing like brimstone behind his mask. He bared his teeth at her with the ferocity of a cornered animal and snarled, "What is the meaning of this?"

"I was asked to deliver that message to you." She retreated a step away from him. "That's all I know." Gooseflesh sprouted across her skin as a terrifying need to escape pulsed through her. A voice screamed inside her head to run... *Turn and run!* She took another step back. "Good evening, Lord—"

His hand shot out and grabbed her arm before she could flee. He jerked her hard against him and menacingly lowered his head toward hers. His breath fanned hot across her face. "What in the *hell* is this?"

Sydney shoved at him, but she couldn't budge him or yank her arm free from his iron grip. He reeked of whiskey and the dank musk of sweat and sex, and her stomach lurched with disgust and terror. "Let go of me!"

"Who are you?" He reached up to claw his fat fingers at her mask and tear it away.

She ducked her head. She couldn't let him see her face! If he knew who she was, she would be dead. Braxton would kill her himself for daring to blackmail him before Scepter had the chance.

He reached toward her again. She sank her teeth into his fingers, so deep she tasted the crunch of bone and flesh.

With a scream of pain, he wrenched his hand free from her mouth. Blood dripped down his hand. "Goddamn bitch!"

He slapped her. Her head snapped back, and a cry tore from her.

"Who sent you?" He shook her.

"I don't know!"

He raised his hand to strike her again—

"Let her go," a deep voice said calmly from behind her.

She glanced over her shoulder, and her heart leapt into her throat.

Nate.

He stood in the middle of the path only a few feet away. His black clothes and chestnut hair blended into the dark shadows. His right hand rested over the back of his left, and the muscles in his shoulders tensed beneath his jacket, ready to spring.

Braxton yanked her back to him as she tried to wrench her arm away. "This is none of your concern."

"Let her go."

"Piss off!"

Nate's eyes narrowed behind the mask with a look so murderous it stole her breath away.

"Let her go," he ground out through clenched teeth, "and I'll let you live."

Braxton laughed. As if taunting the panther, he squeezed her arm tighter until she cried out.

Nate lunged as he pulled a knife from his sleeve. He caught the general across the chin with his left fist and slashed with the knife in his right.

Braxton shoved Sydney toward Nate to use her body to block the knife.

But Nate was quicker. He grabbed her around the waist with one arm to break her fall and slide her protectively behind him while he brandished the knife with the other.

The sharp blade forced the general into the thorny branches of the bower.

"Stay away from her, you bastard," Nate snarled between gritted teeth and slowly backed away with Sydney behind him, one guarded step at a time. The knife glinted a warning in the faint moonlight. "If you come after her again, I'll gut you where you stand."

The general clenched his fists, but he wisely stayed where he was. "She and I aren't through with this."

"Oh yes, you are."

As they stepped backward up the dark path, Nate kept the knife in front of him, ready to kill Braxton if he made a move in their direction. The pounding of blood in her ears deafened her, and her lungs panted to catch her breath. All of her shook, terrified. Yet her grip on the back of his jacket remained as strong as a vise. She was desperate to keep in contact with him and assure herself that he wouldn't leave her.

They reached the spot where the path emptied into the lawn near the terrace. The general remained hidden in the darkness of the rear garden. Behind them at the house, the party had grown busier and louder with even more people crowded inside and spilling out onto the terrace where they might see the two of them. Nate slipped the knife back into the sheath hidden up his left sleeve. Then he took her hand and laced his fingers securely through hers.

He ordered, "Come on."

He led her inside the house and through the ballroom, forcing her to run to keep up with his long strides, but a man hurrying a woman from the room was such a common occurrence at the viscount's parties that they drew no attention. They raced through the grand doors of the ballroom's main entrance and out into the stair hall.

"That way!" She pointed toward the front door.

But Nate led her in the opposite direction. He hurried her down the hallway and into the first empty alcove they reached. He flung the curtain closed behind them, sealing them into shadowy darkness, then yanked off his mask to pull in deep breaths of air.

She sank back against the wall as her knees went boneless beneath her. Her hand pressed hard against her roiling stomach. Oh God—she was going to be sick!

He took her elbow to steady her. "Are you all right?"

"I'm fine." She choked out the lie even as a throbbing heat rose from her cheek where the general had struck her. To come so close to being seriously hurt, or worse—she shuddered.

Nate placed his hands on the wall on either side of her and rested his forehead against hers. He squeezed his eyes shut as his entire body shook, and he pulled in deep breaths to steady himself.

Fear and relief warred inside her. If he hadn't appeared when he did, if he hadn't been able to stop Braxton, if he hadn't understood her summons tonight and not arrived at the party at all… She owed him her life.

"Nate," she whispered. When he didn't answer, she cupped his face in her hands and leaned up to touch her lips to his, to soothe and comfort both of them.

A groan tore from his throat, and he hungrily devoured her simple kiss. He swallowed her gasp of surprise as his lips molded against hers and claimed her mouth with a fierce heat that left her weak and throbbing.

Her arms encircled his neck, and she surrendered to the need to be close to this brave man who left her quivering at all he represented. Not just the breathtaking masculinity of him even as his large body pressed hard into hers and pinned her against the wall until she moaned with surrender, but also the goodness in him and the pain she so desperately wanted to ease.

Her fingers dug into the soft hair at his nape to clench his short curls in her fist and pull his head down closer to her. Even now, with his arms sliding down her body to her waist, he still wasn't close enough. She increased the hungry ferocity of the kiss, then gasped with pleasured surprise when he yanked her hips forward against his.

Electricity sparked through her. This was what she'd wanted since the moment she saw him at Barton's, when she first suspected how exquisite being in his arms could be. Now that she was in them, she didn't want to stop.

With a whimpered invitation, she arched herself against him.

His tongue licked back and forth across the seam of her lips. She opened her mouth to welcome him, only for him to shove between her lips so quickly and greedily that she lost her breath. When she responded in kind and slid her tongue across his, his lips closed around hers and sucked. The sensation pulled up the heat from between her legs and flared it through her body, straight out the ends of her hair.

Never…*never* had she been kissed like this. And she never wanted it to stop.

Seemingly, neither did Nate. With one hand pressed at the small of her back to keep her hips tight against his, he slid the other up her side. He captured her breast and caressed her through her bodice until she moaned. But even that touch wasn't enough to satisfy the need growing inside her. She wanted him to touch her everywhere, run his mouth across every inch of her body, and leave wet, hot tingles in his wake.

God help her, she wanted him inside her, stroking her body with his and possessing her completely.

With a shaking hand, she reached down to raise her skirt. "Nate," she panted breathlessly, "touch me."

He stiffened. Then he lowered his hands and shifted away.

No! She threw an arm around his neck, desperate to keep him from leaving her and to keep his hands on her body and his mouth on hers. She needed him too much to let go. She hadn't felt this aroused since Michael—no, she'd *never* felt this alive, this electric, as she did with Nate. He made her want to shamelessly beg for the pleasures she knew only he was capable of giving her, pleasures in which they would both find comfort and release. If only they'd let themselves.

"I want you to touch me," she whispered, and his gaze fell to her mouth when her tongue darted out to lick her lips. "Please, Nate."

"I can't." His voice was a barely controlled rasp.

"Because the night we met you said you'd never accept a lady's pleasure in an alcove?" When she freed a button on his waistcoat, she thrilled at the tremor that pulsed through him. "I want you, and I don't care where it happens." Another button loosened…and another… She wanted to do far more to him than just make him tremble. "But I do plan on holding you to your promise."

Her hands opened his waistcoat, then drifted lower toward his trousers. His breath came ragged beneath her seeking fingers, but he made no move to stop her. "What promise was that?"

She smiled wickedly. "That it will last much longer than a few minutes."

When she caressed her lips against his jaw, she prayed he couldn't feel her nervousness. She never thought she'd have the courage to seduce a man like this, but with Nate, it came naturally. With him, she was free to be bold. Undressing him felt right and good. So very, *very* good…

"Baroness," he protested gently, "we have to stop."

She nibbled at the corner of his mouth and sighed at the taste of him. *Delicious.* "No, we don't."

"We can't." His hands tightened on her upper arms. "*I* can't."

She stilled. Confusion poured through her. She searched his face for answers but saw only the same heated desire she felt herself. "You don't want to touch me?"

"Of course I want to touch you," he growled with frustration.

"Then why won't you?"

"Because I won't stop with just a touch."

"Good," she purred with relief and leaned in to kiss him again, "because I don't want you to stop."

He held her away. In the shadows, she saw guilt darken

his face and shutter away the desire she'd seen there just heartbeats ago. But it wasn't guilt at taking her in an alcove instead of in a proper bed.

No, it was guilt over another woman. The one he refused to betray, even now.

Her shoulders slumped in defeat. He'd rejected her before, but this time was different. This time, she knew she'd never be able to win. Even if he surrendered to her, she might have his body, but that other woman possessed his heart. No matter what Sydney did now, no matter how hard she begged or pleaded or seduced…

She would lose.

She dropped her hands away from him and leaned back against the wall, careful not to touch him. If she did, she might just scream.

"I frustrate you, don't I?" She rasped out the terrible truth, "You want me, and yet you think you'll be betraying another woman by giving yourself to me."

She felt every muscle in his body tense even from a foot away. His eyes flickered darkly, and for a moment, she thought he wouldn't answer—

"Yes." The quiet admission tore from him.

And ripped straight through her. He might as well have stabbed her with his knife.

Trying not to let the pain of her shattering heart register on her face, she nodded slowly. "I should go home now. We're done here." She risked reaching out to fasten his waistcoat, which she'd rumpled earlier in her rush to undress him. "And you must go on to St Giles."

"Sydney." The plaintive sound of her name on his lips was a sweet torture. "Please understand. It isn't—"

"No," she interjected before he could say something else to hurt her. "I understand far better than you realize."

She secured the last button but lingered with her hand on his chest, smoothing over the black brocade. Even now she wanted to keep touching him, even as unshed tears stung her eyes.

Reluctantly, she pulled her fingers away.

Leaving him to conquer his own demons was the right thing to do. She knew that. But dear God, why did it have to hurt so much?

"I want you, Nate," she confessed. Her slender shoulders conceded the truth of that with a small shrug. "And you can have me."

An alcove, a horse stable, a carriage—she didn't care where because she desperately craved him, this man who set her world on fire.

Yet she wouldn't allow him to wound her again.

She dropped her hands away. "But I won't be second to any woman."

Thirteen

SYDNEY SAT WITH HER FEET TUCKED BENEATH HER AND watched the small fire in her bedroom fade into ashes as the hours drew on.

Outside, the dark sky had given way first to the purples and then to the blues of early dawn. Now even those last remnants had disappeared into the pinks and yellows of full sunrise as the sun peeked over the edge of London and completely banished the night. The city was waking around her, with maids beginning to stir in homes across Mayfair and delivery men and chimney sweeps making their way down familiar alleys.

Inside, though, Sydney couldn't find the energy to start her day or even to fall into bed to try for sleep. There was no point. Each time she tried to close her eyes, she saw Nate's face and the guilt he carried.

She'd removed the red satin costume as soon as she'd reached home, then bathed away the gold dust on her skin, replaced the gown with plain pastel muslin, and pulled her dark hair into a simple knot at her nape. She'd done everything she could to wipe away the empty fantasy of the evening and make herself as ordinary as possible—the complete antithesis of Lady Flame. Yet a part of her would always think of Nate as her Lord Panther and remember him dancing with her as if he thought she were the most beautiful woman in the world, coming to her rescue like a knight in shining armor, and kissing her as if he needed her as much as he needed air to breathe.

She couldn't slip away from those memories as easily as slipping out of a dress.

Now she sat in front of the fire and waited for a man who would never appear at her doorstep.

Her shoulders slumped. What a fool she was to cling to the hope that Nate would change his mind and seek her out! But she couldn't help herself. Yet as each hour slipped past, she realized he wasn't coming. And truly, why would he? He knew the place in St Giles where the gunpowder would be delivered, which meant he would be there to arrest the men who came to collect it. His mission would end, and he'd have no more need of her.

He'd blown into her life with the intensity of a summer storm but one that would prove heartbreakingly fleeting. When he was gone, just like rainwater soaking into the earth, no proof would exist that he'd ever been there at all.

But wasn't that what she wanted—a man who could satisfy her needs but not steal her independence?

What her *heart* wanted, however...

Well, that could never matter. To surrender her heart meant surrendering control, and she would never surrender control of her life again. Not to any man.

Not even to Nate.

A soft scratch at the door interrupted her thoughts. She

looked up as Mrs. Hodges slipped quietly into the room with a small tray in her hands and the morning *Times* tucked beneath her arm. The graying housekeeper had always been more attentive to Sydney than her own maid—for that matter, than her own mother. The woman usually greeted her in the drawing room where Sydney preferred to take breakfast. But this morning, Mrs. Hodges had somehow intuited that Sydney wasn't feeling up to breakfasting downstairs, just as she had known that Sydney was wide awake at dawn when she usually slept past ten.

"Good morning, Mrs. Hodges." Sydney's tired voice was drained from more than a simple lack of sleep.

"I had a feeling you might be up early this morning, my lady," the housekeeper explained as she set the food on the little table beside Sydney's chair. "So I brought up a tray in case you were peckish."

Sydney smiled faintly, more grateful than she would admit at the woman's kind lies. It was obvious from the still-made bed that she hadn't been to sleep at all let alone gotten up early. Likewise, Cook had piled enough food on the tray to feed a small army, as evidenced by the pot of chocolate, thick slices of warm toast, and fresh marmalade. Comfort food, all of it, right down to the small bowl of strawberries and cream—her favorite.

Her eyes stung at the kindness, and she hoarsely whispered, "Thank you."

"Of course, ma'am." Instead of leaving, though, Mrs. Hodges bent in front of the fireplace and set to stoking the banked coals even though starting the morning fire was not her responsibility. "You know, my lady, Danby and I realized last night that you hadn't been to the theatre lately. We thought you might want to know that Shakespeare is playing at the Drury Lane. *Measure for Measure.* We know it's one of your favorites."

"Indeed." She blinked away the blurriness in her eyes at her servants' concern. "Then perhaps I shall attend tonight."

Mrs. Hodges paused while poking aimlessly at the coals. "We've also noticed, ma'am, that recently you haven't done most of what you normally do. The theatre being just one."

A lump formed in Sydney's throat. What the housekeeper really wanted to know, without daring to ask, was if she was all right. The servants were worried about her, apparently, and Mrs. Hodges had been the one sent to inquire, using the theatre as a delicate excuse to tell her that everyone had noticed she wasn't behaving like herself.

"You and Danby are correct," Sydney admitted. "I have not been…enjoying the theatre of late as I normally do." She watched as the housekeeper rose to her feet and wiped her hands across her apron. "But I have a suspicion that I'll be a regular theatregoer again soon."

"Glad to hear it." Mrs. Hodges poured a cup of hot chocolate and frowned as she handed it to Sydney. "Although, if I might say so, without overstepping…" She took a deep breath and hurried on, heedless if she were truly overstepping or not. "I've been employed here now for two years, ever since Lord Rowland died."

"Yes." Sydney had replaced all of Rowland's servants immediately upon his death. She didn't want anyone around who had proven more loyal to her late husband than to her. "And I would be lost without you."

Mrs. Hodges's cheeks pinked. "You are kind to say so, ma'am." Without asking, she handed Sydney a napkin from the tray and a piece of toast, as if she were comforting a small child. "Me, Danby, and the others—we're grateful to work here. Very grateful." She paused. "We just worry sometimes. That is…we would be lost without you, too, ma'am."

Sydney stared down into her hot chocolate through tear-blurred eyes, afraid she might cry. "No need to worry about me. In fact, I'm beginning to feel like my old self already."

To prove it, she forced a smile, although she was certain it looked strained.

Mrs. Hodges relaxed her shoulders, visibly relieved that their small household would be back to normal again soon. "Shall I call for your maid?"

"No, let her sleep." After all, there was no reason to hurry with her morning routine. Not today.

"Very well." Mrs. Hodges retreated toward the door. "Enjoy your breakfast, my lady."

Enjoy your breakfast. Enjoy the theatre. Enjoy your life… How on earth was she supposed to do that when she had no idea any longer how to actually live?

"Mrs. Hodges?" Sydney asked suddenly. Her feet slipped to the floor as she sat up.

The housekeeper turned back. "Yes, ma'am?"

"Was there ever a Mr. Hodges?"

The housekeeper paused. It wasn't an odd question since

all housekeepers were addressed as Missus whether they'd married or not, but it *was* one that employers never asked.

"There was, my lady." She took a slow step back into the room. "My Paul. We were married for two decades before the Lord took him to heaven. We had a lovely child, too, to show for it."

A child... Sydney's fingers tightened around the cup. "A son?"

"A daughter named Lucy, ma'am. Beautiful and as stubborn as her father. She has her own wee ones now to fret over."

Sydney smiled wistfully. "It was a love match?"

"Very much. Both our families were surprised when Paulie asked for my hand. We'd grown up in the same village, and he'd spent every day pulling my braids and tormenting me. But he paid for it." She forced an exaggerated sigh, yet Sydney could hear the love in her voice. "He paid dearly every day for twenty years!"

Sydney laughed softly, then frowned into her chocolate. "Would you ever consider marrying again?"

"Oh no, my lady! Those days are over for me. But if I were young and lively again, like you, I would certainly consider it."

Sydney fixed her eyes on the cup. "But to surrender your life again to another's control..."

Mrs. Hodges snorted. "Says who?"

Sydney looked up in surprise. "Well, the law, for one. And the church."

"And in *my* opinion, neither one has any business governing my marriage!"

Sydney's eyes widened at the blasphemy of the

housekeeper's comment. Then she shook her head. If only it were that simple. "A husband would have the right to control me and all my property, to make all the decisions in my life, and to do as he pleased. Even if I gave him my heart, to give up my freedom like that..."

Her voice trailed off, and she briefly closed her eyes against the fear of losing herself, of once again being held captive like a bird in a cage.

"If he is the right man, my lady," Mrs. Hodges assured her gently, "you won't mind giving up control."

Sydney wasn't so certain.

"Although, if he is the *right* man," the housekeeper continued, "he won't try to control you in the first place."

If only she could believe that! "But how do you know if—"

The brass knocker pounded fiercely against the front door. Its booming reverberated through the silent house.

"Heavens!" Mrs. Hodges startled. "Who on earth could that be at such an early hour and knocking to wake the dead?"

Sydney knew. She jumped to her feet and ran from the room, down the stairs, and into the foyer. Although the kitchen maids would have been stirring downstairs, starting the first fires and preparing for breakfast, the house itself was still closed for the night, her butler and footmen still asleep. So she reached to throw the lock herself as she cast caution aside, grabbed the handle, and flung open the door—

Her heart stopped. "Nate."

But he wasn't alone. He stood with his arm around the neck of a young soldier and a pistol pointed at the man's head.

A blond man wearing all black stood just behind them. Like Nate, he possessed the same confident bearing, muscular build, and imperial air of a soldier. The stranger glanced over his shoulder and kept his hand beneath his jacket on the pistol Sydney suspected was hidden beneath.

But it was the sight of blood that tore a gasp from her. A deep gash bled from Nate's forearm as he pressed it against the soldier's neck. Another cut at his temple trickled blood down the side of his face.

Her hand flew up to her mouth. "Oh God, you're hurt!"

"Let us inside," he calmly ordered.

Nodding dumbly, she stepped aside to let all three men pass, then followed as they charged through the house. Nate peered into every room they passed. He finally decided on the dining room and pulled the soldier inside.

"What happened?" Sydney followed them into the room.

"The delivery went wrong." Nate shoved the soldier into a chair at the table and pointed the gun at his chest. "Your home was closer than the Armory."

"Armory? I don't understand."

"My lady, I heard the front door and—" Disheveled in his rush to dress and hurry from his room, her butler, Danby, halted in the doorway and stared at the scene in front of him. "What on earth…?"

"There's been an accident, but everything will be fine," she assured him, stepping in front of him and blocking his entrance. The last thing Nate needed was an anxious butler fussing over scuffmarks on the dining room floor. "Fetch hot water and some towels, quickly!" Her eyes flicked toward the blood seeping from Nate's arm into his jacket sleeve, and she pressed her hand against her sickening stomach. "Ask Mrs. Hodges to bring her sewing kit and Cook's jar of kitchen salve."

"And a length of rope," Nate added, his eyes never leaving the soldier at the end of his pistol.

Danby gaped, his mouth opening and closing like a fish's. The normally stoic butler was too shocked to move.

Sydney touched his arm to gain his attention. "Go— bring all of it. Quickly!"

Nodding, he scurried away and paused only to pull a half-dressed footman with him down the hallway toward the rear stairs.

Worry that Nate had once again recklessly endangered himself flared inside her, and she rounded on him. "What happened?"

He calmly threw a glance over his shoulder at the other man. "May I introduce you to Clayton Elliott? Clayton, this is Lady Rowland."

When no further explanation was given of the man's identity, she pressed in a low voice, "Who *is* he?"

"A friend." He turned his hazel eyes solemnly on her. "You can trust him with your life."

Mr. Elliott paused in checking the latches on the room's shutters only long enough to nod his head politely at her. "My lady."

"But this one—" Nate's eyes narrowed in contempt at the young soldier. "He's a traitor who put your life at risk. Didn't you, Baker?"

The soldier glared murderously at him. A black mark formed around his eye to go with the red bruise on his chin, and blood stained his uniform. She knew... *Nate's* blood.

Sydney's heart thudded. "What do you mean?"

"General Braxton's delivery in St Giles went wrong," Nate explained. "Someone told them to expect us, so Scepter's men were waiting there to ambush us when we arrived. Our soldiers put up a fight, but their men got away."

"How did they know you'd be there?" She glanced across the room at Mr. Elliott, wondering how much this man knew about Nate's mission and how freely she could speak in front of him. She lowered her voice. "You didn't even know until I told you at the party."

"It was my fault," Nate answered tightly. "I'd asked Baker to watch your house."

As cold understanding seeped through her, she shrank farther away from the young soldier. "He was watching the house when the boy arrived with the message for Braxton, wasn't he?" Her mouth was suddenly dry, yet a metallic taste of fear covered her tongue. "That's why you didn't know about it."

"He was also guarding you the morning I found that thug in your garden. He let that man through so he could threaten you in your own home."

The fierce shaking in her hands spread into the rest of her as she put all the pieces together. "He was the man in the horse stables, wasn't he?"

"Most likely."

She reached for the back of a nearby chair to steady

herself. "They didn't want you to know about the message to Braxton so you couldn't stop them."

He grimaced. "I wouldn't have known if you hadn't sent me the party invitation."

"I'm so sorry." Her throat tightened until her voice was barely a whisper.

Nate shook his head. "I should have known Scepter could get to anyone, even the Horse Guards."

Danby hurried into the room with a length of rope, several towels, and a jar of salve. Mrs. Hodges followed behind with a kettle of hot water in one hand and her sewing kit in the other.

Sydney straightened her spine. *Thank God.* She now had something to do to take her mind off the night's events.

"Put the hot water and towels over there." She pointed at the end of the table as she organized the two servants. "Mrs. Hodges, would you start up a fire? And, Danby, please bring the oil lamp from the entry hall. We'll need as much light as we can get."

"What are you doing?" Nate frowned at her as Mr. Elliott took the length of rope from Danby and set about tightly tying the soldier's hands together.

"You're hurt," she explained. Now that the soldier couldn't attack, she slowly removed the pistol from Nate's hand and very carefully laid it on the sideboard. Then she took his shoulders and steered him gently down into the chair at the head of the table. "Your wounds need to be dressed."

"And most likely sewed up," Mr. Elliott put in after one last hard tug on the rope to make certain Baker couldn't escape. "I'll do it."

Nate raised a hand to stop him from reaching for the sewing kit. "Lady Rowland will do it." He pinned Sydney beneath his grim gaze. "Won't you, Baroness?"

That was a challenge if ever she'd heard one. But she certainly wasn't going to back down, even if she had to bite her tongue to keep from blurting out her insistence to let Mr. Elliott do it. She'd never bandaged a wound in her life, never sewn up anything more than a loose hem at a ball. And now...skin. Her head swam with sudden dizziness, yet she couldn't refuse. The last thing she'd do was show any cowardice in front of him.

Even though she was certain she'd blanched white, she rasped out, "I will."

Mr. Elliott yanked Baker to his feet. "We'll be leaving, then." With a nod at Sydney and a hard look leveled at Nate, he pushed the soldier toward the door. "Send word through St James when you can. He'll know where to find me."

Nate nodded, and Mr. Elliott left the house, harshly shoving the soldier along with him.

Danby carried in the lamp and set it where Sydney directed at the end of the table. He turned up the wick until it blazed, and she quietly thanked him. Along with the bright fire, the lamp would cast enough light for her to clearly see Nate's wounds even with the shutters closed.

"Danby," Sydney called out as the butler and housekeeper began to slip from the room.

"Yes, my lady?"

"Double-check all the locks and shutters around the house." She solemnly met his concerned eyes. "Close the house to visitors. *No one* is allowed inside or out unless I give permission, including our own staff, and post pairs of footmen and the grooms outside the basement doors and those leading to the terrace to make certain no one slips in."

"Yes, ma'am."

She turned toward the housekeeper. "Mrs. Hodges, ask Cook to make up a breakfast tray for Captain Reed." Her eyes glanced down at Nate's bloody arm. *God's mercy*. She darted her gaze back to the two servants before she sickened herself from the sight of the wound and the mounting unease churning in her stomach at the thought of sewing it closed. "Bring a large pot of tea, please. Very hot and lots of it. And hurry with it."

"Aye, ma'am," Mrs. Hodges answered.

Danby closed the door after them, leaving her alone with Nate.

She fought to keep from wringing her hands. Now that orders were given and the household set into action, she didn't know what to do with herself. She faced Nate with a deep breath.

He dryly arched a brow. "Tea solves everything, does it?"

"Of course." She forced a haughty sniff despite her nervousness and pulled a chair up next to his, close enough to reach his arm. "We *are* English."

He laughed and accidentally jostled his arm. With a sharp gasp, he panted down the pain through clenched teeth.

"Here." She reached for his jacket lapels. "Let's take this off first."

He carefully shrugged his shoulders to help her remove the jacket.

Sydney froze at the sight of the bloodied shirtsleeve. A slash of a knife had ripped through the lawn. Beneath it, a long gash sliced down his forearm and bled bright red.

Oh, she could never do this! Already her hands shook, and she'd yet to touch him.

"Perhaps," she said as she started to rise, "we should call a surgeon."

With his good hand, he reached for her arm to stop her. "I trust you, Baroness. Besides, something tells me you'll be gentler."

"Don't count on it," she muttered as she sank back onto the chair.

His lips twitched. He nodded toward the sewing kit. "Let's get started then."

She opened the kit and stared inside. She was at a complete loss for what to do next. "I don't know…"

"Take the scissors," he explained calmly, "and cut off the sleeve above my elbow."

She did as instructed and cut through the cloth around his hard bicep, then carefully slid the sleeve down his arm. Blood had already dried into the lawn where the sleeve lay over the cut and almost glued the fabric into the wound. She gently worked it free, but fresh, bright blood sprang up in her wake. Beneath her fingertips, she felt every wince of pain and sharp inhalation he took through gritted teeth, each one a small slice into her heart.

"What happened to you?" she whispered, desperate to distract herself.

"One of the men had a knife," he explained evenly. "He was too fast, and I was too slow."

She glared at him. His self-deprecation was not humorous. He'd been in real danger, might very well have been much more seriously hurt or perhaps even killed, and now he was joking?

Her hands shook, and she pulled them back. "Nate—"

"Sydney, I will be fine," he interrupted. "I've had worse."

He'd had *worse*? "That's not reassuring."

"Makes *me* feel better," he mumbled.

Infuriating man! Her hands clenched into frustrated fists. He had no idea how much he'd frightened her tonight, how much she worried whenever he risked his life so recklessly—she could throttle him for it.

"Do you always put yourself into harm's way like this?" She ticked off on her fingers. "Leaping into my carriage the night we met, then the runaway landau, that man in the garden, General Braxton at the party—now this."

"It was all necessary."

"Well, stop doing it." *Stop endangering yourself! And stop terrifying me.*

"We're in the middle of this now. I have to do whatever it takes to finish the mission." He held her gaze intently as if he knew more than he was saying. "And to protect you." Apparently deciding that was enough explanation, he frowned down at his arm. "This is really nothing."

She didn't believe that for a second.

"You'll have to clean the cut before you stitch it," he explained quietly, bringing her attention back to the task.

Her stomach lurched at the idea, and she pressed her hand against her belly to calm herself before she cast up her accounts. Yet she gave a jerking nod and summoned her courage. She poured some hot water from the kettle into a bowl and soaked a towel in the water, then wrung it out.

He clenched his teeth as she carefully and methodically dabbed the towel against his forearm.

After several minutes, he nodded sharply. "That's good. Now sew it up."

She reluctantly reached for the needle and spool of thread from the sewing kit. This was going to hurt him. Terribly.

"I don't have any whiskey in the house to dull the pain," she said, delaying the inevitable. "I can send one of the footmen to—"

"Just sew it." He clenched his hand into a fist. "But no more stitches than necessary, all right?"

She bit her lip. The trust he placed in her—she trembled from the enormity of it. Yet the irony of their situation made her want to laugh because he didn't trust her enough to give himself to her, and she couldn't trust him enough to reveal her past. What a pair! Brave in facing physical pain, but cowards with pains of the heart.

Pushing her troubled thoughts away, she concentrated on the thread and needle. "That man who was with you... who is he?"

"General Clayton Elliott."

She shot him a no-nonsense glance. "Who *is* he?"

"Undersecretary for the Home Office."

"He's working with you to stop Scepter?"

"Yes."

"And St James? He mentioned the earl."

"He's my half brother."

His *brother*? Good Lord...

At her silence, he asked, "You didn't know?"

"No." She didn't look at him as she threaded the needle. "I'd heard vague rumors, but...what sane person believes society rumors?"

Yet now, having seen the two of them together, she no longer doubted the gossip. The two men resembled each other greatly, with both possessing the same eyes and hard jaws, the same broad shoulders, the same flaring tempers and confident posturing. They were far more alike than either man would admit.

She tied off the end of the thread as if preparing to do nothing more than fix a snagged bit of lace. "You're working together, too?"

"Not anymore. He was wounded when the Everett School burned down. Now he only gives advice." He muttered, "Lots and lots of unwanted advice."

A smile teased at her lips. Knowing St James as she did, she didn't doubt that. "Did you know about him before this?"

"Yes."

The single word was uttered with such finality she knew not to pry further, no matter how curious she was. So she nodded and bent over his arm to continue with her ghastly sewing.

Pressing together the two sides of the long gash with her fingers, she held her breath and pushed the needle through his skin. The resistance beneath the needle's point gave way with a sickening pop.

Nate flinched.

She froze, mid stitch.

"Go on," he ordered through clenched teeth. "I can take it if you can."

She swallowed. "I'm not certain I can."

"Oh yes, you can." His deep voice softened. "You're so much braver than you give yourself credit for."

She held his gaze for a moment, wishing she felt the courage he claimed he saw in her. Then she inhaled a deep breath, dropped her attention back to the wound, and slowly pulled the thread through to draw up the two sides of the cut.

He flinched with each pass of the needle and the careful tightening of the thread that bound the wound, but his stony face showed no emotion, his teeth clenched hard and his hands pulled into fists.

"I'm sorry," she breathed, so softly she wasn't certain he could hear her and uncertain herself for what exactly she was apologizing...the wound or prying into his past. But she knew she'd hurt him.

"It's nothing," he returned, yet his breathless whisper matched hers.

After an eternity of the grisly work, she finished the last stitch and tied off the thread, careful not to jostle his arm any more than she had to. His arm was whole again but scarlet with blood, already purple and blue, and swollen with bruising. She wiped away the remaining droplets of blood clinging to his skin and noticed how white his forearm was, how black the thread against it.

She applied the salve that Cook used to dull the pain of burns, then ripped away a long strip from one of the kitchen towels and wrapped it around his arm to protect the stitches and stop the bleeding from the needle pricks. She had nothing at hand to secure the bandage, so she reached beneath her skirt.

Nate watched her curiously as she pulled off the blue ribbon that held her stocking in place. It would be the perfect—if decidedly feminine—bandage tie. She wrapped the ribbon around his arm and tied it off with a knot.

Exhaling a long, deep sigh of relief, she lowered her hands away and sat back in her chair.

He inspected his arm. "Nicely done, Baroness."

She smiled faintly at that obvious lie. But the terrible ordeal was finished. *Thank heavens.* Only then did she realize that teardrops clung to her lashes.

She wiped them away with the back of her hand and reached for a clean towel to wet it in the hot water and gently wipe the blood away from the tiny cut at his temple. It wasn't deep or wide enough for stitches. *Thank God.* She didn't think she could survive sewing up a second wound. She reached for the jar of Cook's salve and smeared a dollop onto her fingertip.

"You'll need to change the bandage on your arm every day." She frowned at the tiny cut on his head as she applied the salve, but her thoughts focused on larger, unseen wounds that couldn't be healed with thread and bandages. How did she heal those? "*Every* day," she emphasized. "I don't care what the leeches say. Soiled bandages simply cannot be—"

"You have to leave London."

She froze, her fingers stilling at his temple as her eyes lowered to meet his. "Pardon?"

"You have to stay away until all this is over," he explained solemnly. "Clayton and I will make certain you're hidden somewhere safe."

She wiped her trembling hands on the towel, then folded them on her lap. God help her, they were shaking worse than when she'd sewn up his arm.

She'd known this moment would come, when the men who had been blackmailing her would finally attempt to kill her. But she'd never expected to feel this powerless, this helpless... Once more, her life had been ripped from her control.

"Scepter knows you revealed Braxton's message to me," he continued. "You're too much of a risk for them now."

"But I don't know anything!"

"Perhaps your Robert does." An unexpected harshness laced his voice.

The trembling in her hands now shook all of her. "No. That's im—"

"Or maybe Robert's directly involved with them, and that's how they knew what to use to blackmail you."

"Oh, Nate, you're so wrong." She forced herself to fight against the fear squeezing her heart, not for herself but for Robert... "I let you believe, but—but it's not what you think." She dropped her gaze to her hands and twisted them in her skirt. She couldn't look him in the eyes when she admitted the truth. "Robert isn't my lover."

"Then who is he?"

She answered so softly that the words were nearly silent on her trembling lips. "Robert is my son."

Fourteen

Her son.

Sydney's words pierced into Nate as painfully as the slash throbbing in his forearm.

Robert was her child? All this time, he'd been convinced Robert was her lover, and that was why she'd risked her life to protect him.

But a child...

Impossible. There were no signs of a boy, not once in all the days he'd been guarding her. Lady Agnes had never mentioned a baby; neither had St James and Olivia Everett.

Yet the pain in her eyes—

The cold realization seeped over him like ice water. They hadn't told him because none of them knew. The boy hadn't been missing from her life for just the past few weeks since Scepter had been blackmailing her. He'd been absent for far longer than that.

He narrowed his eyes on her. "Where is he?"

A stricken expression darkened her face. "In Warwickshire. I have a country house there."

The confusion inside him gave way to complete disbelief. "Why isn't he in London with you?"

"Because I can't have him here. He isn't—" She wrapped

her fingers in her skirt to keep her hands from shaking and finished, "He isn't Rowland's son. The scandal that would happen if anyone found out…"

She swallowed hard, unwilling to put words to her fears.

As she began to rise from her chair, he clasped her arm and stopped her. "*Why* isn't he in London?"

Unexpected anger flared in his gut. Situations like hers happened all the time among ladies of the *ton* who got with child. They would place the baby with distant relatives to raise as their own, then return to society a few months later as if nothing had happened.

But Sydney wasn't one of those women. She was brave and generous, independent and strong, and she couldn't have cared less about scandal.

Or so he'd thought.

Apparently, he didn't know her at all.

He clenched his jaw. "Your son deserves your love and protection."

"He has both." She tried to pull her arm away, but he refused to let her go. Not now, not when she had a great deal of explaining to do. In frustration, she added, "I bought a farm in the country where he lives with a wonderful governess. He has toys, books, friends—for God's sake, he even has a pony!" Her anger matched his own. "I have given him everything he needs."

His eyes locked with hers as he accused quietly, "Except his mother."

"He has me," she said firmly, as if trying to convince herself as much as him. "As much of myself as I can give."

This time when she pulled away, he let her go, but not before he saw her glistening tears.

She slipped off the chair and crossed the room to the fireplace to stare down at the flames. Her arms folded over her chest like a shield. At that moment, she appeared so fragile and vulnerable that he feared a harsh word would shatter her. Anguish for her rose inside him, and although he was too ashamed to admit it, so did a deep jealousy.

Fate had given her what it had so cruelly ripped away from him. Yet she chose to reject the joy and love of her son, simply because she feared scandal. "You should be with him."

She silently shook her head. Squeezing her eyes shut, she reached for the locket at her neck and folded her fingers around it.

He shoved himself away from the table and winced at the pain shooting up his arm. Yet it was nothing compared to the pain he'd carried for the past three years. "You should be the one raising him, not some governess who—"

"I wanted to!" she cried out, her emotional restraint breaking. "They wouldn't let me!"

She hung her head in her hands and sobbed openly. A sound of such utter desolation and helplessness tore from her that Nate's heart broke.

He went to her and slipped his good arm around her to draw her against him. "Sydney, tell me about your son." He placed a tender kiss to her temple in desperation to comfort her. "Help me to understand."

At his soft pleas, she stilled against him, except for her

hands which clasped at his chest as if she were afraid he might leave her.

But he had no intention of going anywhere.

"I wanted to keep him with me," she confessed in little more than a soft breath. "They'd told me that I could... But it was all a lie."

Large tears rolled freely down her cheeks, and she buried her face in shame and pain against his shoulder. He placed his hand against the back of her head to silently encourage her to let the sobs come and purge the pain.

"I begged them to let me keep him." Her whispers were muffled against his shoulder, but his heart heard every word. "He was only three days old. I only had him for three days..." The choked words poured out between body-racking sobs. "They pulled him from my arms, and they... I couldn't stop them!"

His arm tightened around her. *Dear God...* "Who took him?"

"My parents." Her hands increased their hold on him, and she pulled in a ragged breath as she admitted, "Robert was Michael's baby." She lifted her head from his shoulder but didn't raise her eyes to meet his. Her lashes were wet and spiked with tears. "We were engaged and in love, and we... I found out three weeks after he died that I was increasing." Her gaze trained at his chest as she confessed, barely louder than a breath, "I was eighteen, and I wanted to die."

Raw grief for her overwhelmed him. Eighteen... *Christ.* Barely more than a child herself.

"My parents took me away to the country," she continued in a hoarse rasp, "to a rented house where they told all the servants that I was their niece and that my husband was a soldier who was away in the wars. I stayed there for my confinement." Her trembling lips formed the silent words as she corrected herself. "My imprisonment."

He nuzzled his mouth against her hair. "You didn't try to run away?"

"I was too ill to flee, too upset over losing Michael, and I had no money of my own, no other relatives…nowhere to go even if I'd had the strength."

"Surely, Berkley's family would have helped."

She shook her head, her beautiful face contorting with shame. "I wrote to them about the baby, but they didn't believe me. Or if they did, they wanted no part of a bastard child. And I had no proof Michael was the father."

"But you were engaged."

"That didn't matter to them. Michael's family could easily have started rumors that I was a woman of loose morals and had been with other men. After all, society already viewed my family as upstart cits with scandalous ties to the Americans."

"You married Rowland after Robert was born." On the very day her mourning period ended for Berkley, according to Lady Agnes. "Why didn't you marry him before and give your son a legitimate birth?"

That was what unmarried society daughters did when they found themselves with child. They married a man who claimed the baby as his and raised it as his own.

"Rowland refused to marry me until after the baby was born. He'd rather have let the barony die than risk another man's son inheriting his title."

Ignoring his own wound, he wrapped both arms around her in an attempt to comfort her. "Yet you still married him."

"Because he still wanted money, and my parents still wanted a title." She twisted his waistcoat in her fingers, focusing her attention on his chest. "Because I had no choice." She whispered, so softly he could barely hear her, "They told me that if I married him, we could fabricate a story of how Robert was an orphaned relation with no place else to go, and eventually, I could bring him home with me. But if I refused to marry Rowland—" The words strangled in her throat, her pain still fresh even after all these years. "Then they would place him in an orphanage, and I'd never be able to find him."

His heart knew what happened next... "They put him into an orphanage anyway."

Her jerking nod confirmed it. "My parents made other arrangements with Rowland behind my back. He had no intention of ever letting me raise Robbie. That was my punishment for choosing Michael over him." The expression of grief on her face was so desolate, so tragic that it ripped his breath away. "And my parents wanted a titled son-in-law more than they wanted their grandson."

His heart shattered for the eighteen-year-old girl who had been so alone, so lost in her grief and betrayed by the people who should have loved her most. Good God, the hell she'd gone through... But he latched on to what would bring her solace—"Yet you found him."

She raised her eyes to meet his. But it wasn't hope or happiness he saw in those green depths, only endless self-recrimination and guilt.

"Two years ago. When Rowland died, I hired investigators to find Robert. He was almost four years old then, still in an orphanage. I petitioned to become his legal guardian and removed him from that awful place." Her voice took on a sense of determination and duty, yet it wasn't enough to expel the pain. "Now he's in a house where he's safe and cared for, where he will have a fine education, all the comforts he could ever want, and a chance at a good life."

She slipped out of his arms and moved away. He didn't try to stop her. She needed space now as much as she'd needed to be in his embrace only moments ago.

Nate watched her closely. He tried to imagine her as that frightened and grieving eighteen-year-old girl who'd had her life and all her dreams ripped away. She'd been thrust under the control of a husband who only wanted her for her money, under the command of parents so desperate to become part of the *ton* that they'd sold their own daughter and abandoned their grandson.

So much of her life had been sacrificed to the flames that it was a wonder she'd managed to survive at all let alone come out the other side with such strength and determination in every aspect of her life. Except one.

Her son.

A hollow sadness ached in his chest for her. "But he doesn't know you're his mother, does he?"

"No, and he never will. He thinks he's a distant Rowland relative, and that's how it will stay." She took another step away from him, as if she were afraid he might reach for her again. "This is the best I can do for him."

"You can do more. You can be a full mother to him." *You can love him.* "But you're afraid of scandal. That's why you're denying him a mother and you your own son because you care what the damned *ton* thinks."

"Yes, I fear scandal—for *him*." She clenched her fist against her bosom as she admitted guiltily, "What kind of life could he have if people knew the truth about him? I would never allow him to suffer like that." She protectively grasped her locket. "Robert just turned six. His governess sends me regular updates and occasionally a drawing or some other kind of keepsake from him." She hesitated as if wondering if she could trust Nate with a precious secret. "This one is my most treasured."

She held up the locket, then flicked the tiny latch and opened it to reveal a curl of dark blond hair secured with a tiny blue ribbon.

Nate's hand shook as he gently stroked the soft hair. She wore this locket always, he knew, keeping it close to her heart. Yet it wasn't grief for her that pierced him as he stared at the memento but envy. That she should have even this small, tiny bit of her son when he had nothing of his own.

He dropped his hand away.

"Even if I could," she whispered with her attention riveted to the locket, "it's too late now."

"It's not." He was desperate for her to realize that she could still make amends, still find absolution and forgiveness. "Your son is alive." That was all that mattered. "You can still be part of his life. He's old enough now to—"

"No." She gave a fierce shake of her head. "I won't hurt him again! That's what it would do if I brought him into my life, and I would *never* harm him." Catching her breath, she admitted, "I will do anything to keep him safe. *Anything*. Including never being his mother."

A primal ferocity radiated from her, like a lioness protecting her cub. With a flash of horrible clarity, Nate suddenly understood every bit of her role with Scepter, why she'd played a part in threatening Henry Everett, and why she'd been so desperate to deliver the message to Braxton. Not to save her own life but to save her son's.

"That's what Scepter used to blackmail you," he murmured, afraid to speak it any louder. "Not threats of revealing his existence but threats to his life."

She nodded. "I thought I could protect him. But now…" Pressing the back of her hand against her mouth, a pained shudder swept through her. When she found her voice again, it emerged raw and frightened. "They're going to kill him, aren't they? Because of what I've done, because I told you about Braxton."

"I will *not* let them harm your son, I promise you." Just as he wouldn't let them harm the mother. He gritted his teeth at the pain in his arm as he pulled on his bloodied jacket. "I'll go to Warwickshire to make certain he's safe and—"

"I'm coming with you." She rushed to the door and called out for Danby. "You're not leaving me behind."

"Oh yes, I am." He took her arm and led her back from the hall. "I'll send for St James. He'll come for you this morning, then move you out of the city as soon as he can. First, though, he has to resolve matters about General Braxton."

She froze. "Why?"

He hesitated to tell her. She was already upset, but he couldn't keep the truth from her. Keeping secrets had already put both her life and her son's in danger. "Braxton's dead. He died this morning in the attack."

Her face drained to a ghostly pale, and she reached for a chair to steady herself. "And the meaning behind his blackmail message—Bois Saint-Louis?"

He shook his head. "I'm hoping Clayton Elliott can find out. Otherwise, we're at a dead end again." He frowned grimly. "Except for you."

Her eyes locked with his. "Am I still nothing to you but bait for your trap?"

Nate clenched his jaw. He didn't know how to answer without hurting at least one of them.

Danby scurried into the room, huffing and puffing from running at her call. "My lady?"

"Have my carriage brought around," she ordered. "Ask the lead groom for a change of clothes for the captain. They're about the same size. And send my maid up to my rooms to pack a bag. I need to leave immediately."

He bowed and retreated toward the door, his round face red from the exertion of the morning's events. "Yes, my lady."

"Danby, stay that order." Nate stopped the retreating butler with a cutting glance. Then he turned back to the woman at the heart of all his troubles. "You are not leaving this house."

He expected her to argue with him or at least jab her chin stubbornly into the air. Instead, her lips parted softly, and a deep vulnerability glistened in her eyes.

Damnation...the soft side of her was more effective against him than her fierce arguments.

"Please, Nate," she whispered. Her fingers clenched at his bicep as if he were the only anchor left to her in the world. "This is all my fault, and I have to make certain Robert's safe. I couldn't live with myself if something happened to him because of me. Can you understand?"

Nate's chest sank. He couldn't argue against that. In exasperation, he demanded, "Can you sit a horse?"

"Expertly."

"Astride?"

She nodded, and his shoulders slumped. He knew when he was beaten.

"Disregard the order for the carriage," he commanded Danby. "Have the groom saddle her horse instead, with a proper saddle, too, and not some damned sidesaddle. And *you*." He settled a hard look on her. He would brook no argument about this. "Get dressed for riding. Wear those boys' clothes you donned for your midnight visit to the Horse Guards, and put a greatcoat over you this time."

She turned to a stunned Danby who glanced nervously between the two of them, not knowing which one's orders to follow. "You heard the captain." She shooed the butler from the room. "Go—quickly!"

Danby ran from the room toward the rear stables, although Nate suspected his speed was more to flee from the tension between the two of them than to give orders to the grooms.

As Sydney began to leave, Nate took her arm and pulled her against him until her soft body melted against his.

"We're going to ride hard," he warned, his mouth so close to hers that her warm breath tickled his lips. "If you slow me down, I *will* leave you behind."

"I certainly hope you do." Her eyes glistened again, this time with gratitude. "You're saving Robert's life. I can't thank you enough."

"You can thank me by ending the lies." Including the ones she was telling herself. "*All* of them."

Nate released her and stalked from the room.

———————

Less than twenty minutes later, their two horses waited at the front gate, saddled and ready to ride. Nate had changed into the groom's work shirt and jacket and was now carefully checking the saddle girths and bridles one more time to make certain they were secure. He trusted no one, not even the staff inside Sydney's own house.

Taking her with him was madness, but he knew one thing for certain about Lady Rowland—when she set her mind to something, heaven help the man who tried to stop her.

Sydney rushed from the house and down the steps toward him. "I'm ready!"

She wore the stable boy's clothes and boots beneath a groom's greatcoat that was too large for her. With her hair pulled up beneath the wide-brimmed hat, she once more looked like the tempting ghost who had appeared to him at the Horse Guards.

He sucked in a deep breath. *Heaven help me.*

With a grimace, Nate swiped down with his hand to grab a fistful of mud from the ground.

"Look at me," he ordered.

She sputtered speechlessly as he smeared it across her face. "What are you *doing*?"

"I've told you before, Baroness." He grabbed her by the waist and flung her up onto the saddle, where she landed in a very unladylike position with her round bottom pointed up toward the sky. "You're too damned beautiful to be mistaken for a boy."

Unable to resist, he slapped her playfully on the bottom.

She scrambled to throw over her leg to sit up. Then she stared at him, stunned, as if she couldn't decide whether he'd just complimented her or insulted her. And Nate was damned himself if he knew which.

He clasped her wrist and pulled her down across the horse's neck until her face was level with his as he stood on the ground beside her. Her breath came in fast, excited little pants that sweetly tickled his lips. Even now, amid the dangers threatening them, he still yearned for her.

For a long moment, they simply stared at each other, like two opponents sizing up the competition before a fight. Nate had the growing suspicion that before this escapade with Sydney Rowland was over, they would share one hell of a brawl.

"You've changed your mind about me, then, haven't you?" she whispered, drawing his gaze to her full lips. "You must think I'm innocent if you're willing to help me like this."

"Yes," he admitted grudgingly, "I do."

"And have you changed your mind about…the other?"

Nate knew exactly what she meant.

He'd never met a woman like her. Courageous and daring, stubborn and insolent, pushing away the people she should have held dear…yet so full of confidence, so gut-achingly beautiful and alluring even in boys' clothing with mud dirtying her face. He simply could not fathom her.

More, she wanted *him*, this woman who refused to be second to any other.

"Her name was Sarah," he told her quietly, answering her question the only way he knew how.

Her lips parted with a delicate, puzzled frown. "Pardon?"

"She was my wife." He drew a deep breath, held it for a moment as he steadied himself, then let go in a jerky exhale. "She died three years ago, and it was my fault."

Fifteen

NATE STOPPED HIS HORSE AND POINTED INTO THE darkness. "There."

Fatigued after a long day of riding, Sydney forced her tired eyes to follow his outstretched arm to a small cottage at the edge of the woods. It sat back from the narrow road snaking away from the end of the sleepy village they'd just ridden through.

"We're stopping there for the night," he told her and lifted his gaze skyward toward the sunset's last purples and reds.

They'd left her town house in London nearly twelve hours—and three pairs of horses—earlier, riding hard in near silence and stopping only to change mounts and gobble down a quick meal before riding on. They'd made good progress and were now over halfway to Oakwood Manor, where Robert lived with his governess. But they were both tired, and it would be madness to continue in the darkness with worsening roads, the scent of rain lingering coldly in the air, and the threat of highwaymen behind every tree.

Truth be told, she was exhausted, and her body was sore and stiff from the saddle and a lack of sleep from the night before. The thought of stopping for a few hours' rest made tears of relief gather at her lashes. The ride had been excruciating, but she'd kept up with Nate all day in the chase he'd led across the English countryside, just as she'd keep up with him again tomorrow.

Somehow.

"Is that part of an inn?" she asked, hoping beyond hope for hot food and water.

"No." He kicked his horse and sent it down the lane.

Sydney shook her head at his taciturn behavior and trotted after. He'd been distant all day.

He rode his horse beneath the small lean-to at the side of the cottage and slipped to the ground, then caught the reins of her mare as she rode up. When she slid off the horse, she winced at the stab of pain that shot up her backside.

He frowned. "Are you all right?"

"Just a bit tender," she answered grudgingly, unwilling to admit to even this small weakness for fear he'd send her back to London.

He said nothing to that, just as he'd said little to her all day, and turned to unsaddle the horses. He avoided eye contact with her and kept his back toward her. His silence hadn't bothered her much during the ride; she'd been too busy focusing on her horse and on worrying about Robert. But now, it grated.

She drew a deep breath. "Nate, why didn't you—"

"There should be oats in that bin." He nodded toward a barrel at the rear of the lean-to. "Pour in a scoop for each of them, and get water from the barrel over there."

Then he turned his back to her again.

She did as he asked. After all, she knew she'd get nowhere pressing him now about what he'd told her in London. But he *would* tell her more eventually. She wouldn't let him keep his silence about that.

By the time she'd finished pouring the feed and water into the troughs, he'd stripped the tack from both horses and tied them to the manger. The two horses were ready for a well-deserved night's rest. So was Sydney.

"This way." He guided her through the darkness to the front of the cottage. Instead of pounding on the door, though, he reached down into a broken clay pot and withdrew a key. The lock turned, and he swung the door open.

"Wait here."

He disappeared into the dark cottage, and Sydney peered after him as she tried to discern what he was doing but failed. After a few moments came the sound of metal striking flint, followed by a bright spark, then the catch of a flame. The fire slowly blossomed in the hearth with a small glow.

Closing the door behind her, she was drawn inside the wattle-and-daub cottage as he deftly built up the fire. Its soft light revealed a tiny but comfortably furnished house of one room downstairs and narrow wooden steps leading up to what she assumed was a bedroom beneath the rafters.

"Will this do for the night?" he asked and tossed two more logs onto the fire.

The comfort and warmth of a fire after such a hard, cold day… She sighed out, "Perfectly." She glanced around. "But whose cottage is this?"

He rocked back onto his heels and wiped his dusty hands on his thighs. "Mine."

"Yours?" She couldn't possibly have heard him correctly.

"You think I live only in an army barracks, Baroness?" He crooked a brow in her direction.

"Well...yes."

His lips curled into a wry smile. "Mostly, perhaps."

He stood and reached for a pot hanging on the swing hook beside the hearth. He carried it to a barrel at the end of the long cupboard in the corner.

"We're on the estate of the Earl of Buckley. My mother works in the manor house at Buckhurst Park." He placed the pot beneath the spout and twisted it open until water poured from the barrel into the pot. "Most of the time, she stays at the manor house. It's easier for her to sleep there instead of making the trek from the village every day as she did when I was a boy. But I keep this cottage just in case she wants to use it and for whenever I come to visit."

"Keep it?" she repeated with a confused frown.

He returned the pot to the hearth and set it to boil. "I pay rent to Buckley for it."

That made no sense. "But it's a tenancy, and your mother works for him."

"And as part of her pay, she's given a narrow bed in an attic room that she shares with two other maids in the manor house. No landowner worth his salt would ever give unmarried help a cottage to themselves when he can extract rent for it." He opened the cupboard bins and withdrew an armful of root vegetables, then dumped them onto the table.

"At least Buckley lets it to me cheaply." His mouth twisted distastefully. "He likes to brag that his tenant is the hero of Toulouse."

Nate let him, she knew, for his mother's sake. Yet it surely pricked his pride to subject himself to that in order to secure a lower lease price, something he'd need with only his captain's commission for income.

Soldier, hero, dedicated son, illegitimate half brother to an earl...he was proving to be far more complicated than she'd first assumed that night at Barton's when he sat beside her and piqued her interest by being the complete opposite of every other man in the room. She hadn't realized until right now, though, exactly how different he was, and not just from the men at Barton's but from every other man she'd ever known.

"The Home Office has promised reward money for stopping Scepter," he admitted quietly. "Not much, I'm sure, but if I sell my commission, there should be enough between the two to permanently secure a better cottage where she can be pensioned." He muttered beneath his breath, "Somewhere far away from here."

Sell his commission? But his position in the army meant everything to him—his identity, his career, his future. "You can't!"

Both of his brows raised in surprise.

"I mean—" An embarrassed blush heated her cheeks. Heavens, she'd overstepped. His commission was his to do with as he pleased, including selling it, and how busybody of her to stick her nose into his business where it didn't belong…even if he would be making a grand mistake. "I mean, you can't leave this place. You grew up here."

"Yes, I did. Which is why I want to leave it behind." He tossed her an apple, and she easily caught it. As easily as he switched topics with, "I don't suppose you know how to cook."

So…he didn't want to talk about his childhood home. He didn't want to talk about his father or brother. And from the all-day silence following his announcement about his late wife, he didn't want to talk about her either.

Was there anything he was willing to share about himself? Or did he simply not trust her the same way he expected her to trust him?

Conceding the conversation to him—momentarily—she shook her head. "Not even tea."

As an heiress, there was no point in learning to cook. For that matter, there was little point in learning anything that didn't directly relate to catching a high-ranking husband. But now, when she thought about all the hours she'd spent practicing the pianoforte and learning to watercolor, she felt like a fool. She should have been in the kitchens instead for all the good those husband-hunting skills did her.

"Then I'm afraid it's army stew for you tonight, Baroness." He pulled out his knife to chunk up the vegetables and tossed them into the pot on the fire.

Sydney watched him work. This was how he must have looked in camp on the Peninsula, rugged yet making do without complaint. But the man who now cut up vegetables for a stew was the same one who had shone so brightly in his evening finery when he approached her at Barton's. He'd taken her breath away then. And he did so now, too.

He gestured over his shoulder with the blade. "There's a bottle of whiskey in the sideboard. Fetch it, will you? We'll need it to choke down the stew."

Snapping out of her reverie, she retrieved it. The liquor shimmered golden in the firelight as she splashed it into a pair of mugs, then held one out for him when he'd finished with the vegetables.

He mumbled his thanks and sank onto a chair at the small table, with no place else to sit save for a wooden settle on the other side of the fireplace. The rest of the room was just as sparsely furnished, with various cabinets and cupboards against the walls and a thick, tightly woven hearth rug covering the rough floorboards. Yet the place felt cozy, warm, and welcoming, and more like a real home than her grand London town house. She felt safe here.

Yet ghosts haunted this place.

She sat down across from him, cupped the mug between her palms, and stared awkwardly into it. Her heart pounded at what she was about to do. Was this what soldiers felt like before they charged into the fray?

She gathered her courage and blurted out, "Did you and Sarah live here?"

He froze, the mug raised halfway to his lips. She held her breath and waited for him to tell her to mind her own damn business.

Instead, he quietly answered, "No," and raised the mug up to his mouth for a large swallow of whiskey.

After a long stretch of silence when it became clear he wasn't going to willingly disclose anything more, Sydney gently pressed, "Where did you live?"

His eyes flicked across the table to hers, then just as quickly darted away. "I was in the Guards when we married, so she lived with her parents on a small farm about five miles from here. I stayed there whenever I came home on leave, which wasn't often."

"How long were you married?" Her fingers tightened around the mug. She had no business prying into his life like this, yet she desperately needed to know. If she was going to depend upon Nate, then she needed to trust him completely, and this woman was keeping him from her, all the way from the grave.

"Two years." He finished the mug of whiskey in a single, gasping gulp. "You think I'm a fool to mourn for a woman longer than she was part of my life?"

"No," she assured him softly. She'd lost her fiancé of less than three months over seven years ago, and her heart still missed him. Perhaps it always would. "You must have loved her a great deal."

"Very much." But he'd paused before he answered, and Sydney suspected he was attempting to persuade himself as much as her. Then he confessed, "Not enough."

Her heart lodged itself in her throat. "You weren't happy?"

"We were happy in our marriage." He leveled his gaze at her across the table and accused, "But you weren't."

The change in conversation took her by breathless surprise. She knew why he'd asked—he wasn't going to pour out his heart alone. Tonight, they were in this together. If she wanted to learn his secrets, she would have to share hers.

"No, I wasn't." Despite a defensive stiffening of her spine, she answered honestly, "I hated every day of it. We never shared a marriage bed, and I never mourned for him, not one day."

He stared at her for a long moment as if deciding whether to believe her. "Yet you remained faithful to him."

She gave a slow shake of her head in correction. "I remained faithful to Michael. My fidelity in my marriage was simply an overlap."

"But you took a lover after your husband died."

"Not a lover. It was only for one night. I was so very lonely, and I needed to feel wanted and alive. That was all it was." She needed him to understand the difference. "I'll always love Michael, but I no longer mourn." She paused. "But you haven't stopped mourning your wife, have you, Nate?"

Avoiding her eyes, he reached for the bottle and refilled his mug. "My past is more complicated than yours, Baroness."

"We both lost people we loved," she insisted gently. She understood his grief because it was the same pain she'd suffered and somehow managed to survive. She wanted to help him do the same. "People we thought we'd have with us for the rest of our lives, but we can't—"

"Sarah died in childbirth."

Her heart stopped. She fixed her eyes on him and noted every detail of his face, every change in his expression no matter how slight. His face remained emotionless, but the sudden grief she felt for him was excruciating.

"I was away on the Peninsula," he continued quietly. "When I received word that Sarah was having problems, I came as quickly as I could, but I was too late."

"Nate," she breathed. Her lips were barely able to form his name. "I'm so sorry."

He gave no indication that he heard her and continued to stare dully into the mug. "By the time I reached home, Sarah was dead, and the baby died a few days later." He tossed back the whiskey, then shoved the empty cup away as if all the drink in the world would never be enough to ease his pain. His hazel eyes glistened as they rose to meet hers. "I had a son."

She inhaled sharply, and her hand flew to her chest as his words sliced into her. She blinked rapidly, unable to stop her tears. *Good God.* He'd lost his son...

"It wasn't your fault." Her voice strangled as she repeated his words to her from that morning.

He gave a single, sharp nod, but was he truly agreeing or simply making the motion? "For years, I thought it was because I wasn't there when she needed me, because I put my army career before my wife." He paused before admitting, "My life ended that day."

"I know," she whispered. "When they told me Michael was dead, I wanted to die myself." Only now, seven years later, was she finally beginning to feel alive again.

She slowly reached across the table and covered his hand with hers.

He stiffened. Then he accepted the solace she offered and laced his fingers through hers.

"You still mourn her and your son," she continued, so low the words were nearly lost beneath the crackle of the fire.

"I grieve for them, certainly." He traced his thumb over the backs of her fingers, and she trembled as he said quietly, "But mourning...I don't know anymore."

"Yet you don't want to betray their memory." She looked down at their joined hands, and they blurred beneath her burning eyes. "Even now, simply talking with me like this, you feel as if you're betraying your wife."

His thumb stilled. "That's the problem, because I don't feel that it should be a betrayal, not anymore. That I should have the right to start living for the future."

He released her hand and leaned back in the chair. Whatever small moment of connection they'd discovered dissolved away. He reached across the table not for her hand but for the whiskey bottle.

"But wanting to move on, wanting to live when she'll never again..." Not bothering to pour the whiskey into the mug, he raised the bottle straight to his lips. "*That's* why it feels as if I'm betraying her." He wiped the back of his hand across his mouth. "And for the life of me, I don't know how to move past that."

Sixteen

NATE SLUMPED LOW AGAINST THE STRAIGHT BACK OF the wooden settle and grimaced into the fire.

Sydney was upstairs in the bedroom. Even now, he could hear her moving across the creaking floorboards. She'd been there for the past hour after they'd finished a dinner nearly as silent as the day's ride. He'd carried up hot water for her so she could bathe away the mud still smeared across her face and the layer of dust she'd picked up from the road. Then he left her, prepared to spend the night on the rug in front of the fire. Alone.

Not that he didn't want her. From the moment he met her, he'd wondered what it would be like to be with her, to trail his mouth across her naked flesh and experience her body's excited response to his.

Now he also wanted to simply hold her in his arms, safe and protected, and watch her as she slept.

But he'd never let himself do either.

Blowing out a harsh breath, he stripped off the borrowed jacket, along with the waistcoat and shirt beneath, and let his braces dangle around his hips. He didn't care if she came downstairs and found him half-naked. No need for modesty now. He'd already bared his soul to her by telling her about Sarah. What was a bared body compared to that?

He yanked off a boot with a muttered curse and placed it on the floor.

Last night at the party, she'd wanted to seduce him in the alcove, and he'd very nearly let her. After tonight, though, he wouldn't blame her if she never wanted to speak to him again, because he sure as hell didn't know how to feel about her. Except that he still wanted her.

The second boot dropped.

He leaned forward, elbows on knees. Keeping himself from Sydney wasn't about Sarah, not anymore. He'd realized that at the masquerade when he'd seen Braxton strike her. Hot rage flashed through him that anyone would dare harm her, and he realized then that saving her had become more than just stopping Scepter.

He'd been willing to give his life for hers.

At that moment, everything changed. He no longer felt a sense of betrayal toward Sarah. That guilt vanished, and with its parting, he'd felt as if he'd lost his wife all over again.

Shoving himself to his feet, he stalked across the cottage to the washbasin on the kitchen dresser and splashed cold water over himself. He threw back his head and let the bracing water run down his bare chest, dampen his breeches, and drip onto his bare feet. Only when he shivered beneath the cold wash did he finally reach for a towel to dry himself.

But even that chilly drenching wasn't enough to drive away the growing heat in his gut.

Worse, he also found himself enjoying the time he spent with her. Unpredictable, alluring, challenging…she was anything but boring. More—she understood him the way no one else did. She knew the same deep love and the inconsolable grief as he did. More important, though, she knew how to live on afterward. He prayed she could teach him how to do that, too. Because the alternative...

No. There was no alternative.

He needed to live again. Sarah would have wanted that. She wouldn't have wanted him to withdraw from the world and spend the rest of his life living like a monk.

But was he ready for Sydney?

He raked his fingers through his damp hair. Regardless, this tension between them had to end. Boundaries had to be established to put both of them firmly back into their rightful places as nothing more than mission assets. *Tonight.*

He bounded up the stairs with a fierce determination to make her understand. After all, Sydney was an intelligent, logical woman. He would simply explain to her that although he found her extremely attractive and would very much enjoy being her lover, they were from different worlds and had no future. Therefore, they needed to end their flirtations with all due haste.

Yes, that was exactly what he would tell her. No more delving into pasts and secrets, no more guilt and misunderstandings, no more distractions—

He froze on the top stair.

She stood in the soft light of a single candle as she brushed her sable hair, wearing nothing but one of his old shirts. The white cotton hung down to just above her knees and revealed shapely calves and bare feet beneath, and the wide neck hung off one shoulder, baring its creamy smoothness to the candlelight. All of her was casual and soft, all ready for a warm bed.

He was unable to tear his eyes away from her. Neither could he ignore the sudden pulsing in his groin as he hardened at the sight of her. All the frustration he'd carried inside since they'd met transformed into white hot desire. He wanted her, she wanted him, and he would no longer be betraying Sarah.

It was suddenly that simple.

She looked up and gave a soft inhalation of surprise at his unexpected appearance, and that little breath twined through him straight down to his core. Immediately, tension flashed like a crackle of electricity on the air between them.

"Nate..." His name was a pleading whisper.

He reached her in a single stride, pulled her against his chest, and seized her mouth beneath his.

With a low moan of capitulation, she dropped the brush to the floor and wrapped her arms around his neck to press herself as close as possible. The warmth of her body reached him through the cotton shirt, as did the softness of her breasts and thighs as she molded herself against him.

He tore his mouth away from hers and growled as he left openmouthed kisses across her throat. "You're wearing my shirt."

"I forgot to pack my night rail," she panted out, "and I couldn't find one of your mother's."

Thank God for that. He ran his hands down her body. She quivered everywhere he touched, and his cock throbbed painfully in response.

She dug her fingertips into the bare muscles of his shoulders and back, then shivered deliciously when he took her earlobe between his teeth and nipped a warning that tonight he would not be gentle.

"When I saw you standing there," she whispered and arched her neck to give him access as he grazed his teeth down her throat, "I thought you'd come up to say you'd made a mistake, that you were still mourning—"

"Hush."

He cupped her cheek in his palm and tilted her face up to silence her doubts with a kiss. Not just any kiss, but one with a singular focus as his tongue slid between her lips to ravish her mouth the way he planned on ravishing her body.

When a low moan swelled up from inside her, he slid his mouth away from hers and licked his way across her bare shoulder. He wanted to devour her.

"I haven't been with a woman in years, Sydney," he muttered against her flesh despite the bruise to his pride. "I might not be able to last very long the first time."

"The first..." She blinked, then swallowed. Hard. "All right."

He ran his hands over her body again. But this time when he reached her thighs, he fisted the tail of the shirt and pulled it up, over her head, and off. He dropped it away to the floor.

Gloriously naked, his temptress stood perfectly still and let his eyes hungrily take their fill of her, from her taut pink nipples down the long stretch of legs to her bare toes and back again.

She was beautiful. And tonight, she would finally be his.

He touched his fingertips to her red lips to outline their fullness, then trailed his hand down her throat and over her spiking pulse as it throbbed wildly. His hand slipped into the valley between her full breasts, lower across her stomach to her navel, and then lower still into the curls guarding her sex.

He slid his fingers possessively between her legs as his mouth captured hers in a demanding kiss that left her panting for breath.

He groaned against her lips. "You're wet."

"Yes," she murmured as her arms snaked around his neck to keep herself pressed against him.

"For me." An army captain, a bastard son...a man who could offer nothing more special tonight than a straw mattress and coarse sheets.

"Yes." A heated whimper rose on her lips. "Oh, very much yes..."

He placed openmouthed kisses against her throat and felt the spike of her pulse against his lips. Each heartbeat shot through him all the way down to the tip of his aching cock. "I want you, Baroness."

She ground her hips against his erection to signal that tonight, body to body, she was his equal in every way. "Then have me."

He scooped her into his arms, carried her to the bed, and followed down after her. He shed his trousers even as his mouth found her breasts and suckled hard, pulling her nipples deep into his mouth.

She welcomed his roughness by arching herself beneath him with a shuddering moan. Her fingers twisted into his hair and pressed his head harder against her, and her thighs spread wide beneath him as he settled into the cradle of her hips.

"Now," she begged and writhed beneath him. "I can't wait. Now, Nate, please!"

He reached between them to position his cock against her, and he buried his throbbing tip in her slick outer folds. Claiming her mouth with his, he plunged inside her and swallowed her cry of pleasure.

He shuddered at the exquisite feel of her. He wasn't prepared for the overwhelming sensation of her body accepting his, the delicious heat and softness that enveloped him, or the way her sex clenched tightly around him. And when he began to stroke his hips against hers...*bliss*.

She dug her fingernails into his buttocks to urge him to go faster and deeper, and her hips rose up beneath his to meet each hard thrust. He groaned. There was nothing gentle about what they were doing. This wasn't making love. This was sex. Raw and primal. Animal. Each desperate for the other, they craved release and demanded satisfaction.

She reached up to grab the headboard for leverage and locked her ankles together at the small of his back. She cried out his name as her body bucked beneath his. Her thighs quivered around him but never loosened their hold as sudden release swept over her.

Nate lost his breath as her spasm of pleasure flowed into him. The sensation overwhelmed him, and for a moment, he lost all thought. All he knew was this moment with her. His hips ground against hers in his need to sink as deeply as possible into her tight warmth, to possess her completely—

Before he could regain thought, he poured himself into her as she clung to him. Sweet release spasmed through him as he clenched his buttocks to spill every last bit of himself inside her, and the sensation shook him to his core.

He collapsed on top of her. He rested his forehead against her shoulder and fought for breath as he struggled to calm his speeding heart. Beneath him, her body shook with each residual pulse of pleasure that passed through her.

She wrapped her arms around his neck and held him pressed tightly to her, her legs still encircling his waist. She didn't move, not even to shift her hips away and slip his spent length from her warmth. Instead, she kept him inside her as if she, too, didn't want the moment to end.

"Sydney, I'm sorry," he rasped out, his eyes still shut. "I lost control. I didn't mean to—"

"Shh," she whispered and silenced him with a brush of her fingertips across his temple. Her soothing touch now was as gentle as her body had been fierce only moments before, her silent caresses dispelling all notions of any kind of regret.

Nate knew then that no part of him, body or soul, had escaped being branded by her tonight, and he trembled.

Seventeen

SYDNEY FROWNED. NATE STOOD A FEW FEET AWAY FROM her in the drawing room at Oakwood Manor, but he might as well have been a thousand miles away.

Last night, the need inside her had set free the pent-up demons inside him. And oh, what an encounter! The night had been simply amazing, both more thrillingly passionate and deeply comfortable than she'd ever imagined making love could be.

Yet she woke at dawn to find him gone from bed, already dressed and saddling the horses. The same tensions as before still lingered between them, and she knew he thought he'd betrayed his late wife. Sydney had somehow found the strength to move past her mourning for Michael, but her hopes were dashed that Nate had done the same.

He'd maintained a painful silence yet again today, somehow even more withdrawn than before. The only time he'd spoken to her was when they stopped at a village before reaching Oakwood so she could change into the day dress she'd brought with her and he could rent a carriage to give the appearance of a proper, if wholly unexpected, arrival. But once they were back on the road, the silence resumed.

Truly, though, she had no reason to feel so bereft. Last night was exactly what she'd wanted—to be in his arms without surrendering control of her life. Her heart was still safely her own, her life still hers to manage.

So why was her stomach now tied in knots? Why did her heart skip every time she glanced at him and caught him staring back? Why did she long to caress his cheek? Even now, she had to bite her bottom lip to keep from telling him how wonderful he was, how unlike any man she'd ever met before, including Michael.

As if he could feel the heat of her confused stare, he glanced up and met her gaze across the room. He held her eyes for only a moment before turning back to the window.

Frustration flared inside her. This silence between them could *not* go on. She refused to let him withdraw from her, not after all they'd shared.

She gathered her courage and asked, "What are we going to do?"

"We'll stay here tonight and rest," he answered. He faced her but kept his distance. "Tomorrow at dawn, we'll take Robert and head north to the Scottish border. I have a friend there who can take him in and protect him. Then we'll find a hiding spot for you."

Her eyes never left his. "That's not what I meant."

He turned back toward the window and quietly admitted, "I know."

With that, the divide between them grew even wider.

After several minutes of painful, awkward silence, he finally moved away from the window and circled the room.

His attention focused on the paintings on the walls, on the fine furnishings…on everything but her.

"So." He glanced around the large room whose only purpose was the comfort of guests, which was ironic since there were never any guests at Oakwood. "You bought this place for Robert."

He wanted to talk about the farm? She frowned, confused. This wasn't the conversation she wanted to have, the one they *needed* to have. But at least he was speaking to her again.

"Two years ago." Her shoulders slowly relaxed. "Robert was four and had just left the orphanage. He needed a stable home."

She'd known nothing about farms or country houses then except that they seemed like a wonderful place for boys to be raised, amid fields and woods where they could run and play. More, Oakwood Manor sat just far enough away from London that she wouldn't be able to impulsively travel here whenever the temptation struck her, which had entered her mind almost constantly in recent weeks.

"How big?"

She blinked at the unexpected question. "Pardon?"

"How big is the farm?"

"One thousand acres, roughly," she answered, feeling an inexplicable awkwardness now at the questioning, wondering where this was leading. "It's not a grand estate."

"Tenants?"

"No." That was one of the reasons she'd purchased this particular farm. There were fewer people connected to it who might grow suspicious that Robert lived here alone with only his governess and a handful of servants.

She stole another nervous glance toward the door. Where was Miss Jenner? The governess should have been here by now to greet them.

"And the house?" He rolled his eyes toward the ceiling at the painting that luxuriously covered the plaster. A scene from Greek mythology with the nine Muses playing in a sunny glade, the decoration was a far cry from the wooden beams and plain plaster of Nate's comfortable cottage.

An embarrassed blush heated her cheeks at all this opulence in a home for one little boy. "Thirty rooms or so, I'd imagine. But I'm certain most of them are closed off and never used."

His gaze dropped to hers and pinned her where she stood. "You've never been here before."

It was an accusation, not a question.

"No," she answered defensively. "But I keep a dependable household staff who run and care for the farm."

He said nothing for a moment, and she held her breath as she waited for the question she knew was poised next on the tip of his tongue... *Do you really think a big house and servants can make up for your absence?* She could hear his deep voice whispering it inside her head, filling her with fresh guilt.

Of course it couldn't. But if she couldn't be a true mother, then she could provide a safe, happy place for Robert to grow up. She could be a good mother in that much at least.

Instead of asking the question, though, Nate turned away.

His attention drifted to the collection of curios in the corner cabinet. "And you hired the governess?"

"Yes. Miss Jenner worked for Lord Hawking's nephew. The marquess recommended her very highly." Unease rose inside her at his string of probing questions, at the governess's failure to appear more quickly, and most of all, at the impending moment when she would meet her son. Her heart pounded so hard with trepidation that her rib cage ached. "I had an estate agent find the property, and Miss Jenner hired the staff. Mr. Beasley oversees the stables, the gardens, and everything without. Mrs. Larkin is the housekeeper and tends to everything within. There are also two maids of all work and a cook to help keep the house and more men to help outside with the stables and gardens. The house doesn't require a large staff."

"No one else who has access to the farm or house?"

"Only a few of the villagers who make deliveries or repairs...that sort of thing." Her eyes widened. She suddenly realized why he was asking all these questions. "You don't trust the staff."

He folded his arms over his chest. "Right now, I don't trust anyone."

"No, you don't, do you?" Then she added softly, her voice solemn, "Not even me."

His strong shoulders slumped beneath the rough tan jacket. "Sydney, please understand." He blew out a harsh breath as he ran his fingers through his hair in open frustration. At least he had the decency this time not to pretend he didn't know what she meant. "I need time to think and sort through everything—"

The door opened, and a plain young woman walked into the room. Her brown hair was pulled back into a tight bun, and her eyes were hidden behind a pair of spectacles. She wore a simple dress made of worsted wool, the style plain and unassuming. Her gaze landed on Sydney, and she began to smile pleasantly until she noticed Nate on the far side of the room. Her smile froze in place, only for a moment, but enough to register her surprise.

"Good afternoon." Her voice was as quiet and unremarkable as the rest of her. Finishing her smile, she curtsied. "I'm Miss Jenner, Robert's governess. Welcome to Oakwood Manor, Lady Rowland."

Sydney returned the greeting with a faint nod and an awkward smile. She'd always felt uncomfortable with the formalities her courtesy title brought, borne as it was on the back of a marriage she had loathed and dearly paid for. "Thank you, Miss Jenner. It's a pleasure to meet you."

The woman's eyes drifted to Nate.

"Captain Reed," Sydney said as he stepped forward, "may I introduce you to Miss Caroline Jenner, Robert's governess. Miss Jenner, this is Captain Nate Reed." She searched for the proper way to describe him. "My...escort."

He made no visible reaction to that except for a polite incline of his head to Miss Jenner.

"I hope we're not inconveniencing the household by arriving without notice," Sydney apologized. "I regret that we were unable to send word ahead."

Miss Jenner smiled that away. "Not at all, my lady. We're delighted at your visit. Will you also be staying with us, then?"

Sydney nodded. "But only—"

"Yes, we will," Nate interrupted quickly and touched a hand lightly to her arm to silence her.

Sydney's throat tightened. He didn't trust the staff enough to inform them that they would be leaving at dawn and taking Robert with them. Not even Miss Jenner.

"I'll ask Mrs. Larkin to prepare rooms for you," Miss Jenner said. "And how long will you be staying at Oakwood, ma'am?"

An honest question asked only so that the cook and housekeeper could make plans. But Sydney had no idea how to answer and darted her gaze to Nate for rescue.

"Most likely only for the sennight, if that's no trouble." Nate gave her one of his most charming smiles. "Oakwood was along our route from London, and it offered a more accommodating stay than an inn. Lady Rowland thought it would be prudent to take time to inspect the property while we're here."

Miss Jenner nodded. "Of course."

But what else would the little governess say? Her manners were too proper to comment upon the peculiar circumstances of her employer's unexpected visit in a rented carriage with a soldier, no less, and without so much as a maid accompanying them. Or luggage.

"We'll make certain your stay is comfortable." Miss Jenner hesitated, barely a pause at all, but Sydney noticed. "There's a wonderful dressmaker and tailor in the village, ma'am. If you're in need of anything during your stay, I'm certain they'll be able to provide it. A general mercantile, too, should you or Captain Reed want anything that we don't have here at Oakwood."

"Thank you," Sydney sighed out gratefully. She liked this woman. Miss Jenner was sharp and paid attention to details, yet a pleasantness exuded from her despite her well-guarded answers.

The governess hesitated again, and this time a troubled frown finally cracked her carefully held countenance. "Forgive me, but I wasn't expecting— Is something wrong with Oakwood, my lady?"

"No, of course not. You're doing a fine job here, by all appearances." Sydney glanced quickly at Nate, shaking her head more forcefully than she intended and certain her cheeks had paled. "We were just...traveling from London because...because..."

"Because Lady Rowland has business in Birmingham at one of her parents' mills that requires her attention," Nate interjected smoothly. "We weren't intending to stay here, but this afternoon, when she noticed how close we would be, I suggested we stop."

Sydney nodded, knowing to play along. "Yes." She forced a smile to cover the lie. "We thought it would be nice to—"

"Miss Jenner!" a young voice shouted from the hallway, followed by the thumping of running feet. "Miss Jenner, where are you?"

The air ripped from Sydney's lungs, and her heart lurched into her throat. She wasn't ready for this! She hadn't given herself time to prepare or to—

The door flung open, and a small boy ran inside.

Robert.

Eighteen

NATE'S GAZE FLEW TO SYDNEY'S FACE. SHE'D GONE instantly white as the young boy burst into the room with all the subtlety of a cavalry charge. She stiffened as he bounced toward them. Her hand flew to the gold locket at her throat, her eyes widening with... Good Lord, was that *fear*?

"Walk, please," Miss Jenner scolded gently, and the boy immediately slowed. "Remember what I told you. A gentleman never runs inside the house."

"Yes, miss." He nodded automatically, obviously having heard the admonishment several times before. Even though he'd slowed, he still came at a half-trotting walk, and excitement over the news that Oakwood had visitors glowed on his face. From what Nate had gathered, he and Sydney were the first official visitors Oakwood had ever had.

The boy's attention landed on Sydney, and he frowned. "Hello..."

That unsure greeting caused her breathing to come so fast and shallow that Nate worried she might faint.

Then his big, blue eyes flicked to Nate. His blossoming grin clearly declared that he found Nate's soldier's bearing far more interesting than some strange lady. "Who are *you*?"

"Robbie." Miss Jenner shushed him with a gentle hand

on his shoulder. "Gentlemen are never rude to their guests. Introductions before questions, please."

He heaved a heavy sigh and rolled his eyes in boyhood exaggeration. "Very well."

He approached Nate first, and his gaze swept curiously over him. Sydney's own eyes were glued to the boy and every move the towheaded youngster made.

"Welcome to Oakwood Manor, sir." He gave a well-practiced nod of his head to match his well-practiced speech. "I am Robert Michael Rowland, and I live here. It is a pleasure to make your acquaintance."

Nate suppressed the amused twitching of his lips at the boy's precociousness and returned his nod. "And mine to meet you, sir." He gave the lad a smart salute. "I am Captain Nate Reed of His Majesty's Horse Guards."

"Truly?" The boy's eyes widened like saucers, and his voice filled with awe. "A Horse Guard?"

"Truly," Nate confirmed confidentially. Then, before the boy's excitement could burst loose and have him bouncing around the room again, Nate gestured toward Sydney and gave her a proper bow from the waist as an example for Robert to do the same. "And may I introduce you to Lady Rowland? My lady," he said in a low but reassuring voice, "this is Robert Rowland."

"Robert *Michael* Rowland," the boy corrected and shot an irritated scowl at Nate. Apparently, his awe for soldiers only went so far. Then he stared up at Sydney and scrunched his nose as he studied her. "Are you really a lady?"

Sydney drew a deep breath, her eyes glistening, and nodded as she choked out, "Yes."

"Oh," the boy whispered. This time, his voice didn't hold the same awe he'd shown toward Nate but raw curiosity. Then he held out his hand for her in greeting. She hesitated, then gingerly slipped her fingers into his, and he made great show of giving a sweeping bow over her hand. He was a miniature gentleman in the making. "My lady, it is a pleasure to make your acquaintance."

Robert took a quick glance toward Miss Jenner to check if he'd made the introductions properly, and at a nod of approval by his governess, he beamed proudly and released Sydney's hand. It happened only for a heartbeat, but Nate would have sworn he saw Sydney's fingers tighten around the boy's to keep his hand in hers for just a moment longer.

Then she pulled away and wrapped her empty hand in her skirt.

"Lady Rowland and Captain Reed are traveling from London," Miss Jenner explained to Robert. "They will be our guests at Oakwood for the next week, and you will be their host."

"Good," he confirmed. "I should like to have guests." The boy looked up at Sydney as if intuitively knowing that the baroness was the most important person in the room and outranked a captain. Then he gave her a puzzled frown as if also intuiting more between them than mere host and guest. "Have you been here before?"

"No," she whispered.

"You seem familiar…but I don't remember you." He gave another curious tilt of his head and deepening of his puzzled frown. "Have we met before?"

"Once." She blinked rapidly and knelt down to bring her face level with his. "A very long time ago when you were just a baby."

He stuck out his chest with boyish pride. "I'm six years old."

"I know." She gave him an uncertain smile. "You'll be all grown up soon."

"I *am* grown up," he protested with a touch of pique and jutted his chin into the air.

Nate stared at the boy, and his gut tightened. Despite the dark blond hair and blue eyes, with his chin angled upward like that... Dear Lord, he looked just like Sydney.

"I study lessons now upstairs in the nursery, *real* lessons with books and blackboards. I can count to one hundred, and I know all my letters and numbers. And"—Robert leaned toward her as if sharing a deep secret—"Miss Jenner is teaching me to speak French!"

"Is she?" Sydney's voice hitched.

He nodded with excitement. "So we'll be able to talk in secret, and Mrs. Larkin and Mr. Beasley won't be able to understand us!"

"My, that's a fine thing for a gentleman to know." Sydney leaned closer as if sharing a secret of her own, and she reached up tentatively to brush at his blond hair as it lay against his temple. "I know French, too."

Robert looked at her warily, suspicious that anyone else might be able to share in the secret he kept with Miss Jenner. "Well, we don't actually *speak* French yet."

Then he stepped back out of her reach, and her hand fell empty to her side.

Something inside Nate's chest shattered as the boy turned away from her and approached him instead. He watched Sydney's reaction, and his heart burned with sympathy and concern for her.

But her attention was still rapt on her son, her green eyes bright with unshed tears. He'd never seen her more vulnerable than at that moment.

"Did you bring your warhorse with you, Captain?" Robert asked.

"No, sir." He tore his eyes away from Sydney to the boy. "I left him in London at the Horse Guards."

"Well, I have a pony, and I'm a very fine rider. I can trot and canter, and Beasley has promised to teach me to jump!"

"*Mr.* Beasley," Miss Jenner corrected, doing her best to fade from the group and not look at Sydney, who was dripping emotion as she stared at her son.

"Mr. Beasley," Robert repeated automatically. "Someday I'm going to be a dragoon and fight for the Horse Guards, too!"

"We can always use a good man like you," Nate said.

Excitement lit the boy's round face. "Will you ride with me tomorrow, Captain, if it's not raining?"

Nate sent a look toward Sydney to seek her permission to lie to her son as he had every intention of being on the road to Scotland by then. But her eyes never left Robert. "Yes, sir. I would be happy to."

The boy cheered.

"Now that introductions have been made," Miss Jenner said as she placed her hand on Robert's shoulder to gain his attention and stop him from jumping up and down in excitement, "you must leave your guests to settle into their rooms, and you need to go to the breakfast room to eat your dinner." The governess glanced quickly at Sydney as a self-reprimand darkened the woman's face. "Robert takes all his meals in the breakfast room, my lady," she explained as Sydney finally rose from her knees where she'd been kneeling since talking to the boy. "I know it's unusual. But it doesn't seem necessary for him to take his meals in the nursery any longer, and the dining room is too big for just the two of us. That is, unless you'd prefer we followed tradition, even in your absence."

"The breakfast room is fine," Sydney answered, deferring to the governess. "You know what's best for Robert."

Nate narrowed his eyes sharply.

"Thank you, ma'am. We'll make certain not to bother you and the captain unduly while you're here."

Sydney gave a curt but absent nod because her attention was still focused on Robert. And on the way Miss Jenner continued to rest her hand possessively on the boy's shoulder.

"Go along, then, Robert," Miss Jenner ordered.

"Yes, miss!" He turned on his heels and ran toward the door with the same enthusiasm and energy he'd had when he'd entered.

"Walk, please." Miss Jenner turned back toward them. Finding Sydney's gaze staring at the door after the boy, she swiftly slid her smile to Nate. "My apologies. Robbie can be a bit of a handful."

"No apologies necessary," he assured her, but his concern for Sydney grew with each heartbeat. "It's been a long day.

Perhaps we can be shown to our rooms now." He lowered his voice as he added, "And send up a hot bath for her ladyship. I'm certain she'll want to freshen up before dinner."

"Of course," Miss Jenner answered in the same quiet voice. She gestured toward the door. "If you'll follow me, please."

Miss Jenner preceded them from the room. Distracted, Sydney walked after her, with Nate following closely behind.

When they reached the door, he took Sydney's elbow and stopped her.

"Wait," he ordered beneath his breath. Then he said louder to the governess as she stood in the hall, "I need to speak to Lady Rowland. We'll only be a moment."

He closed the door to give them privacy, not caring that he'd just broken half a dozen rules of propriety.

Sydney didn't move except to squeeze shut her eyes and inhale deeply, as if willing her racing heart to calm and her breath to come normally again.

He gently took her shoulders and turned her to face him, and with his hand at her chin, he tilted her face until she had no choice but to look at him. Regret and sadness glistened in her eyes. But more emotion swirled inside her from the encounter with her son that even now had her trembling…

Fear.

Impossible. How could a woman so brave and confident in all other aspects of her life be afraid of a small boy?

No, he realized grimly. Not afraid of the child—

She was afraid to be his mother. So afraid, in fact, that she was letting another woman raise him in her place.

"Miss Jenner is only his governess," he reminded her.

Sydney would be a wonderful mother to the boy if she only let herself. "But *you* are his mother. You need to make the decisions for him, not her, and you need to be with him."

She shook her head. "No one can ever know who he really is. The scandal, all that gossip…"

Lies. All of it.

"When have you ever cared what the *ton* thought of you?" He cajolingly stroked her cheek with his thumb. "Tell me the truth now. Why are you afraid to be around Robert?"

Her lips parted. "Pardon?"

"You're not afraid of scandal. Not a woman like you." He couldn't resist placing a reassuring kiss to her lips. "Besides, a mother who loves her son would find ways around that."

Her lips had trembled beneath his, but he wasn't arrogant enough to believe her reaction was desire. "I don't know what you mean."

"Trust me." He somehow resisted the desperate ache to pull her to him and soothe away in his arms the doubt and pain that hurt her. "For once, *trust me.*"

She blinked rapidly as the first tears began to cling to her lashes, and she admitted, "I don't know how to be a good mother." A strangled sound of fear and hopelessness came from her. Her hand went to her mouth as if to physically force back fresh cries. "Dear God, Nate—*my* own mother did this to me!" Desolate anguish rang through her voice as she whispered between her fingers, "How am I supposed to be a good mother when she…"

He dropped his hands to his sides as the icy truth tumbled over him. She didn't fear scandal and a ruined reputation.

She feared herself.

His heart shattered for her. "Sydney..."

She pulled in a long breath as she admitted what he knew to be her deepest fear, the primary reason she kept the boy out of her life and away from her heart—"I don't know how to be a good mother. That's why I can't be with him."

"You can learn," he assured her gently. "It's not too late."

"And if he hates me for giving him up?" The words choked from her. "If he can't forgive me or refuses to accept me as his mother?" She shook her head, and at her sides, she clenched and unclenched her hands in frustration and grief. "I'll have lost him all over again. If I have to bear that, too, after everything else..." Her voice trailed off into a strangled shudder. "I won't survive it."

"Baroness," he murmured, "you're far stronger than you know."

He slipped his arms around her and drew her close. She melted against him and turned her head to nuzzle her cheek against his shoulder. At her vulnerable gesture, he tightened his hold around her and lowered his mouth to her hair.

"You have to tell him the truth," he urged.

Her trembling hands clutched at his lapels. "And if not knowing is better in the end?"

"It isn't." He knew firsthand the truth of that with his own father.

Slowly, she stepped out of his arms. "I-I need time. I can't—not right now." Each shake of her head was a jerking refusal. "I just can't!"

She stood before him pale, shaking, and anguished, and

he summoned all his restraint not to grab her back into his arms and kiss her until he made all her pain and fear vanish. But he knew it wouldn't work. For once, he couldn't help her.

She'd have to find her way to her son by herself.

"Before I change his life again," she whispered, barely louder than a breath, "I need to be certain I'm doing what's best for him. And right now—" A single tear fell down her cheek. "Right now, I'm not certain that having me for his mother is best."

Nineteen

In the darkness of the first-floor hallway, her feet padded silently on the carpet runner as Sydney made her way carefully toward her room. The house was still and quiet around her except for the chimes of the long-case clock in the front foyer as it struck eleven o'clock.

She hadn't meant to retire so late. After all, today had been a long, exhausting day on the heels of a wonderful, exhausting night. She was bone-tired and needed rest. But she hadn't been able to drag herself away from Robbie.

After a reserved and awkward dinner in the formal dining room with just she and Nate, Caroline Jenner passed along an invitation from Robbie, asking his guests up to the nursery to join him for his evening chocolate and biscuits. Sydney had gone eagerly despite her pounding heart, with an introspective Nate following slowly behind.

She hadn't expected to feel such a pull toward a child she hadn't seen in six years, yet she loved him, and far more than she realized until she saw him come running inside the drawing room that afternoon.

By the time he ran back out, she knew her life would never be the same.

It had been a bittersweet few hours in the nursery tonight.

She played with Robbie on the floor with his toys and listened to him tell her about his life on the farm, and she simply could not get enough of him. Nate excused himself early to retire to his room, but Sydney remained long after the chocolate tray was taken away and Robbie had changed into his nightshirt. Miss Jenner let Sydney put him into bed, tuck him beneath the covers, and read one last bedtime story to him from a large book of fairy tales he kept on his bedside table. Sydney prolonged the evening by remaining until he fell asleep. Even then, with his blond head resting peacefully on the pillow, she lingered at his bedside to simply watch him sleep.

She reached her room and slipped inside. Thankfully, one of the maids had already prepared it for the night. The satin coverlet had been turned down, and a small fire burned low in the fireplace, its soft glow heating the room against the cold night. On the stand beside the bed sat a glass and a bottle of port.

She gave a grateful yet tired smile as she crossed the room to pour herself a drink. Mrs. Larkin had thought of everything she might—

"Sydney."

The low voice slid heatedly down her spine.

Nate.

She whirled around to find him leaning back against the closed door. The handsome devil must have slipped into the room behind her without a sound. He was in his shirtsleeves with his cravat missing and his tan waistcoat unbuttoned. He was half-dressed, completely desirable, and wholly unexpected.

She'd been certain he wouldn't come to her room tonight after what she'd said to him in the drawing room that afternoon. His silence all through dinner had only increased her assurance of that. So had his distance in the nursery, when he'd remained at the side of the room and away from her and Robbie.

Yet here he was, with his hazel eyes gleaming at her so intently that they sent her heart somersaulting. How was it possible that even such a simple look from him had the power to undo her?

She fought down the rising arousal low in her belly and reached for the port to pour out a glass. She did her best to appear as calm as possible. As calm as any proper lady would be upon finding a half-dressed man in her bedroom, that is…the same one who had ripped her breath away last night and shattered her in his arms.

God's mercy. Her hands shook so violently she nearly spilled the port.

She remembered all the delicious things he was capable of doing to her, all of which she would gladly let him do to her again tonight.

Yet he remained on the far side of the room with his back against the door as if he couldn't quite decide whether to come fully inside the room or flee.

That did not portend a good end to the evening. She asked, "What are you doing here?"

"Reconnaissance."

She paused in mid pour to glance over her shoulder at him. "Pardon?"

"Civilian," he chastised teasingly. "While you were upstairs with Robert and Miss Jenner, I searched through the house to find all the doors and stairs, learn the layout of the rooms, and discover where all your servants spend the night. And you should know," he informed her with a quirk of his brow, "they don't all spend the night in their own rooms."

Just as he wasn't in his. Did he plan to spend the night here, or had he only come to update her on his plans and to give her instructions for their departure at dawn?

But she no longer wanted to leave Oakwood.

She held out the glass toward him and waited. If Nate wanted her tonight, he would have to come to her. He would have to accept her as she was, including all her confusions about her son. And about him.

He studied the proffered glass for a long moment. Then he pushed himself away from the door and slowly approached her.

"Apparently," he told her as he accepted the port, "Mr. Beasley is a very busy man."

"*Beasley?*" She couldn't help but laugh at the thought of the balding, ruddy-faced groom and gardener as the farm's resident Casanova. "Your talents are misplaced, Captain." She smiled at him with unabashed amusement. "You should be working for the *ton*'s gossips."

"It could be a second career if this army thing doesn't work out," he said dryly.

She bit back a laugh. This man couldn't be anything else but a soldier.

Without invitation, he slumped into the chair in front of the fire and kicked his long legs out in front of him. He appeared completely at ease and deliciously rumpled. Her thighs clenched at the sight, and she somehow resisted the urge to climb on top of him.

"Nate," she whispered, her pulse speeding. "I want—"

"Miss Caroline Jenner," he interrupted quietly. As he took a sip of the port, his eyes met hers over the rim of the glass. "Do you trust her?"

Her heart fell with rejection. He was only here tonight for business after all.

She shouldn't have been surprised, yet she wasn't prepared for the panging echo of loss inside her or for how she already felt utterly bereft. He'd warned her that his goal was stopping Scepter as soon as possible. Once he put an end to Scepter, he would receive his reward money, and then he was as good as gone from London. And from her life.

Last night, she'd found exactly what she'd wanted— intimacy without losing control of her heart or her independence. So why was her traitorous body still aching for his, her mind still wanting to be challenged by him? And why, oh dear God, *why* did she find herself wanting to surrender to him in more ways than only with her body?

Ignoring her disappointment, she crossed to the armoire and reached behind her back to unfasten the short row of buttons.

"Yes, I do trust her," she answered. "I hired her two years ago, long before the blackmail started."

She shrugged out of the sleeves and bodice, then stepped

out of the skirt and petticoat. Her stays went next, tossed unwanted across the back of a nearby chair.

"She's never given me any reason to doubt her loyalty to me or her dedication to Robert," she added as she hung up the dress and reached to take down her hair.

He paused, the glass raised halfway to his lips. His eyes narrowed on her as she pulled the pins from her hair and shook it free. "What are you doing?"

"It's late, and I'm tired," she explained wearily.

She pulled her long hair over her shoulder and began to loosely braid it. After all, what was the point in remaining dressed if he had no interest in undressing her? She'd have to do it herself.

"If you want to discuss your mission tonight," she told him, "you'll have to do it while I get ready for bed."

He said nothing to that but finished bringing the glass to his mouth.

She took his silence as an invitation to carry on and continued to fix her hair. After all, based on his behavior last night, he would have swept her into his arms and taken her to the bed by now if he wanted to make love.

Obviously, he didn't.

"I needed someone to care for Robert and give him a good education," she explained, "and not just on scholarly subjects but also on how to behave in society. He'll be part of that someday. Oh, he'll have enough money that they'll accept him just the same whether he has manners or not, but I don't want him to feel uncomfortable the way I did."

She finished the braid and reached into the armoire for

the shirt hanging on its hook. Nate's shirt. The same one she'd planned on wearing to bed last night before he stripped it off her, the same one she'd wear in bed tonight. Alone. Her belly sank with bittersweet emotion at the sight of it.

He commented quietly, "You stayed a long while in the nursery this evening."

If she wasn't so irritated at him, she might have teased him about how port made his voice hoarse. Instead, she turned her back to him and pushed the shift off her shoulders and down to the floor around her feet.

"I was enjoying myself and didn't want to leave," she admitted with a bit of embarrassment over revealing her emotions to him but none about displaying her bare backside. He deserved that. "I stayed until Robbie fell asleep."

"He likes you," Nate half whispered.

She paused as she raised her arms into the air to slip the shirt on over her head. His words warmed her more than she had a right to feel. Her fingers tightened on the linen material as it bunched around her shoulders and breasts, and she didn't have the courage to face him as she asked, "Do we have to leave tomorrow? I want one more day with him, Nate. One more day when I can get to know him as the little boy he is before his life is turned upside-down again. Please."

She held her breath, fearing he would refuse and break the fragile bond forming between her and her son.

"All right," he agreed reluctantly. "But only one day."

Her shoulders sagged with relief, and she pulled the shirt down into place around her thighs.

"Thank you." She was more grateful for this opportunity with Robbie than she wanted to admit, even to herself.

"Do you still think you can part with him, then, even after tonight?"

Emotion tightened her throat. Hadn't she been wondering the same thing herself since the moment Robbie ran into the drawing room?

She slowly propped her foot on the stool of her dressing table and lifted the hem of the shirt to midthigh so she could untie her stocking and roll it down her leg. Could she ever be Robbie's mother, a true and proper and *good* mother to a boy who didn't even know who she was? Especially when she had no good mother of her own to model herself after?

"I don't know," she whispered honestly.

Nate gave no counter to that. Most likely, he still didn't understand the decision she'd struggled with to keep Robbie at Oakwood rather than with her in London. After all, Nate had a good mother who had been willing to sacrifice everything to keep her son with her, a mother he could respect and emulate. Of course he wouldn't understand. He *couldn't*.

Yet she let a wistful smile tug at her lips as she slipped the stocking from her toes and dropped it to the floor. A soft laugh passed her lips. "Did you see the way Robert introduced himself to—"

The words choked on her tongue as she glanced up at Nate and froze. He was staring at her bare leg with a wolfish hunger in his eyes as if he wanted to devour her.

God help her… *Yes. Please do.*

"Take off the other stocking, Sydney," he ordered quietly,

but the husky purr of his voice shivered through her like the rumble of distant thunder.

She did as he commanded, placed her left leg on the stool, and reached beneath the hem of the shirt for her stocking. This time, she slid her palms along her leg as she pushed up the shirt, far higher than before, and revealed to his eyes a long stretch of bare thigh. And this time, when she untied the ribbon and rolled the stocking down her leg, her fingers brushed slowly down her calf as the tantalizing heat of his gaze prickled over her skin and formed goose bumps in its wake.

The stocking fell away to the floor.

His gaze drifted along the front of her body until it met hers. "Loosen your hair."

Her fingers trembled as she performed his bidding and undid the braid she'd just woven.

"Now shake it out."

She reached her hands up into her hair and ran her fingers through it to free the thick strands and let them cascade down her back. Every move she made was watched closely by his hazel eyes, whose intense gaze stirred a damp heat between her thighs. She shouldn't like this as much as she did, being ordered about and controlled, yet his raw desire aroused her until she shook from it, until she would have gladly followed any order he gave as long as he kept looking at her.

"Come here, Baroness."

Unable to stop herself because she simply wanted him too much, she went to him. "I've told you," she scolded, although her voice was thick with need, "you shouldn't call me baroness."

"And I've told you." He sat up and placed the unwanted port onto the side table. "Someone as strong, independent, and beautiful as you…deserves to be worshipped."

Pleasure warmed through her even as she corrected, "That's not what you said."

"Didn't I?" He feigned ignorance but couldn't stop a sly smile from curving his sensuous lips.

She knelt on the floor between his knees. Her hands rested on his thighs as she tilted back her head to gaze up at him, and what she saw stole her breath away. Heat and arousal, longing and need—surely the same raw desire she glimpsed on his face was mirrored on her own.

"You still want me," she whispered with surprise.

He trailed his fingertips across her cheek. "I've wanted you since the moment I saw you sitting at that faro table."

"But this morning when you weren't in bed…" She shook her head. What was she supposed to believe—the desire for her that had him trembling or the distance he kept putting between them?

"I needed time to think." He brushed his hand down her front and caressed her breast through the cotton shirt. It was a gesture both possessive and deliciously arousing. "Sometimes, you confuse the hell out of me."

She arched into his touch as her body begged for more. Ironically, confusion was the one emotion she no longer felt about him. With Nate she was certain…certain that no man had ever made her feel this way before, that no other man ever would again.

When she was with him, she became a complete woman,

a daring and courageous fighter to conquer the world and a seductress to rule his body. He made her feel beautiful, protected, free. Important. For the first time in her life, she felt as if she truly mattered. Not her money, her courtesy title, or her family's connections, but *her*. She'd loved Michael and always would, but he had never made her feel the way she did when she was with Nate.

She wanted to love him, to let him into her heart the way she had with Michael, yet not enough to let him have reign over her to hurt her the way she'd been hurt before. She could give him her body, but she could never surrender her independence.

She rubbed her cheek against his thigh, unable to find the words to explain all that to him.

"I didn't know what to make of you." He gently stroked her hair. "When I met you, I knew there had to be more to you than what you showed the world, a vulnerability you revealed to no one."

"Except you," she admitted with a tremble of fear at exposing her emotions.

"Except me." He pulled at the shoulder of the cotton shirt. "Take this off, Baroness, and let me see you again. *All* of you."

She succumbed with a shiver to both her desire for him and her fear of losing control. "If I'm a baroness," she reminded him as she slid her hands tantalizingly up and down his thighs, her fingertips sinking into the hard muscle beneath his breeches, "then I outrank you, Captain." Her hands moved up to where his breeches were already tented, and she brushed her fingertips over his hard erection, then teased him by moving her hands away. "Which means I give the orders, and you do *my* bidding."

He gave a throaty but strained laugh. "And if I refuse?"

"Court-martial." She stroked slowly back up his thighs. This time, she cupped him against her palm through the fabric and elicited a sharp inhalation from him. "I might even have to put you in irons for punishment."

She'd hoped for another laugh from him at that double entendre. Instead, he clenched his teeth as his cock jumped against her hand. Already he was fully aroused, large, and heavy. His reaction flamed the need licking inside her and emboldened her.

"Take off your waistcoat," she commanded.

To her delight, he shrugged it off his shoulders and tossed it away. She yanked his shirt out of his waistband and slipped her hands beneath it. She explored the hard ridges of his stomach, and his muscles rippled beneath her seeking fingertips.

"Good," she purred.

His breath came fast and shallow, and his heartbeat raced beneath her fingers as she reached higher up his front to touch his chest.

"Now remove your shirt."

Pulling down his braces, he tugged it off over his head and dropped it to the floor. He was bare from the waist up, with his arousal very evident from the waist down.

Unable to touch him enough to satisfy the growing need inside her, she rubbed her hand over his chest and stroked the warm skin stretched smooth over the hard muscles beneath. She paused to flick her fingertips over his flat nipples and reveled in the tremor that pulsed through him at such a simple touch.

"*Very* good, Captain."

"Sydney." Her name was a warning growl at his lips.

She was pressing her luck, she knew, by poking at a sleeping lion. But the temptress inside her was enjoying this too much to stop. "And my next order…you will let me kiss you. Everywhere."

He shuddered his acquiescence, and with her pulse racing, Sydney leaned forward to place her mouth against his chest. He trembled beneath the delight of her lips on his body, of her tongue tasting his flesh. She followed with her mouth everywhere her hands had caressed him before. Then she dared to close her lips over his nipple and suck.

He buried his hands in her hair but didn't set her away. Not even when she kissed lower across his abdomen, then lower to swirl her tongue teasingly inside his navel, and then lower still…

She unfastened his fall and freed him from the tight material. Sweet Lord, he was magnificent, and she shamelessly licked her lips at the sight of him.

"Sydney." This time, her name emerged as a pleading groan.

She brushed her fingertips along his hard length, mesmerized by the combination of soft skin and steely hardness. Her thighs clenched at the memory of having him inside her last night, stroking her from within, and filling her completely with man and heat and need. When he'd driven himself to release inside her, the exquisite sensation had simply torn her breath away.

She moaned and lowered her head to close her lips around him.

Gently but persistently, she drew him deeper into her mouth and swirled her tongue around his engorged tip. Soft groans came from him and encouraged her to be even bolder, even more wanton and free, so she fluttered her fingertips along his shaft in a teasing caress as her mouth increased the intensity of its sucking.

He rolled back his head and whispered incoherently. His hands tightened in her hair, tangling her strands around his fingers and fisting her waves against his palms.

Excitement pulsed through her, and she thrilled with the power she held over him. Her hand tightened around his length and stroked, and each caress made his body shake harder until a bead formed at the tiny slit at his tip. She licked it away. He tasted of masculine salty sweetness. *Delicious.*

But it was only a small taste, and she craved more.

She took him deep into her mouth. A moan of aching arousal rose from her throat when his cock flexed against her tongue. She suckled hard, her lips firm and relentless around him, as her tongue flicked and swirled over his swollen tip.

He groaned with each strong pull of her lips. He was close to release, and so was she from simply having her mouth on him. Her own body quivered, and evidence of her arousal for him soaked the throbbing folds between her legs. She felt the restraint in him begin to give. He would lose control at any moment and come inside her mouth, surrendering control to her.

As if reading her mind, he took her by the shoulders and

pulled her up onto his lap. She fell against his bare chest as her legs straddled him.

He placed his hot mouth against her ear and rasped out in a half order, half warning, "You first."

Oh yes! Love me…please love me… But before her trembling lips could moan out the words, his large hands encircled her waist and pulled her forward against the tip of his cock. He thrust his hips up hard and buried himself deep inside her.

"Nate!" she cried out as she was swept up into the sweet, rocking rhythm engulfing them. She pulsed her hips against his to meet each exquisite rise and fall beneath her.

He grabbed the hem of her shirt and lifted it up her body, over her head and off, baring her breasts to him. His mouth swooped to capture one, and even as she continued to buck her hips against his, he suckled at her nipple with the same determined ferocity that she had sucked at him.

She shuddered with a gasping breath as she arched in his arms. So close…her body was so close to shattering, her heart so close to breaking.

He'd sworn to protect her, but who could protect her from him? All her life, she'd opened her heart and been hurt. To Rowland, who promised in front of the bishop always to love and honor her only to degrade her with his prostitutes and insults, sometimes with his fists. To her parents, who sold her for a title. To Michael, who told her he loved her but then hurt her most of all by dying and leaving her behind.

After all that, if she gave her heart to Nate and he broke it too, how would she ever survive?

She wrapped her arms around his neck so she could raise and lower herself against him in her own rhythm, her own controlled pace. He wanted her to surrender, but despite digging her fingernails into his shoulders with want and need, she simply couldn't. She would surrender her body but never her heart.

His hands went to her hips to guide her, and he shifted forward to bring himself to the edge of the chair.

"Take it," he growled against her ear, once more giving her orders but ones she'd gladly obey. "Take all the pleasure you want."

With a soft cry, she bore down on him and did exactly as he wanted. Her hips bucked wildly against his as she bounced over him, and her ankles locked together at the small of his back for leverage. Each thrust of her hips was delicious, each of his groans the most erotic sound she'd ever heard.

"That's it, darling...just like that." He rested his forehead against her shoulder, briefly shutting his eyes against the pleasure she brought him by claiming her own. But instead of trying to wrench control away from her now, he let her go, granting her the freedom to move—to make love to him— however she wanted.

Her chest tightened even as fire licked at her toes. He'd changed the rules on her, and the realization terrified her. Somewhere between ordering her to undress and this moment, he'd managed to maneuver her into believing she was in control when each passing heartbeat only brought her closer to surrendering. Each movement to wrest control from him only made her want to give him even more.

He thrust up hard beneath her, plunging himself impossibly deep inside her. Once, twice—with a last driving push, he groaned and stood. He lifted her from the chair with him, and she was forced to wrap her body around his to keep from sliding to the floor. Never leaving her tight warmth, he carried her to the bed, placed her onto the mattress, and followed down on top of her.

He whispered her name with so much affection and respect that he overwhelmed her.

A sob tore from her, and her arms tightened around him as she felt herself begin to fall. But the only man in the world who could catch her was the same one sending her over the edge.

She shattered in his arms.

Her heart followed a single beat later.

Twenty

"DAMNATION, BARONESS." NATE SCOWLED AS HE REACHED up to rub his shoulder. "I think you left claw marks."

Smiling wickedly at him, she handed over the bottle of port she'd slid out of the bed to fetch.

He sat back against the pillows propped along the headboard and gave her a long, leisurely look that made her blood boil. Again. They were both naked, having shed what little was left of his clothes. Now, he lay across her bed as if he had no intention of going anywhere until dawn.

She certainly hoped he didn't.

Heavens, what a magnificent sight he was. Even now, lying naked in the bed with his manhood resting against his thigh, he was impressive. And the things he could do...*oh my*.

Before the night was over, she hoped he would do those things to her again.

She crawled back into bed and curled up against his side. She was unable to resist the magnetic pull of him, and even now her body ached with sweet anticipation of making love again. Her hand brushed over his broad chest, and she smiled at the way his muscles quivered beneath her fingertips.

She placed a shy kiss to his chest. Sex had never been like

this before. Oh, it had been nice. Michael had been so gentle, so tender... In truth, she could barely remember now what it felt like to be with Michael, except that she knew she'd been loved. But never had she cried out so helplessly with him the way she did with Nate, and she'd certainly never had the urge to scratch him.

A bubble of laughter escaped her.

"What is it?" he asked and brushed his hand leisurely along her side.

She lifted up to smile at him. "I was just thinking about how amazing you—" She froze, her eyes focusing on his forearm. "You're bleeding."

His gaze flicked dismissively at his arm, then back to her. "Your fault."

She scrambled off the bed and snatched up the discarded shirt on the floor. She jabbed a finger at his arm. "How is that my fault?"

"You distracted me, and I didn't realize I'd strained it." He opened his arms. "Come here and distract me again."

She gave him a scowl to tell him what she thought of that idea, then ripped a strip of cloth from the bottom of the shirt and gestured at him. "Hold out your arm so I can tend to it."

Without complaint, he did as she asked. She sat on the bed next to him to untie the soiled bandage.

"If you tore out my stitches, Nate Reed, I swear I'll put them back with nails and glue until—" She paused as sudden suspicion raced through her. He was being accommodating. *Too* accommodating. Her eyes narrowed. "Why are you cooperating so easily all of a sudden?"

He shrugged. "If a naked nurse wants to put her hands on me, who am I to stop her?" When she opened her mouth to give him the biting retort he deserved, he added, "Besides, you just made that shirt shorter. Which means it will only be a greater distraction when you put it on again tomorrow night."

She slid him a narrowed glance as she carefully applied the new wrap around his forearm. "What makes you think I'll wear that shirt again?"

"Because you wore it to seduce me two nights in a row."

"I didn't seduce you. *You* seduced m—"

Realizing what she was about to say, she clamped her mouth shut. Her lips pressed together with an irritated *hmph* at the flash of self-pleased triumph on his face.

She tied off the fresh bandage. "Are you always so arrogant after bedding a woman?"

He rakishly grinned and eased back against the headboard. "Let's do it again and find out."

She smacked him with a pillow.

She moved to slide off the bed, but he grabbed her, flipped her onto her back, and pinned her beneath his large body. Before she could protest, he touched his lips to hers in a kiss so gentle that it made her eyes sting.

"You are so beautiful," he whispered, his hazel eyes flickering gold in the dying firelight.

Her throat tightened at the tender compliment. With all her irritation at him seeping away, she reached up to caress his cheek and felt the rough stubble of midnight beard beneath her fingertips. He simply took her breath away.

He stroked his hands leisurely down her body, taking the

time to explore her the way he hadn't done before in their earlier rush to possess each other. Her flesh prickled with heat everywhere he touched, and a sweet ache for him blossomed anew between her thighs.

As if knowing exactly how her body was responding, he caressed between her legs and smiled when she whimpered.

"You like being touched here." It was not a question.

"Oh yes." With a sigh, she relaxed beneath his hand.

"Good," he murmured, then brushed his lips so lightly over hers that it was barely a kiss at all. "Because I like touching you."

Closing her eyes, she surrendered to the delicious slide of his hand between her thighs. All her senses focused right there at his fingertips and at the heat radiating out from them as they gently delved into her soft folds, making her tingle and throb in anticipation with each deepening stroke. Oh, his touch was simply heavenly!

Except...little ridges snagged against her fingertips as she ran her hands over his bare back. She'd not noticed them before, having been too distracted by what else he'd been doing to her each time they were naked together. Now that they had time to explore each other, though, her curiosity got the better of her.

"Nate?"

"Hmm?"

"How did you get these scars?" She trailed her hand over his shoulder blade. When she sewed up his arm, he said he'd experienced worse... "Were you hurt in battle?"

His fingers stilled against her. Slowly, he pulled away and leaned up over her on his good forearm to stare down at her.

"I told you," he reminded her quietly. The length of his

body still pressed against hers, but suddenly, he felt miles away. "The baby came early."

"What does that have to do with your back?"

His expression remained stony blank, and the hazel depths of his eyes turned distant. "I was on the Peninsula when I received word that Sarah was having problems. I didn't have leave to return to England, but I went anyway."

Her brow furrowed. "I don't understand."

"I deserted."

Icy realization sank through her. If he deserted, then... No, that couldn't be—

"You were flogged?" she whispered, horrified. The words barely formed a sound on her stunned lips.

His face remained inscrutable. "Yes. When I returned to the regiment."

She blinked hard, barely able to breathe beneath the fresh grief that gripped her, yet his handsome face still blurred as tears welled in her eyes. She choked out, "How could they..."

"I deserved it." His own voice was emotionless. "I deserted my position and left my men. I should have gone in front of a firing squad. The flogging was lenient."

No. It had to have been hell. The thought of Nate being tied to a post while one of his fellow officers took a whip to his bare back when he'd only left to be with his wife, to find her already dead and his baby dying—

A tear slipped down her face. She couldn't hold back her anguish.

"Don't cry for me, Baroness." He reached up to gently wipe it away with his thumb. "I don't deserve your tears."

"I'm not crying for you," she whispered as more sobs followed the first. From the softening of his mouth and eyes at that, she knew he didn't understand and thought she was lying. But she wasn't. She wasn't crying in pity but in blinding fury at his commanding officers. They didn't deserve to have him among their ranks. "Why did you go back, knowing what they would do to you?"

He answered solemnly, "Because I wanted to die."

Her eyes widened, aghast. Surely, he couldn't have meant... But when Michael died, she'd wanted to follow him into the grave. Nate undoubtedly felt the same.

"No," she whispered and slid her hand behind his neck to pull him back down on top of her where he belonged. "No, I won't let you—"

"Sydney." Her name was a painful objection. "It was a long time ago. Don't let it upset you now."

"But you're still doing it." She slapped him on the shoulder with her palm as her anger bubbled to the surface. "Stop it! Stop risking your life so recklessly—"

He caught her hand and brought it up to his lips to kiss it. She inhaled a shuddering breath at the surprisingly affectionate gesture. He had suffered so much, yet even now, he was attempting to comfort her. Her heart ached and swelled, both grieving and caring for him in turns. It was unfathomable how he could make her feel this deeply when only a few weeks ago she barely felt alive at all.

"Don't be upset." He placed another kiss in her palm. "I can't bear it."

When he touched his lips to hers to soothe away her

pain, she had to blink rapidly to keep fresh tears from falling.

She whispered his name and placed her hand against his chest. She needed to feel his heartbeat beneath her fingertips—proof that he was safe and alive. And for the moment, that he was hers.

He tucked a stray curl behind her ear and forced out a crooked grin. "Do you need to be distracted, darling?"

She gave a short laugh through her tears at his bittersweet teasing. She knew he was attempting to turn her attention away from the conversation, just as he always did whenever the topic became too painful for him. This time, though, he did it for her.

He reached for the bottle of port on the bedside table. "Did you know," he mused as he dribbled drops of the sweet liquor onto her breasts, "that you smell like oranges and cloves?"

She caught her breath at the wet sensation on her warm skin. "I…what?"

He chuckled softly at her bewilderment as he set the bottle aside. He drew his fingertip through the droplets on her left breast to slowly smear them across her flesh. "Which makes me wonder…"

She trembled as he traced over her hard nipple and made it draw up tight. "Wonder what?" she prompted when he fell silent. He'd turned his attention to the right nipple and teased the port over it as he'd done to the left.

"If you also taste like oranges and cloves."

She moaned as his mouth descended to her breast. His tongue licked along the same slow circle as his fingertip, then lapped at the port still clinging to her skin like a giant cat enjoying a lick of cream.

She dug her fingers through his silky hair and arched her back to lift herself harder against him and deeper into his mouth. The pull of his lips shot through her, and she shivered heatedly all the way down to her toes. He was right. She desperately needed his distractions.

"Sweet Lord, you *do* taste like oranges and cloves," he murmured with feigned incredulity against her breast. When he nuzzled his cheek against her, his midnight beard scraped gently against her sensitive nipple. "Which makes me wonder…"

The wanton inside her made her pant out, "Wonder what?"

"If you taste like oranges and cloves everywhere."

He slid down the front of her body, nibbling and licking as he went. When he reached the junction of her legs, she surrendered with a sigh and spread herself wide.

He placed his mouth against her, and her sigh transformed into a whimper. Her fingernails dug into his shoulders as he kissed her in the most wicked way she could imagine, and she could barely keep still beneath his teasing lips and tongue. The intimate kisses he gave her were unlike anything she'd ever known. What he was doing to her was scandalous, wanton, wicked…and oh so very, *very* good.

He teased at her with his mouth and took swirling licks across her damp folds. She ached for more, so much that she shook beneath his ministrations. Every time his mouth grazed against that most sensitive point buried in her folds, she thought she would burst with pleasure.

Then the kisses changed, becoming harder and deeper...
hungrier. His tongue plunged into her. A shuddering gasp
tore from her lips, and she lifted her hips off the mattress to
meet each thrilling thrust of his tongue inside her.

When she could hardly bear the feel of his mouth against
her any longer, his name emerged as a soft plea for mercy on
her lips. He answered her cry by closing his mouth around
her aching nub and sucking hard.

She broke with a soft cry. Pleasure cascaded over her
in throbbing waves, and she had no more strength than to
lie boneless and let it seep over her. Never—*never* would
another man ever make her feel like this.

He moved back up her body with the same attention
he'd given her when he'd moved down it. When he reached
her lips, the kiss he gave her held so much tenderness that it
shook her to her soul.

"Nate?" she whispered.

"Yes, darling?" He placed a delicate kiss on her nipple.

"Please don't leave me tonight." Her fingers trembled as
they stroked over his chest. "I couldn't bear it."

———

Nate stilled, his mouth lingering against her warm skin. Her
soft plea nearly undid him.

He closed his eyes. The frantic urgency to make love to
her that had consumed him earlier was gone now, replaced by
something deeper, something tender...something that confused the hell out of him but that he knew his heart wanted.

He felt a soft tickle against his cheek.

He looked down to find her staring uncertainly at him, with her fingertip caressing lovingly along the side of his face. When he gazed into her emerald-green depths, he was lost.

"I'm not going anywhere until dawn," he said quietly.

Her arms circled his shoulders, and she buried her face against his neck, as if to hide the happiness that small concession brought her. Could she feel his heartbeat against her lips, the quickening of his pulse, the heating of his blood? Did she realize what she did to him, how she laid waste to his senses and left him helpless?

Even now, she had him shaking.

He rolled onto his side and brought her up against him, her back to his front, and folded his large body protectively around hers.

She nestled against him. Now that she was in his arms, the fatigue of the last few days—and nights—overcame her, and her eyes closed heavily.

He lost track of time as they lay together silently like that, long enough that the fire died away. When he reached for the blanket to cover her to keep her warm, she responded with a half-asleep sigh.

"You're exhausted," he murmured. His chest tugged with concern, and not without a little guilt, that he was the reason she was so spent.

"Just…a little…tired."

He grinned at her lie and nuzzled his cheek against her bare shoulder.

He listened as her breathing grew deep and even, and her

body softened against his. She drifted in and out of dreamy unconsciousness. Soon, she'd be asleep in his arms.

"Go to sleep, darling," he assured her. "I'll watch over you."

"You…always…" she whispered in words slurred from fatigue, "do."

Her sleep-fogged mind meant in London, those nights when he'd kept guard in her garden. Those same nights that now seemed so very long ago. His smile faded. "I won't let anyone harm you or Robert, I promise."

She lay still, her breathing so soft and even that he thought she'd already fallen asleep. But when he brushed his lips against the back of her neck, she trembled.

"I…can't…" Her quiet voice trailed off as she hovered on the precipice of sleep, completely unaware of what she was saying.

She was exhausted, barely able to hold on to consciousness and make sense with her whisperings. But he couldn't resist asking, "Can't what, darling?"

"Love…you." The words were a soft breath on the darkness, so faint he almost couldn't hear her, but his heart heard every word. "But…I do…"

Then she fell asleep with a sigh. Her body went limp against his as unconsciousness finally overcame her.

Not moving a muscle, Nate watched her sleep in the darkness. She breathed deep and even in his arms, but he had no idea how to slow the sudden somersaulting of his heart or free the tightening knot in his throat.

Love? *Impossible.*

This was not the plan he'd had for his life just a few weeks ago when Clayton Elliott first approached him to take on this mission. Then, he'd only wanted to earn the reward money, settle down in the countryside, and perhaps become one of those gentlemen farmers who turned up in London once every five or so years whenever they managed to break away from the ongoing demands of their wheat and their wool. After a long decade of war and army life, he'd wanted only calm and peace, relaxation, and retirement.

Nothing about Sydney Rowland was calm or peaceful and certainly not relaxing. Especially not with a six-year-old son in tow.

Yet he couldn't imagine his life without her now. To give Sydney up and return to how he'd lived before he met her, to that darkness and those long stretches of loneliness, to that shadow of a life without emotion or hope—

No. He could never live like that again. It would end him. Unconsciously, his arms tightened around her, as if he might lose her right then.

But dear God, was he ready for this?

Twenty-One

FAMISHED, SYDNEY PUT SECONDS ONTO HER BREAKFAST plate. Well, she supposed, a substantial appetite *was* what came of a night of amazing sex.

No, it wasn't just the sex, she considered as she placed one last strawberry from the sideboard onto her plate and turned toward the table to rejoin Robbie and Miss Jenner. Being with Nate was incredible; she couldn't deny that. It was as if their two bodies were made for each other.

Yet being with him was so much more than just physical attraction. He made her happy even when he wasn't touching her. It was...well, very special. *That* she knew for certain even if she couldn't put words to it, and she suspected so did Nate, although he left her room at dawn. This time, though, his leaving was so he would be out of her room before an unsuspecting maid entered and found a naked man in her bed. A very impressive naked man who—

"Are you all right?" Robbie frowned at her.

She choked as her gaze flew across the table to him. "Pardon?"

"Are you ill?" The boy tilted his head as he studied her curiously. "You look feverish."

She turned her heated face away before his innocent scrutiny could make her flush grow even deeper. "I'm fine."

"You've been distracted."

"*What?*" she sputtered, gaping at the boy.

Robbie shrugged and stirred at his eggs with his fork. "You haven't been paying attention all during breakfast."

"Oh. That." She forced a smile, but her stomach twisted until she wasn't hungry anymore. *Good heavens*, if she couldn't fool a six-year-old about her true feelings for Nate Reed, how on earth would she ever be able to keep fooling the man himself? "It's nothing. It's…just a little warm in here, that's all."

From the suspicious knitting of his young brow, he clearly didn't believe her. Yet he was old enough to know to let adult matters drop and turned his full attention to the egg moat he'd built around an unwanted piece of sausage.

Beside him, Miss Jenner didn't seem to notice the exchange at all. She stared down at her untouched food and idly pushed a kipper around her plate with her fork. The governess had invited Sydney to join them for breakfast instead of taking a tray in her room, and Sydney had eagerly accepted. The small meal was another opportunity to spend time with Robbie, as if it were any other normal morning.

But Miss Jenner had also been distracted. Her pale complexion contrasted sharply against the dark circles beneath her eyes as if she hadn't slept well last night. Or at all.

Yet she'd had the thoughtful foresight that morning to bring Sydney one of her dresses. A very pretty light-blue muslin day dress so Sydney would have fresh clothes to wear until more things could be purchased for her from the dressmaker in the village.

Rather, things that would *not* be purchased. Fresh guilt pricked her. She and Nate let everyone at Oakwood believe they would be staying on for several more days when they'd actually planned to flee north with Robbie as soon as tomorrow morning.

Would he cry at being swept away by strangers, his life once more in turmoil? But she had today at least to spend time with him like a normal boy, happy and safe, before they sped him away from his home. She planned on making the most of it.

Sydney leaned across the table to offer him her strawberry. She smiled as he took it from her fingers and popped it into his mouth. His cheeks puffed out like a chipmunk's.

"What shall we do today, hmm?" she asked.

"The captain promised to ride with me," he mumbled around the large berry between chews. "I can't wait to show him Agamemnon!"

She blinked. "Agamemnon?"

"My pony. Aggie's a fine one and very spirited. Beasley's promised to teach me to jump." He shot a quick glance at Miss Jenner, expecting to be corrected, but when no correction came from the preoccupied governess, he beamed and began to swing his legs beneath the chair. Obviously, in addition to running, swinging one's legs was something else gentlemen did not do in the house. "When I get old enough, Beasley said he'd teach me to drive a team!"

"My, isn't that something?" Then she asked hopefully, "Would you like it if I joined you and the captain for your ride?"

He scowled. "Ladies don't ride!"

"Some of us do." She longed to show him how well she could ride. Inexplicably, she wanted him to be proud of her, even though he had no idea who she was.

Stilling, he sent a puzzled glance at Miss Jenner. Except for the elderly Mrs. Larkin and the handful of maids in the house, the mousey governess comprised the only female role model in his life, and most likely Miss Jenner didn't ride.

"No, I don't think so." He swung his legs again in wide arcs beneath the chair. "I'd rather ride with the captain by myself. Just him and me and Aggie."

Her throat tightened. She was unprepared for the pierce of that rejection, yet she somehow kept her smile from faltering. "All right. Just the men, then."

He nodded as if that resolved all the problems about ladies on horseback. "Just the men."

"Perhaps we can play a game later in the garden."

That pricked his interest. "A game? What kind?"

"How about pall-mall?" That sounded like a fine idea. There must be a set somewhere at the house.

"Pall-mall?" He scrunched up his face. "I don't know that game."

"I can show you how to play." Her heart leapt at the thought that she might be able to teach her son anything, even a simple game. "It's great fun, I promise."

His mouth screwed up dubiously. "I don't know…"

"You get to hit balls with mallets," she tempted in a flagrant attempt at boy bribery. Boys liked to hit things, she'd been told. What could be better than whacking with mallets?

His face lit up. "Truly?"

"Truly."

He laughed. "Deuces!"

"Robbie." Miss Jenner finally broke free from her reverie and frowned at him, although Sydney suspected the frown had been on her face before the boy's excited outburst. "Voices down, please. And I've told you before, gentlemen do not use that word."

"Yes, miss."

"Please stop fidgeting."

"Yes, miss."

Sydney ached with jealousy as she watched the interaction between the two. Miss Jenner knew more about being a mother and raising a child than she did, and she'd given birth to the boy. Was it too late for her? Could she ever learn to be the proper mother Robbie deserved?

Or would she be a terrible mother, just like her own?

Her hands trembled, and she dropped them to her lap to hide them before Robbie noticed. He tended to notice everything.

"We're going to smash things with hammers!" Robbie announced.

Miss Jenner went impossibly paler and looked toward Sydney for explanation. "Beg pardon?"

"Not hammers, Robbie, but mallets," Sydney explained self-consciously. "Pall-mall."

"Oh." Miss Jenner breathed a sigh of relief. "Of course."

An uncomfortable silence fell over the table.

Sydney awkwardly placed her napkin beside her plate. Oh, how she wished Nate were here! He always interacted so easily with Robbie, proving to her that he was the natural-born parent she wasn't.

Her chest squeezed with a flicker of grief for him. His own son would have been just three years younger than Robbie if the boy had lived. When she looked at her son, she was reminded of Michael and the pain of losing him. What did Nate see when he looked at Robbie?

"I'm pleased that my dress fits you, my lady."

Sydney glanced up at Miss Jenner. It was her turn to be caught in distraction. "Oh, yes. Thank you so much for letting me borrow it. I'll make certain the dressmaker creates another one for you, along with anything else you need. I think it's time you had a new wardrobe."

The governess's cheeks flushed with an expression that crossed embarrassment with horror. "It's not necessary, I assure you."

"I insist. It's the least I can do for your generosity." Sydney did not mean the dress nor the hospitality during their stay. She meant being granted access to Robbie.

Sydney had never told Miss Jenner the truth about Robbie's birth or how he was related to her. But the governess was sharp, and Sydney was certain she'd figured it out. Children born to women who could not keep them were certainly not uncommon among the *ton* and were usually sent off to distant relatives to be raised as their own.

The unwanted children of the *ton*'s men fared much worse. They were usually abandoned to foundling hospitals by mothers who had no choice but to surrender their babies. Rarely did the mothers keep them as Nate's had done. Even rarer still were the children who managed to raise themselves above their illegitimate station. But Nate had done just that. It was one more complicated facet to his life that elicited both wonder and admiration from her.

"Very well," Miss Jenner conceded. "If it pleases you, ma'am."

"It does." She smiled through the tightening knot of emotion in her throat. "It pleases me a great deal."

Miss Jenner followed Sydney's gaze to the boy. "I'm glad to hear it."

Robbie glanced back and forth between the two women. The private conversation floated above his head, so he simply reached for another strawberry and popped it into his mouth.

Twenty-Two

"Stay up out of the saddle as you take the jump, but don't lean across his neck," Nate instructed Robbie as the boy trotted his gray Shetland pony around the rear lawn in a wide circle toward a small jump not more than a foot off the ground. His young face was set with grim determination. "Keep your shoulders straight."

The boy nodded, but his full attention was on the trotting pony beneath him who, thankfully, seemed about as excitable as a sleeping vicar. Despite his name, the animal was a mild-mannered, frighteningly rotund, and very lazy beast who wouldn't have broken into a run if someone shot off a pistol at its rear.

"Whenever you're ready," Nate encouraged, "ride him a few yards out, then circle back toward the jump, point him at it, and go."

Robbie nodded. His hands gripped the reins so tightly for this momentous event that his knuckles showed white. Nate knew without having to glance her way that so did the knuckles of the baroness as she sat on a blanket beneath the chestnut tree at the edge of the lawn and breathlessly watched her son's first jump.

The woman—and her sleep-induced, contradictory

confession that she loved him—should have terrified him. Yet oddly enough, she didn't.

She certainly confused the hell out of him, though. Half the time, he didn't know whether he wanted to throttle her or laugh with her, but always he wanted her. She had him thinking in circles, and holding her in his arms last night while she slept was almost as pleasurable as being inside her. Most confusing of all, she hadn't run away when he told her about Sarah, the baby, and the flogging. Any other woman would have done exactly that.

She couldn't love him, yet she did, even if she couldn't admit it in the light of day.

Just as she obviously loved her son yet couldn't admit that either.

As the pony trotted slowly toward the little jump, Nate found himself not knowing where to look—at the boy to see his reaction or at the woman who loved him to see hers.

The pony lumbered across the lawn, reached the low jump, and trotted over it, barely breaking stride.

Nate blinked. Did the shaggy beast even realize the pole was there at all? But Robbie shouted with excitement, bouncing so hard on his saddle that Nate began to hurry forward to steady him, only to stop dead when Robbie jumped to the ground and ran across the lawn to Sydney, threw his arms around her neck, and hugged her.

Nate's heart thudded as he held his breath and waited for her reaction.

Sydney hesitated as if she didn't know quite what to do. Then she raised her arms and hugged him back. She pulled him tightly to her and buried her face against his little shoulder. When she raised her head, her eyes found Nate across the lawn and held his gaze, even as she whispered something into the boy's ear.

Robbie nodded. Then he released her to run back. He slid to a stop in front of Nate and sharply saluted.

Nate returned the salute. "Very good, sir," he told the boy, aware of Sydney's gaze still on the pair of them. Her close attention warmed him.

"Thank you, Captain!" He bounced up and down. "It was deuces!"

"So it was." He gave the boy a grin of approval.

"What next?"

"You do it again. Practice makes perfect." He signaled to Mr. Beasley, and the man set about raising the pole. "This time, higher."

"Higher?" the boy squeaked out.

"Just a bit." Not even half a foot, but enough that this time, the shaggy pony might actually jump. "If you're going to be a proper dragoon, sir, then you need to learn to ride your mount across all kinds of terrain and all kinds of jumps."

"How high?" Nate detected a trace of nervousness in Robbie's voice.

"Eventually, higher than your head."

The boy's eyes grew impossibly large at that.

"But for today," Nate assured him, "I don't think we should worry poor Aggie about jumping that high."

Behind them, the pony munched on a daisy. The yellow

flower dangled from the side of his mouth when he raised his head to look at them.

"Yes," the boy agreed, his face suddenly serious with relief. "Aggie needs to work up to it."

"Wise man, Robert." Keeping a serious expression on his face so he wouldn't reveal his amusement, Nate tousled the boy's hair. "Now, mount your horse, and do it from the ground the way I taught you."

"Yes, sir! Like a real dragoon."

Nate nodded. "There are no mounting blocks in the middle of a battlefield."

Robbie laughed and ran back to Aggie, who heaved a great sigh as the boy approached but stood perfectly still as Robbie scrambled gracelessly up the side of the saddle and found his seat. He pressed his heels into the pony's sides as Nate had instructed and practiced guiding the Shetland with just his heels back into a slow circle toward the jump.

Sydney rose from her blanket and brushed her hands down her skirt. The borrowed blue dress hung shapelessly on her, but Sydney could have worn a burlap sack and Nate would have thought her stunning...except that she was shaking in it. He could see the emotion dripping from her all the way across the lawn where he stood.

"Captain Reed." She started toward the stables. "Might I have a private word with you, please?"

Christ. She was angry that he'd raised the jump, and now he was going to get an earful about unnecessarily endangering the boy, although how anyone could be endangered on that lump of a pony he had no idea. He'd seen sleeping lambs less docile than that woolly beast.

But instead of rolling his eyes, he felt a happy tug at his heart because she was fussing over Robbie. He knew then that Sydney was never going to let the boy go, that she would open her life to him and be a loving, smothering mother. The good mother she'd claimed she didn't know how to be.

He forced back a smile. "Yes, ma'am." With a call toward Beasley and Miss Jenner to keep close watch on Robbie as the plodding pony circled the lawn, he fell into step behind her.

When they reached the stables, she hesitated and glanced around.

He frowned. "What's wrong?"

"Nothing. I just… In here."

She opened the feed room door and led him inside, seeking extra privacy despite Robbie being on the far side of the stable yard and out of hearing distance.

"I saw how you were with Robbie." She closed the door behind them. Her hands were still shaking. "When you were showing him how to ride and jump."

He frowned. "If you think I wasn't teaching him properly, then—"

"No." She pressed herself against him and fisted his waistcoat in her hands. Her eyes glistened. "I think you were simply marvelous."

"Sydney," he whispered tenderly at the unexpected compliment.

"Kiss me," she ordered, although her words emerged as a soft plea.

"Gladly." He lowered his head and captured her mouth beneath his.

———————

Sydney leaned into his embrace to show him with her body what she couldn't say with words. That he was the most amazing man she'd ever met. That his kindness toward another man's son left her trembling. That as she'd watched the two of them together, she knew she was in love with him. She didn't want to be, yet she was—helplessly, hopelessly in love.

She slid the tip of her tongue across his bottom lip to coax him to open to her. When he did, she plunged inside to experience all of his kiss, to imprint on her mind the deliciousness of him.

She shivered as his hands caressed her and touched her lovingly through her borrowed dress.

"Burlap," he murmured appreciatively.

Her eyes fluttered open, and the raw emotion she saw in his hazel depths stole her breath away. "Bur—what?"

Chuckling, he captured her mouth beneath his in a hot, openmouthed kiss that left her breathless and aching. Instead of increasing in ferocity with desire, though, his kiss softened until it was affectionate and gentle yet just as intense as before.

She sighed at his tenderness. Having experienced the same man at his most fiercely passionate in her bed, she loved both contradictory sides of him, the hard façade of a soldier and the compassionate man beneath.

Breaking the kiss, he wrapped his arms around her and drew her against him so he could nuzzle his cheek against her hair. "I know."

She smiled, happier than she'd been in years. Perhaps ever. "Know what?"

"That you love me." He smiled against her hair. "And I'm pretty certain I love you, too."

Her heart stopped. "*What* did you say?"

Leaning back just far enough to look down at her, he grinned. "Are you really going to make me repeat it?"

Her mouth fell open as she stepped away to put enough distance between them so she could breathe again. "You…" How on earth—what he'd said—that he— "*What?*"

With a faint chuckle, he stroked his thumb against her cheek. "While you might not think that you can love me, I'm pretty certain you can. And do."

Panic kicked up inside her, and she scowled. "Once again, you've missed your mark." She crossed her arms over her chest in futile protection against the truth. "To think that I'm in love with you and that you—"

"I heard you say it last night as you were falling asleep. That you can't love me, but you do."

Oh God… "I was asleep—it was a dream! It meant nothing."

"You're beautiful, Baroness, even when you're lying to yourself." His gaze turned solemn. "Just as you're still trying to convince yourself that you can't be a good mother to Robbie. But I watched you today, and you love that boy." He took a single step to close the distance between them. "It might take you a while to figure out the nuances of mothering, but it's a natural part of you. You're never going to be able to let him out of your life now that he's in it."

"It isn't that simple." Not with either of the two males now in her life.

"Yes, it is." He gazed softly down at her, his expression somber, and he guessed, "You're afraid to openly love anyone, aren't you?"

"What an absurd notion." To accuse her of not loving when she'd loved so deeply that she'd wanted to die... Oh, he was so *very* wrong! "I loved Michael and announced it to the world."

"Yes, you did," he challenged with a slightly provoking arch of a brow. "You loved him, and he died. You loved your parents, and they betrayed you. You loved your baby, and he was taken from you." He faintly shook his head. "Now you're afraid to love anyone else because you think they'll be stripped away from you, too, and you'll be left alone again." He paused. "Including me."

"You don't know—"

"I've seen you with Robbie, yet you still refuse to admit that you want him with you." He stepped forward and took her back into his arms, then lowered his head to caress his mouth along her jaw and murmured into her ear, "And I've seen you at your most bare and vulnerable, yet you still won't share your heart with me."

She closed her eyes against the anguished tremor that swept through her.

He had no idea of what she'd been through...the

gut-wrenching grief over losing Michael and Robbie and those horrible days when she wanted to die herself. Her parents' betrayal and abandonment. All the humiliation heaped upon her by Rowland and the terrible happiness she felt when he died. And now, the attraction she felt for Nate, so overwhelming and frightening that it shook her to her soul.

"Because it terrifies me." Her chest constricted so sharply at the soft admission that she could barely breathe. "How could *you* hear what I said last night and not be just as frightened?"

"Because I care about you," he answered simply. "And I'm not going anywhere."

"You can't promise that." Her tear-blurred eyes stung as she traced her fingers down his forearm and the wound beneath to make her point.

"Perhaps not. Perhaps some things are beyond our control." Grief deepened his voice. "Perhaps that's why we need to seize what happiness we can while we're able to, and damn the tomorrows to come."

If only it were that simple! "I can't—" she choked out. "I can't surrender control of my life. Not again."

"I'm not asking for that." He cupped her cheek against his palm. "I love you, Sydney. I only wish you'd let yourself say the same to me."

The loving touch of his lips to hers as he lowered his head and kissed her sliced into her heart. It was too much to bear, and a tear rolled down her cheek.

"If I give you my heart," she whispered, "if it's broken again..."

"I will never intentionally hurt you." He gently kissed away the tear, and when his mouth returned to hers, she tasted the saltiness on his lips. "I meant every word when I swore to protect you and Robbie." He took her chin in his fingers and raised her face until she looked into his eyes. "Do you love me, Sydney? The truth."

She hesitated, knowing that once the word left her lips, there would be no going back… "Yes."

He traced a fingertip across her cheek. "Then say it."

"But Michael," she whispered, barely more than a breath, "and Sarah…"

"I will always love Sarah, and you will always love Michael." A fresh tear rolled down her face, and he caught it against his thumb. "But life—and love—goes on, my darling. They would want that for us. We both know that, and we need to accept it."

A sob broke from her, and she clung to him, his arms going tightly around her and pressing her close. She buried her face against his chest and wept harder than she had since the day the Countess of Wyeth told her that Michael was dead, since the day her parents took Robert from her arms. She was unaware of how long she sobbed in his arms and of the soothing words of comfort and love Nate whispered in her ear, but slowly, she felt a wetness on her neck even through her own grief.

Nate's tears.

At that moment, her heart surrendered completely.

Rising onto her tiptoes, she whispered against his lips, "I love you, Nate… I love you."

Twenty-Three

NATE LEANED AGAINST THE STABLE WALL AND INHALED A jerking breath.

Sydney was gone now. She'd headed back to her blanket beneath the chestnut tree as if nothing had happened between them, as if they hadn't just admitted to loving each other. He'd wanted to keep her with him, to continue to comfort and reassure her, yet he'd had no choice but to send her back to the garden. The last thing either of them needed was for a particularly curious boy to find his mother in a cramped feed room with a man and rumpled clothes.

He also needed a moment alone to collect himself and figure out what to do next. Yet he was just as emotionally roiled now as he'd been fifteen minutes ago when she slipped from the stables.

Sydney loved him. He'd coerced the confession from her, yet he suffered no guilt or regret over it. In order to protect her, he had to make her realize that opening her heart again was the only way to save herself, even if it meant the possibility of pain. For both of them. Yet she was in his life now, in his arms, and in his heart. He had no intention of ever letting her go.

He stared down at his hands. They were shaking, and he

had no idea how to make them stop. The army prepared a man for all the wrong things.

A clatter of hooves sounded from the front drive.

Nate walked outside into the stable yard. Squinting his eyes against the sun, he watched a horse canter toward the house.

Nate recognized the tall, easy posture of the man in the saddle before he drew close enough to see his face— Clayton Elliott. A cold chill raced down his spine. If Clayton was here instead of London, then all hell had broken loose in their mission.

The horse slowed and trotted to a bouncing stop at the stable door. A groom hurried forward to take the reins as Clayton dropped to the ground.

Nate frowned at the condition of the horse, which had been ridden hard. "Unsaddle him and cool him down," he ordered the groom. "Then brush him well and put him into a stall with oats and fresh water." He locked eyes with Clayton. His presence here did not portend good news. "This way."

He gestured for Clayton to follow him into the stable yard where they could speak privately. Despite Sydney's protests to the contrary, Nate trusted no one at Oakwood.

"What's brought you here?" Nate kept his voice low and stood shoulder to shoulder with Clayton, the two men facing in opposite directions like scouts on a battlefield. His thoughts immediately went to the worst. "Did something happen to Olivia Everett or St James?"

"They're both safe." Clayton tugged off his worn riding gloves. "I'm here about Lady Rowland."

Cold dread licked at Nate's boots. "Why?"

"I went to Braxton's residence to search for any connection to Scepter, and I found a written confession the general left on his desk before he went to deliver the explosives."

"Perhaps he suspected he wouldn't live through the night."

"Or perhaps it was the only way he had of leveling vengeance on the unknown blackmailers." Clayton tucked his gloves into his greatcoat's pocket. "In it, he referred to the message Lady Rowland delivered to him."

"Bois Saint-Louis," Nate mumbled. "And?"

"It wasn't a battle in France. It was a small village near New Orleans in America. No more than a crossroads and a scattering of two dozen houses."

"Was?"

"It was caught up in the fighting during the last troubles there. Braxton's men captured the town and destroyed everything…every house and barn, every shop and mill. The villagers were locked inside the church to keep them out of the way, all the shutters and doors barred from the outside." Clayton's eyes followed the movements of the groom as he tended to his tired horse. "The soldiers moved on, but two officers circled back to the church that night. Instead of setting the villagers free, they set fire to the church. The entire village—including women and children—were burned alive."

Good God. The pieces began to fall into place. "Braxton was one of the men who set the fire. That's what Scepter used to blackmail him."

Clayton gave a sharp nod. "If the War Office ever learned of what he'd done, he'd have been stripped of his commission and forced out of the army in disgrace. His career and reputation—his life—would have been ruined."

"How did Scepter learn of it? Braxton was too smart to share damaging secrets like that with anyone."

"He didn't have to share. There was a witness. The other officer who was with him." Clayton slid him a dark look. "Major Jonas Langley."

"Langley?" Nate frowned, unable to place the name.

"Younger brother of Charles Langley, Marquess of Hawking." Clayton squinted into the sun to hide his frown "He was killed a few weeks later in the fighting and never made it home to England. But I think he sent off a letter to his brother about Bois Saint-Louis before he died."

"And Scepter found out from Hawking."

"I think it's more than that. The marquess is the second most important official in Parliament and the lord who would most likely assume leadership if the prime minister were ever assassinated." Clayton paused, but the intensity that radiated from him was palpable. "I think we've finally found one of Scepter's leaders, if not the man directing it all."

"Then you should be in London arresting him." Worry rose inside him. "Why are you here?"

"Because I discovered something else." Clayton wore that same look of grim determination Nate remembered from before every battle they fought against the French. "Aren't the marquess and the baroness close friends? Perhaps close enough that he would know about this place?"

Nate shook his head. "No one knows the boy's true

connection to Lady Rowland." She'd hidden his identity too well for too many years. "All the staff were hired locally two years ago when…"

Nate's blood froze. His mind spun as it made all the connections between the Marquess of Hawking and Sydney. He knew—*Christ*, he knew!

Caroline Jenner. The governess who had once worked for Hawking's family.

"Sydney!" Nate bolted for the rear lawn.

The garden was empty, and the blanket where she'd been sitting was bare. No Robbie on his pony, no Beasley or Miss Jenner. No Sydney.

They were all gone.

"*Sydney!*"

He held his breath and strained to listen. Only silence answered him.

Then—a muffled cry came from the oak trees beyond the lawn. Nate rushed forward and slid his knife from its sheath as Clayton followed behind him, his hand on his pistol.

Beneath the trees, the pony pulled frantically at his bridle as it struggled to free itself from the reins, which had been tied around a low limb. Beasley lay beside him on the ground, tied and gagged. The governess was missing.

Sydney and Robert were gone.

Twenty-Four

A LARGE HAND YANKED OFF THE FLOUR BAG FROM OVER Sydney's head, and she stared into the pockmarked face of the kidnapper who had come after her and Robbie at Oakwood.

Frantically, she darted her gaze around the dimly lit and shuttered one-room cottage where they'd brought her, only letting herself breathe again when her eyes landed on Robbie as he huddled in the corner, terrified but unharmed. *Thank God.*

"You can take the ropes off her," a quiet voice said from behind him.

Miss Jenner.

"She'll be less trouble that way," the woman told the kidnapper. "And she won't run away, not as long as we have the boy."

The governess stood on the other side of the small cottage. Her hands weren't tied, and Sydney couldn't remember the woman screaming with surprise or trying to run away when they'd been attacked. Not once.

No, Miss Jenner had simply stood there beside the blanket while they'd been attacked and held Robbie in her arms as the men surprised Sydney from behind before she could scream. She'd been holding Robbie not to protect him,

Sydney realized now, but to kidnap him. Miss Jenner had known! That was why she'd been so distracted at breakfast, why she'd given Sydney the blue dress to wear...so the kidnapper would know which of the two women to come after.

Sydney narrowed her eyes on the woman she'd entrusted with her son's life. *You bitch.*

The kidnapper pulled a knife from his belt. Sydney shrank back at the flash of metal, only to be jerked forward when he grabbed her tied wrists and pulled them toward him to cut through the bindings.

"Do as we say, an' you can stay free of the ropes," he instructed in a thick Cornwall accent. "Get in the way, an' we'll put 'em back on. With a gag."

Sydney tried to swallow down the terror swirling in her stomach. "I won't be in your way."

He gave a stiff nod, pleased that she was cooperating. He shoved her backward, and she fell onto a narrow wooden bench along the wall. Then he grabbed Robbie by the scruff of his neck and roughly placed him onto the bench beside her.

Sydney grabbed her son into her arms and pressed him protectively against her.

"We'll wait here until dark," he told Miss Jenner.

"Why dark?" Sydney asked as suspicion licked at the backs of her knees.

The man sent her a patronizing smile, the same one the old baron used to give her. "So no one'll see us leave." *...after we've killed you and the boy.*

The words reverberated through Sydney's mind as loudly as if he'd actually uttered them.

She glanced down at Robbie as he sat on the bench beside her, his small form both tied and gagged to keep him from crying and being heard.

Think! She had to think through her fear, to ignore the furious racing of her heart and find a way to free them, to hide, to save Robbie—she *had* to!

"I'll watch the boy," Miss Jenner said as she stepped forward and reached to pull Robbie from Sydney's arms.

"Do not touch him!" Sydney snarled through clenched teeth.

The woman stiffened, momentarily taken aback. Then she relaxed, and a macabre smile stretched her thin lips. "But looking after him is my job. That *is* why you hired me."

"*I* will take care of him." She sent a pleading look past Miss Jenner to the kidnapper, knowing instinctively that he was the one in charge. "At least let me take the blindfold off his eyes. He's terrified with it on. He won't cry so much if he's not as frightened."

The man paused as he considered her logic, then nodded curtly. "Just keep the brat quiet."

He stalked away to a table near the door, then pulled out a deck of cards from his pocket and settled in to play a game of solitaire.

Sydney's stomach sickened at his cold-blooded demeanor. He was simply wasting time until dark when he and Miss Jenner would slit both her throat and Robbie's and use the cover of darkness to make their getaway.

Sydney cooed softly to Robbie as he struggled in terror when he felt her hands at his head. But if she could untie him, then he might just have a chance at running, and if she could distract the kidnapper and Miss Jenner, he might be able to get away. Saving her son's life was all that mattered. Her own life meant nothing in comparison.

With trembling hands, she slipped the blindfold off and forced a comforting smile at Robbie when he blinked open his eyes. Through red-rimmed eyes glistening with fear, he stared for a confused moment before he recognized her. Then he began to cry, his sobs muffled behind the cloth shoved into his mouth.

"Shh, my darling, it's all right." She wrapped her arms around him and pressed him tightly against her.

Miss Jenner reached once more for him.

"*Don't.*" Sydney glared murderously at the woman, her eyes narrowing to such furious slits that Miss Jenner gasped and retreated to the other side of the room.

Sydney cradled Robbie in her arms and rocked him gently as she kissed his hair. When he'd calmed enough that he could hear her soft whispers, she brought her mouth close to his ear.

"Robert, listen carefully to me." She prayed the distress in her voice didn't send him into a fresh bout of crying. "We have to find a way out of here. You have to do exactly as I say. Understand?"

When the boy nodded, she gently cupped his young face in her hands and kissed away the tears on his cheeks. It anguished her to keep him gagged like this, but she knew she couldn't free him completely. Not just yet.

"You must do *exactly* as I say or—" A piece of her heart shattered at having to create more fear inside the already terrified little boy. "Or that man will hurt us."

His eyes widened. From beneath the gag, he cried out loudly enough to catch the attention of the kidnapper, who looked up from his cards.

He scowled at them, furious that the boy had interrupted his game. He slammed his fist onto the table. "Keep him quiet, goddammit!"

Sydney suggested innocently, "Maybe if I untie his hands, he won't struggle so much and he'll be quiet."

"Fine," he snapped out and turned back to his cards. "Just keep the brat's mouth shut."

Miss Jenner narrowed her eyes at Sydney. "I don't think that's such—"

"What's he going to do?" the man interrupted and gestured a handful of cards in their direction. "He's just a baby, for God's sake."

"He's wrong," Sydney whispered into Robbie's ear. "You're not a baby. You're a young man. That's why Captain Reed taught you to jump today. He would never have taught that to anyone who wasn't a brave man."

Her words seemed to mollify Robbie a bit because he stopped struggling enough that she could quickly remove the bindings from his wrists. His loud, terrified cries faded into sniffling sobs.

"And brave men do *not* cry," Sydney lied, her voice quaking as she remembered Nate's tears that morning when he finally let go of Sarah and the guilt he'd carried for the past three years. "So you cannot cry or shout, all right? You must keep quiet and do exactly as I tell you."

He nodded but gave one final, long sniff of a sob.

She'd left the gag for last to make certain his cries were over. She couldn't risk having the kidnapper order Miss Jenner to tie him up again. Or worse.

As soon as the cloth was pulled from his mouth, he threw his arms around her neck and pressed himself as tightly against her as he could. Yet her brave little boy did not cry. Not once.

"You're safe with me, Robert. I *will* protect you always, I promise," she whispered into his ear, meaning every word with all her heart and soul. "Now do as I tell you, and we'll soon be away from here and back home at Oakwood."

He nodded against her neck, and he trembled as he drew a shaking breath. "I'm scared," he whispered.

"So am I."

Her confession seemed to settle him a bit, knowing they were in this together. "Is Captain Reed coming for us?"

Her stomach clenched in a tight knot, which made the sickening inside her belly churn even more. She had no idea where Nate was or if he was safe. He could very well be—

No. She squeezed her eyes shut for a moment against the thought. He'd promised that he wouldn't leave her, and she would put her full faith in that.

"Yes, he is," she lied with every ounce of resolve inside her. "So we have to be ready for him when he comes."

"How?"

Biting her lip, she looked around the cottage. It was empty except for the bench where she sat with Robbie and the table and chairs where Miss Jenner joined the man to play cards. The cupboard doors in the little kitchen had been ripped from their hinges and now hung broken; the glass in the two windows was shattered. The dirt floor was bare except for broken shards of crockery scattered about, and a beam from the ceiling had split apart and fallen down onto the floor, nearly bringing down the roof with it. Even the large stone-and-mortar hearth had crumbled with disuse, and a large rock from its corner lay on the dirt floor.

"I don't know," she admitted honestly, "but I'll think of something."

Robbie nodded, as confident as the frightened little boy could be in a woman he barely knew, and rested his head on her lap. She placed a kiss to his temple and gently stroked his blond hair. The tender gesture comforted her as much as him.

Passing minutes turned into hours, and the slant of sunlight into the cottage through the broken shutter grew longer. Sydney had no idea how long she sat there on the bench trying to think up a plan while Miss Jenner and the kidnapper played at cards. But every passing minute made Sydney's heart speed faster with fear and her hands shake harder.

Soon. She would have to act soon. But whatever she did, she was willing to sacrifice herself to save Robbie.

The stone by the fireplace kept drawing her attention.

It was the size of a large apple. God only knew how long it had lain there, how long the cottage had been abandoned. She had no idea how close the cottage sat to any of its neighbors, in what direction to run, or where to find someone who might be able to help them. All she knew was that she *had* to get Robbie away from here.

It was time to act.

"Can you run fast?" she leaned over and whispered into his ear. "As fast as the wind?"

The boy nodded.

"Good. That's what I need you to do."

His bottom lip quivered. "But Captain Reed is coming."

"Yes, he is, and we need to help him help us. We're going to be his soldiers, all right? I'm going to be the general, and you're going to be a captain, too, just like him, so you're going to follow my orders."

Bright blue eyes scarched her face. "Does Captain Reed follow your orders?"

She grimaced inwardly at that. *Never. He* never *follows my orders.* "Always," she lied. "A good soldier always does exactly as he's told, and *you* are a good soldier."

He nodded and gave her a small salute the way Nate had taught him.

"Here are your orders, Captain Robert." She leaned over to whisper into his ear. "You are going to slowly count to one hundred, just like you did for me in the nursery last night. When you reach one hundred, I want you to very slowly ease off this bench and walk toward that corner over there by the door. Then, wait right there. No matter what happens, stay there. All right?"

He nodded.

"Then when I yell 'Run,' you run for the door as fast as you can, right outside, and into the woods. Keep running like the wind until you can't see the cottage anymore. Then keep running until you see a person or a house, and ask for help. Tell them who you are, and ask them to take you back to Oakwood to Mr. Beasley and Mrs. Larkin, understand?"

He nodded.

"Repeat your orders, Captain."

He leaned to whisper into her ear just as she'd done with him, and his hand reached to hold hers for reassurance. He recited, "I count to one hundred. Then I walk over there."

When he began to point toward the corner, she caught his hand and patted it to hide the gesture.

"And when you say 'Run, Robbie!'" he continued, "I run out the door as fast and as far as I can. Like the wind."

"That's exactly right. Then you keep running until you find someone to help you and ask them to take you home," she insisted. "You *keep running*." Her eyes stung at what might happen to her when she stayed behind to stop the kidnapper, and she blinked rapidly. "No matter what you see or hear, you do *not* stop. Understand?"

He nodded, but his young face pinched in concern. "Where will you and Miss Jenner be?"

"Miss Jenner's staying here." Her throat tightened as her gaze darted to the governess. "But you and I have to leave. When you run, I'm going to run in the other direction just as fast as I can."

"Like the wind?"

"Like the wind," she choked out. "And I'll be waiting at home for you to finish your mission because you are my soldier."

"I thought Captain Reed was your soldier."

Her chest clenched with a blinding pain. Was Nate truly

hers? Would she ever see him again? "He'll be waiting at home for you, too," she deflected and blinked back the stinging tears. She placed a kiss on his forehead and closed her eyes, imprinting on her mind this moment with him, which might prove to be her last. "Now count to one hundred. Slowly."

Then she released him to sit back on the bench, closed her eyes, and pretended to nap.

She heard him pronounce each number as he counted softly beneath his breath, and his legs began to swing with anticipation as he fidgeted on the bench beside her, each number coming faster as he neared one hundred.

On the count of one hundred, he slipped off the bench as she'd instructed and slowly slid along the wall toward the corner where she'd ordered him to wait.

"You!" the kidnapper bellowed. "What the hell are you doing over there?"

Sydney shot to her feet as if startled from sleep. "What is it? What's the matter?"

"Keep that boy on the bench with you," he ordered.

Blinking in confusion, as if she didn't know what was happening, Sydney glanced at Robbie. His bottom lip trembled with the first sign that he was about to break into tears. *Good.* Her chest tore at how frightened he was, but his fear made her plan believable. Right now, that was all that mattered.

"He probably has to relieve himself," she snapped back and moved across the cottage to Robbie, passing by the old hearth. "You've kept us tied up in here all day. He's a little boy. What do you expect?"

The man shoved back from the table and threw in his

cards. Fury contorted his face as he rounded on her. "Get back on the bench, or I'll tie an' gag both o' you!"

Her chin jutted up as she knelt down beside Robbie. "He has to visit the necessary," she argued in her best icy-cold governess's voice.

"He can piss 'is pants fer all—"

"What was that?" Sydney suddenly shrieked and pointed toward the door. "I heard a noise outside. Oh, thank God, someone's come to save us! We're in here!"

She jabbed her finger emphatically and drew their attention away from her. Then she scooped up the stone at her feet and hid it in the folds of her skirt.

Miss Jenner raced to the window. "If someone's out there—"

"Shut up!" the man growled. "There was no noise."

"You'd better go outside and check anyway." Miss Jenner turned her head from side to side for a better view out the window, but her vision was blocked by the shutter at every angle. "If we get caught here with a baroness and that boy, we'll both hang. I want out of this mess alive."

The man's face darkened. Cursing loudly, he stalked to the door. He flung it open but paused in the doorway.

"Go on," Miss Jenner urged. She nodded toward Sydney and Robert. "I'll keep an eye on them."

With a grumble, the kidnapper stepped outside and disappeared from sight as he circled the cottage. Miss Jenner stayed at the window and strained to see outside, lifting up onto her toes for a better view.

Sydney lunged. She grasped the large rock in both hands

and raised it over her head, then slammed it down into the back of Miss Jenner's skull. A sickening thud echoed through the cottage. The woman fell to her knees with a loud moan.

"Run!" Sydney screamed at Robbie.

He flew from the cottage and straight on into the thick woods just as she'd instructed, not slowing down, not looking back. He was following his soldier's orders to the letter and running like the wind.

Sydney dropped the rock and ran. She headed away from Robbie in the opposite direction and yelled at the top of her lungs as she went to catch the attention of the kidnapper. As she'd hoped, the man didn't see Robbie and came after her.

Hitching up her skirt, she ran as fast as she could. She *had* to put as much distance between herself and her son as possible, *had* to draw the killer away from him to give him time to find help. Her legs shook and her lungs burned as she gasped for breath, but somehow she found the inner strength to keep running over the moss-dampened ground beneath the trees and through the undergrowth. Each footstep put more distance between her and Robbie, and even one extra stride might just save his life.

She slowed to risk a glance over her shoulder—the kidnapper wasn't there!

She halted, turned back, and saw him running through the trees in the opposite direction. After Robbie.

"No!" she screamed. The man was too far away. She could never reach him in time if she ran back.

She raised her arms over her head and waved them wildly to get the man's attention.

"I know who you are!" she yelled, her voice screaming itself raw. "I know who you are, and I will tell the authorities!"

The man froze in his steps, then hesitated a moment as if torn between running after Robbie or going back after her. He looked over his shoulder and met her gaze through the trees.

"I will tell them," she promised as loudly as she could, "and you will hang!"

An evil, cold smile spread across his face. Then he started after her.

Sydney fled for her life.

His long strides quickly closed the distance between them even as she darted through the trees and bushes. Her long skirt snagged on the brambly undergrowth and slowed her down, and the fabric ripped as she twisted to free herself and stumble on. She heard heavy footsteps pounding up behind her. Only seconds now, and he would catch her. Only heartbeats—

She snatched up a tree limb from the ground and swung it in a circle with a groan of exertion to strike him on the head as hard as she could. But the rotten limb snapped in two, and the glancing blow only grazed his jaw.

"Bitch!"

He grabbed her arm and twisted hard, and the pain shot up into her shoulder. She fell helplessly to the ground with a scream. He kicked her. She ducked but too late, and his boot caught the side of her head.

With a cry of pain, she fell backward, and he pounced on top of her, straddling her waist and holding her pinned beneath him. She struggled fiercely to free herself, kicking her legs and flailing her arms in violent desperation, but he was too heavy and strong.

He grabbed both her wrists in one large hand and pinned her arms to the ground over her head. Baring his teeth at her, he yanked a knife from his belt and flashed it at her throat.

"I'm gonna kill the boy. I'll find him an' break his little neck. But first, I'm gonna gut you." He pricked the tip of the knife against the flesh at the base of her throat and traced it down her front between her breasts, and she closed her eyes against the terror. "From neck t' belly like a fish."

She heard herself scream, the sound tearing from her throat of its own volition. One last, desperate cry for help—

A pistol shot boomed through the woods. Sydney's eyes flew open.

Above her, the man convulsed as red blood blossomed on his chest. Then he coughed, and bloody spittle dripped from the corner of his mouth. She screamed again as he fell forward on top of her, and she shoved him away with all her strength. He was dead by the time he hit the ground.

Nate stood behind him. A trail of smoke curled from the end of his spent pistol.

Tossing the gun away, he rushed forward and dropped to his knees to pull her into his arms. She clung to him. For several seconds, she was unable to do anything more than gasp for breath.

"Sydney," he rasped hoarsely as he crushed her against him. "Are you all right?"

"Robert!" She craned her neck over his shoulder to see into the woods in the opposite direction where her son had disappeared only moments before. "He ran the other way! You have to save him. You have to—"

"Beasley and Clayton have him," he assured her. "He's safe."

"No!" She pushed against him to free herself and gasped at the wincing pain in her shoulder where the kidnapper had twisted her arm. "Miss Jenner—I left her behind at the cottage." Frantic to find Robbie and keep him safe, she struggled in his arms. "I have to get to Robbie!"

"He's safe," he repeated, cupping her face between his hands to reassure her. "Clayton handed him off to Beasley, and Beasley's taking him straight back to Oakwood. He's protected."

"Clayton?" She stilled as his words slowly sank into her panic-filled brain. "The man who was with you at my town house?"

"He came to Oakwood to warn us but arrived too late." He frowned with dark fury at the cut on her forehead as the trickle of blood seeped down the side of her face. "He helped me find you. We were ready to burst into the cottage when you and Robbie ran out."

"It was Miss Jenner," Sydney told him. "She arranged for the kidnapping. She was going to help kill Robbie and me."

He traced his fingertips gently over her bruised cheek, and his face filled with guilt. "I know."

She grasped desperately at his waistcoat. "She can't be allowed near Robbie. He trusts her, and she—"

"She's been captured and arrested." He placed a kiss to her lips to soothe her. "She can't hurt Robert now."

She gave a soft cry and buried her face into his shoulder

to weep. All the fear bubbled out of her, and her body slowly filled with his strength and solace.

"You're both safe, Sydney," he whispered into her hair, "and everything's going to be all right now." He soothingly stroked his hands over her back. "It's all over."

Twenty-Five

Nate frowned grimly at Clayton as the two men stood outside Oakwood's front door. Sydney and Robbie waited inside the rented carriage at the bottom of the steps, ready to leave.

Behind them, the house was in an uproar. Mrs. Larkin had protested that they were risking their safety traveling on such short notice in the middle of the night. Beasley was following Clayton's orders and searching Miss Jenner's possessions for any evidence to connect her to the kidnapping, while Miss Jenner sat tied in the breakfast room with a rock-shaped lump on her head. One of the grooms had already been dispatched to London to deliver two coded messages. The first message from Clayton asked Lord Sidmouth in the Home Office to have the Marquess of Hawking placed under surveillance until an arrest warrant could be secured for treason and murder. The second message was from Nate to Brandon Pearce, his old friend turned earl, notifying him that Nate was bringing Sydney and Robbie back to the Armory and wanted Pearce's man McTavish there to act as guard.

They needed to be gone from Oakwood as far and as fast as possible, even at the risk of nighttime travel, and he had paid the hired driver and tiger well for it. Even with the small number of staff at Oakwood, that afternoon's events couldn't be kept secret for long.

Nate shook his head, unable to fathom where their mission had brought them. "Why would Hawking do this? He's a marquess, for God's sake. He has a fortune and lands, the ear of the regent—he's one of the most powerful lords in England."

"I don't know," Clayton answered, "but I plan to find out."

"You plan to torture him, you mean."

"Torture, interrogation—who am I to quibble over definitions?" Clayton said dryly with a shrug. "I'll spend the night here, then start back to London with the governess at dawn."

"How should I contact you?"

"Through St James." When Nate didn't reply to that, Clayton asked quietly, "Does it bother you to work this closely with him?"

"No." Nate flipped up the collar of his greatcoat against the night air.

He felt Clayton's gaze swing curiously to him at his curt answer, but his friend wouldn't find any indication of his true feelings about St James's sudden and unwanted presence in his life, nor about the bevy of Sinclair ladies with their desperate desire to make amends with a recognition he'd never pursued nor wanted. Nate wasn't certain himself how he felt about it all.

Clayton continued to stare at him until Nate returned his gaze. Then his old friend coolly arched a brow.

"Sinclair and I are brothers, whether we like it or not," Nate explained simply. There was no emotion in his voice as he said that, no anger or bitterness, although plenty of both simmered inside him. "The past makes not one bit of difference to the present."

"Don't think I believe that for one moment," Clayton said and turned back toward the carriage as the last preparations were made for departure.

Blowing out a hard breath, Nate admitted grudgingly, "The Sinclairs want to recognize me as a son of St James."

He felt Clayton stiffen in surprise, but he didn't dare look at his friend. "Are you going to accept?"

"I don't know."

If Clayton had asked him the same question two days ago, before Sydney admitted to loving him, he would have said no.

Hell no.

But now he had no idea what to do. Recognition would make no difference to the hard life he and his mother had suffered at the hands of the Earl of St James, but it might make a great difference going forward.

Nate shook his head. "But they don't want me. They want the hero of Toulouse." He wasn't prepared for the bitterness of uttering that truth aloud. "They want to welcome a war hero into their fold, not the illegitimate son of an upstairs maid."

"Or perhaps," Clayton countered, "they simply want to do right by you."

"That's what worries me most," Nate muttered, his shoulders slumping.

"Don't let it. The Sinclairs are good people." Slapping Nate on the back with brotherly affection, Clayton turned to head back into the house. "Safe travels," he called out as he bounded up the steps. "See you in London."

Nate looked back at the carriage and squared his shoulders. There would be time later to sort through what the Sinclairs wanted with him.

Now, he had to get Sydney and Robbie to safety.

"Go!" Nate called up to the driver as he swung into the compartment and locked the door. The carriage started forward into the night.

Sydney sat on the bench across from him with Robbie asleep on the seat beside her, his head resting on her lap. She'd wrapped him in a thick blanket to keep him warm against the chilly night, and now she gently stroked his hair and hummed to him in the soft glow of the carriage lamp.

Nate's chest tightened. It was the most beautiful sight he'd ever seen.

Her eyes rose to meet his through the shadows, and she smiled tenderly. "So we're off, then." She softened her voice to keep from waking the sleeping boy. "Where are we going?"

"London."

He'd kept their destination secret from everyone here but Clayton. Even the driver and tiger riding up top knew nothing more than to head east and keep their weapons at the ready. Nate planned on switching out both driver and tiger when they'd reached their first stop, which would be sometime near dawn, then again every time they changed teams. No one they encountered would know where they'd come from, who they were, or where they were going.

"London?" she repeated in surprise, yet she continued to brush her fingers through her son's hair.

"We're needed there." They had no choice. Hawking's arrest warrant wouldn't be issued without Sydney's testimony.

"Will we be safe?"

"I'm taking you to the Armory. It's the safest place I know, and I've asked Brandon Pearce, Earl of Sandhurst, to send his valet to us."

She blinked. "Why would we need a valet?"

Nate's lips crooked into a smile. "Sergeant McTavish is far more than just that."

Callum McTavish had been a trusted and dependable soldier during the wars, serving as aide-de-camp for several high-ranking officers, only to find himself cast out upon the streets after returning home. Brandon Pearce employed him as his valet not because the grisly old sergeant was good at fashion but because the earl knew he could trust McTavish with his life. He was incorruptible and deadly with both gun and bayonet.

"He'll guard you and Robert well," he assured her. "You'll be safe under his care."

"If we're with Sergeant McTavish, where will you be?" The question came in the same soft voice she was using to hum to the boy, but Nate had become so attuned to everything about her that he easily heard the nervousness edging it.

"Arresting the Marquess of Hawking."

Her hand stilled. "Pardon?"

Not wanting to upset her any more than she already was,

he kept his face carefully blank and his tone even. "Clayton traced the message you delivered to General Braxton, and it led back to the marquess. He's working for Scepter. We think he might be their leader."

She stared at him, stunned. "Charles? That's impossible."

Charles. Jealousy bit at him. "Bois Saint-Louis was an incident during the last war with the Americans, a little parish in Louisiana. The entire village was murdered at the hands of Braxton and Hawking's brother. No one else was involved but those two officers."

"But Major Langley is dead," she whispered. Her fingers began to stroke the boy's hair again, but now they trembled. "He died in America. He never came home to England."

"He must have sent off a letter to his brother before he died. It was that secret that was used to blackmail Braxton."

"Lots of soldiers fought in the war. Anyone could have discovered what they'd done."

He leaned forward, elbows on his knees. "Braxton wouldn't have been foolish enough to share that secret with anyone. A general murdering unarmed women and children... The War Office would have stripped him of his commission, and he would have lost all honor and reputation, become an outcast and hated across the empire. No, it had to be Jonas Langley, the junior officer in the incident, who shared the secret, and he shared it with the one man he thought he could trust— his brother. Since he died soon after, it's likely he told no one else, certainly none of the men he served with, for the same reasons as Braxton." He eased back against the squabs. "I know how soldiers think and what's important to them. If any of them found out, they would never have tolerated in silence something so cowardly."

"He *had* to have told someone else. Either that, or Lord Hawking was blackmailed himself into revealing it to Scepter." She dropped her gaze to the sleeping boy on her lap. "Otherwise, what you're suggesting is that the Marquess of Hawking is a revolutionary who wants to overthrow the government, and I simply cannot believe…" She shook her head. "What proof do you have?"

"Henry Everett was a bad mathematician."

Confusion skittered across her face as she tried to follow that jump in logic. "Henry Everett?"

"Was a bad mathematician," he repeated. "It was his sister, Olivia, who solved his equations. Anyone who looked closely at his work would have known that, yet he was invited to join the Royal Society. An invitation he didn't deserve."

She countered quietly, "Lots of men are invited to join the Society who do not deserve it."

"Influential lords and wealthy patrons, not poor school-masters. Yet Everett's invitation came anyway. Hawking would have had the influence to make that happen."

"Any member of the Society could have done that."

He ignored that, knowing there was no point yet in arguing with her until she knew all the facts. "Once the invitation was issued, Everett was strongly encouraged to socialize with the other members, which included evenings spent drinking and gambling at clubs where Hawking was a member."

"Coincidence." But her soft voice lacked conviction. "Many peers keep memberships to clubs they never patronize."

"Where a mathematician good enough for membership to the Royal Academy can never win at the odds?" He shook his head. "His losses ran up as if the tables were rigged against him, because they were. Soon he owed over twelve hundred pounds—a lifetime's earnings for a schoolmaster." He nodded at her. "That's when you became involved. You were blackmailed into buying up Everett's debts because your fortune was large enough that you had ready money at hand, and you had a secret that could be used against you. Your son."

His gaze dropped to Robbie as the boy stirred in his sleep, and her arms tightened protectively around him.

"Then, a few weeks later, you were blackmailed again, this time into demanding that Everett repay you, even though he couldn't."

She slowly shook her head. "Why would Hawking, of all men, do what you're suggesting?"

"Hawking wanted to assassinate the prime minister by blowing up the Admiralty Club, but he needed to know the weakest places in the club's construction to place the explosives for the greatest damage. Once Lord Liverpool was dead, he could assume control of the government himself, then call for the overthrow of the monarchy. When that assassination attempt at the Admiralty failed, he needed the same information to place explosives at Waterloo Bridge to assassinate both the prime minister and the prince regent during the opening ceremony. Luckily, the men of the Armory foiled their plans."

She didn't move, not even to breathe. Her eyes remained trained on his.

"Everett would never have willingly provided that information, so Hawking schemed to run up the man's debts, then blackmailed you into demanding repayment. But Everett had no money to pay you and feared being sent to debtor's prison, with his career ruined, his school and life destroyed. When Scepter conveniently showed up with a job for him, he felt he had no choice but to give them the information they wanted." He paused to let her absorb this new information. "It was never about the money, Sydney. That was simply a means to an end. It was always about where to plant explosives to murder the right people."

If her face wasn't covered by shadows, he was certain he would have seen her turn white. "Henry Everett paid for it with his life," she breathed out, and Nate suspected that her low voice had nothing to do with the sleeping boy. "Because of me."

"No, he didn't," he told her quietly. "Henry Everett is still alive."

"*What?*"

"Everett survived the fire at the school that Scepter set to kill him, and when we rescued him, he told us everything he knew. In exchange, he was spared the gallows and exiled from England, and an unidentified corpse was slipped into the charred remains in his place. The world thinks him dead, but he's alive, most likely somewhere in Spain."

She pressed the back of her hand against her lips, and her shoulders sagged with overwhelming relief. "Thank God."

"But Scepter wasn't done yet in their attempts to assassinate the prime minister and regent. They needed more explosives to carry out their next attempt. General Braxton was blackmailed into providing them, and you were threatened into delivering the orders to him. You know what happened after that."

"But none of that proves Charles Langley is behind Scepter."

"No," he agreed quietly. "But *you* do."

Her eyes grew wide.

"Scepter used Robert to blackmail you into doing their bidding. Hawking knows you're the boy's guardian."

"Yes," she said softly.

"He's the only one who knows, except for the woman he helped you hire." He paused pointedly. "Miss Jenner."

"Yes." This time, the word was nothing but silence on her stunned lips. She blinked hard and lowered her gaze to Robbie as she admitted shamefully, "I know Hawking through my charity work. We sit on several of the same boards and donate to the same children's organizations. Everyone trusts him. So did I." Her arms tightened around the sleeping boy. "When Rowland died, he offered his support, however I needed, and we became close friends. I was finally able to hunt for Robbie, but I needed someone to help me retain investigators to find him, to recommend a lawyer who would draw up a guardianship without asking questions..."

"To hire a governess to care for him," he added quietly. "The woman *he* recommended who was also indebted to his family. The one who soon discovered that Robert was far more to you than the distant relative you claimed."

She blinked rapidly. "Caroline Jenner knew that man was coming after us today," she whispered. "That's why she gave me this dress to wear, why she acted so oddly when we arrived, because...because she was part of it all. I trusted her." Her voice cracked. "I trusted Charles."

His heart ached for her and the guilt that must be consuming her. "Clayton and the Home Office will make certain he can't harm anyone again."

She nodded absently and looked away, first to the sleeping boy on her lap, then out the window at the dark countryside, although Nate knew she could see nothing past the glass except for the dim circle of the lamplight at the front corner of the carriage and blackness beyond. Her fingers plucked in agitation at the fringed edge of the blanket tucked around her son.

"Hawking proposed to me," she breathed out so softly that he could barely hear her above the noise of the carriage wheels rolling beneath them. She didn't look at him, still staring out the window. "I refused."

Nate kept his gaze glued to her profile in the darkness and forced down the anger churning inside him.

"That's why I was blackmailed again, isn't it, even after Henry Everett was reported as dead? He wanted me to turn to him for help, but I didn't. I turned to you. He knew that and couldn't stand it." She swallowed hard to clear her throat.

"When he proposed, I first thought he wanted only…" Her voice trailed off into silence, but she might as well have uttered the words… *Only to bed me.* "But he wanted marriage. When I refused him, he most likely hated me for it."

"I know."

Her head snapped up. Even in the dim light, her eyes glistened brightly with her tears of pain and the betrayal of a dear friend. "How?"

Because I know what it's like to have your love and how much a night of that would mean to any man.

No, not a night. Nate wanted a lifetime with her.

"Because he could have paid a boy from the street to deliver the message to Braxton," he answered instead. "But he wanted to humiliate you for refusing him, so he made you dress in costume like a lightskirt and go to a party that was little more than an orgy. He might have even counted on the general attacking you in the garden."

She pressed the back of her hand against her mouth as if fighting down the urge to be ill. "If you hadn't been there… *Oh, God.*"

"Hawking was probably there at the party, too, watching you from behind a mask. Most likely he wanted to save you from Braxton himself and become a hero to you. A man whose marriage offer you then could not refuse."

Sydney turned her attention back to Robbie, and she brushed the dark blond hair from his forehead. "Hawking thought I was so lonely, so desperate for help, that I would accept his proposal." She inhaled a deep breath. "It was true—I *was* lonely and aching, but I didn't want him. I wanted more. But I never realized how much until I met you that night at Barton's."

"The madman who leapt into your speeding carriage?" he asked wryly.

She smiled faintly at Robbie as he stirred in his sleep. "The man who keeps risking his life to save us."

The man who always will. The sight of her with her son undid him. He knew he would lay down his life for them. *Always.*

Her smile faded into a troubled frown. "This afternoon, I realized how much I love Robert, how much I'm willing to sacrifice for him, and that I want him with me. Just as you've been trying to convince me since London."

"You're his mother, Sydney. He deserves to know who you really are." Nate knew that more than anyone. He didn't want Robbie to go through life with the same doubts he'd suffered about his father. "I'll help you tell him if you'd like."

"Thank you, but no." She gave a slow shake of her head. "I think that's something I want to do with just the two of us, if you don't mind." Pride flickered across her face, and her eyes shone with love. "He showed such bravery during the kidnapping. I told him that he was a captain just like you, that he was my soldier." She smiled at Nate through the darkness. "Although I think he now deserves a field promotion."

"To major?" He arched a brow with mock pique. "He'll outrank me."

She sighed. "So go the fortunes of war."

He laughed, and a tingling warmth filled him. God, how much he loved this woman and the boy she held on her lap!

How much he wanted to hold her in his arms tonight and every night, put children of his own into her womb, and build a home with her. He loved her laughter and her scowls, the way she baited him one moment and then seduced him the next. Lord help him, he even loved the way she ordered him about.

He had loved Sarah and always would, just as Sydney would always love Michael Berkley. Past loves never completely died.

But this woman sitting across from him, humming softly as she stroked her son's hair—she was his future.

"Sydney."

She twirled a blond curl around her finger. "Hmm?"

"Marry me."

Twenty-Six

SYDNEY'S HAND FROZE—ALL OF HER FROZE, EVEN THE breath in her chest. For a long moment, there was no movement inside the tiny compartment, no sound but the roll of the wheels beneath them. Then she slowly raised her eyes to his.

She couldn't have possibly heard him correctly. "Pardon?"

"Marry me, Baroness." He exhaled a heavy breath of resolve, his face serious despite the teasing words. "Make an honest man of me."

"Dear God," she whispered as the shock of what he was asking jolted through her. "You're mad!"

He glanced down at Robbie, she was certain, to make sure the boy was still asleep and not overhearing their conversation. "I'm not one of those men, Sydney, who wants only mistresses and convenient couplings for an evening or two, then goes away without an afterthought. I've always been serious about the women I've invited into my life." His voice was low against the night and its darkness, and it brushed over her skin like soft velvet. "Especially the ones I take into my bed."

She gaped at him. "You can't be serious."

"I'm very serious. When I saw you at the faro table, I

think part of me knew even then that you'd become more to me than just a mission asset, and I knew at the cottage that you were more than just a lover." His eyes glowed intensely, even in the shadows. "*You* are my future, Sydney. I want you to be my wife."

Her voice lowered even as her exasperation grew. "I can't marry you."

"Can't," he pressed quietly, "or won't?"

"Both," she answered honestly. She sagged back against the squabs in frustration. Robbie fussed in his sleep at the movement, and she caressed her hand over his back to soothe him.

Nate leaned forward. "Do you love me?"

"Of course I do."

"Good. Because I love you, too, and I love that little boy of yours. So marry me, Sydney. We'll be a family together, and you and the little major can order me about all you want."

Marry him? She was afraid to look up at him for fear that the blasted man might very well be on his knees in a formal proposal right then.

"I can't." She pressed her hand to her forehead in a futile attempt to stop the throbbing inside her skull that matched the sudden frantic pounding of her heart.

"Why not?"

She gave a frustrated groan. "An army captain and a baroness?"

He shrugged. "The hero of Toulouse and a widow free to do as she pleases."

"Nate," she scolded plaintively. He couldn't possibly be that naïve.

"I don't care about status and position or what society says. Neither do you. So to hell with the lot of them, and let's do what we want. Let's make ourselves happy, now and for the rest of our lives."

"It isn't that simple." Her arms tightened around Robbie, and she choked out, "I have a son by another man."

His voice was a low but insistent purr as he assured her, "I will raise him as if he were my own."

The knot in her throat strangled her so she couldn't answer. She'd seen him interact with Robbie, and she knew he would do exactly that.

Just as she knew that wasn't the real reason she wouldn't marry him.

"We'll give him brothers and sisters to play with, Baroness. A full family of our own." His voice was filled with emotion, and his hands shook, although he tried to steady them by lacing his fingers together between his knees. "I want that with you, Sydney, more than anything."

She closed her eyes tightly against the wonderful temptation he offered to create a real home and family together, the kind she'd once dreamt of having. But *marriage*... Marriage meant surrendering to the power of a husband, to his command and control, socially, financially, and legally. *Always*. She knew well the kind of hell a woman's life could become at the hands of a husband. Rowland had taught her that. Only when she'd become a widow and escaped the humiliation of her marriage, the threats and abuse, had her life truly become hers.

"You taught me that life needs to go on, Sydney," he

cajoled as softly as the night surrounding them. "That it *must* move on. And you need to do the same."

She shook her head. How could she explain her fears to him, an army captain who was used to charging into battle? How could he ever understand the feeling of utter powerlessness and helplessness when a person's life was not her own? Emotional control with Michael, parental control with her mother and father, matrimonial control with Rowland—it made no difference whether the power was freely given or forcibly taken. When a more powerful person could bend another to his will...

"No," she answered with as much resolve as she could muster, even as her heart shattered and a single tear slid down her cheek in the darkness. "I will not marry you."

Silently, he sat back, and his eyes narrowed on her in the shadows. The tension between them pulsed through the tiny compartment like the electricity of an approaching storm.

For a long while, silence stretched between them, broken only by the sound of the horses' hooves and the rolling crush of the carriage wheels against the road. Outside, the carriage lamps were extinguished as the horses picked up speed on the main road, allowing the light of the full moon to guide them. Inside, their faces were washed dark by the shadows.

"We're meant to be together," he said quietly, yet the determination in his voice made her quake. "What we've been through together—the trust we've built between us—that proves it."

Her voice was equally low, matching his in intensity in

this fierce argument being waged in whispers. "To do as you're asking—the implications for both me and Robbie, and for you, too… To lose all I've gained during the last two years—I *won't* go back there."

"I'm not asking you to go back. I'm asking you to go forward."

She was thankful the shadows were too thick for her to see his face and the emotion playing across his handsome features. It would have undone her. Her heart might be losing the battle, but she couldn't afford to lose the war.

"Do you love me, Sydney?" He reached across the compartment to rest his hand on her knee. "The truth."

"Yes," she breathed so softly the word could barely be heard by her own ears.

"And do you believe that I love you?"

"Of course."

He pulled his hand away from her and leaned back against the squabs. "Then this matter is far from over."

And *that* was exactly what frightened her.

Twenty-Seven

London
Two Days Later

SYDNEY FOUND HERSELF STARING AT NATE. AGAIN.

She tore her gaze away from him as he crouched before the massive stone hearth in the octagonal main room of the Armory and stirred up the coals with a poker. She forced her attention back to the book she'd taken from the shelves in a half-hearted attempt to spend the evening reading until she grew sleepy enough to join Robbie upstairs in the bedroom…and to distract herself from knowing Nate would leave the Armory in the morning to hunt down Hawking.

Robbie was being tucked in for the night by Sergeant McTavish. The sergeant was not having an easy job of it, Sydney was certain, given Robbie's uncontrolled excitement at being in the Armory. Although the old structure had been renovated—complete with bedrooms on the tower's second floor, kitchens in the former basement magazine, and all the comforts of a proper manor house—the place had immediately conjured up fantasies of medieval castles and fortresses for the boy. That was to be expected, she supposed, given the crenellated battlements and the twin portcullises that guarded the narrow entryway. A portcullis system that still worked, apparently, given McTavish's stern warnings to Robbie not to dare touch the wooden levers that would send the two spiked gates crashing down.

McTavish watched Robbie like a hawk, never letting him out of his sight—never letting him stray more than ten feet away, in fact. No mean feat given all the pent-up energy bursting out of the boy after two days of being cooped up inside the carriage with only Nate's stories of the army and whatever games Sydney could invent to keep him entertained.

The old sergeant was patient with Robbie, and it was clear from the way Nate greeted the man upon their arrival this evening that he held the same respect for the former enlisted man that he did for Wellington. Perhaps even more. The easy friendship between them made her feel relaxed and safe.

McTavish never asked why Nate was hiding in secret in the Armory with a baroness and her child, nor did Nate volunteer any information. Yet she was keenly aware that the former sergeant suspected something more between them than the story he'd been given—that Nate was simply providing a personal guard for the evening. Just as she suspected that McTavish had volunteered for bedtime duty tonight in order to give the two of them time alone.

But she could have told him to save himself the trouble.

Since she'd refused his proposal in the carriage, Nate had seemed more distant than ever. Most annoyingly—or at least she told herself she was annoyed so she would be angry at him rather than in anguish—he hadn't attempted to kiss her or touch her at all during the remaining hours of the carriage ride.

He still doted on Robbie, even after Sydney had so carefully explained to her son who she was, why she'd finally come for him, and that they would be together always. Nate had reassured the boy that all would be fine, and he did it with as much love as if he were Robbie's father.

But the affection between Sydney and Nate that she'd come to cherish was gone. Its absence left a gaping hole in her heart.

He looked up from the fire and caught her staring.

She dropped her gaze to her book and offered a quick prayer that he didn't see the glistening in her eyes.

"Interesting reading?" he drawled.

"Very."

"Glad to hear it, since you've been on the same page for ten minutes."

She rolled her eyes at him in irritation. Of course he would notice that she hadn't turned the page. "I find this passage particularly fascinating."

He wiped the coal dust from his hands onto his trousers and stood, crossed the room to her, and took the book from her hands. "*Wheat Farming Across the Seasons.*" His lips twitched. "A scintillating read, I'm certain."

With a scowl, she snatched the book back. "I do own a farm, you know."

"You raise sheep."

She lifted her chin. "I'm considering going into the wheat crop."

"So will the sheep," he answered dryly.

As he returned to the fireplace and leaned against the mantel, she resisted the urge to heave the book at him. He was the most frustrating, arrogant, unbelievably—

"Have you changed your mind?" he asked quietly, interrupting her mental tirade.

"About what?" Oh, for goodness' sake! If she wanted to grow wheat—

"Marrying me."

Her breath caught.

Stunned into silence, she didn't know how to answer. She'd thought of little else since he proposed to her, and these past two days of being so close to him and yet a world away had worn on her. She hadn't realized how much she'd come to enjoy his friendship, his nearness, and his attention until they were gone. In only a few hours, *he* would be gone from here, too, and once Hawking was arrested, if she didn't agree to marry him, there would be no reason for him to return.

Nate wasn't Michael, yet she loved him just as much. If not more.

But *marriage*—could she do it? Could she give over her existence so completely again, even to this hero she loved with every ounce of her being?

She cleared her throat and dodged his question. "You hadn't mentioned that since our first night in the carriage. I thought perhaps you'd given up the idea."

He shook his head. "Siege warfare."

She blinked. "Pardon?"

"When the enemy stubbornly digs in and refuses to negotiate, you pull back your forces and wait them out."

He ducked as the book flew through the air at his head.

With a soft chuckle, he picked it up from the floor where it had landed. "That's not a nice way to treat soldiers," he admonished with a clucking of his tongue. Risking another object being aimed at his head, he turned his back to calmly slide the book into place on the shelf. "Or wheat farmers."

He stilled with his hand lingering on the book's spine.

"I'm leaving at dawn to arrest Hawking," he said quietly, not looking at her.

"I know." She wrapped her trembling hands in her skirt so she wouldn't reach for him and beg him to stay.

As he turned to face her, he crossed his arms over his chest as casually as if they were discussing the weather. "I was hoping to have an answer by then."

He already had her answer. But she couldn't bring herself to say it again because this time, she knew, her answer would be final.

As if sensing the turmoil churning inside her, he slowly knelt in front of her chair. "The reason you won't accept my proposal isn't because you don't love me or want to be with me. Anyone could see that with just a glance at you."

She couldn't deny it. If she did, he'd see right through her lie.

"It's more than that." His hazel eyes were solemn as he studied her in the golden glow of the firelight. "You're frightened of marriage, aren't you?"

"No," she answered. That was the God's truth. She wasn't frightened of it—"I'm terrified."

The flicker of dark amusement registering on his face made her chest pang. "So am I," he admitted. "But I'm even more terrified of living without you."

He reached for her knee just as he'd done in the carriage when he'd proposed the first time. But this time she slipped her hand over his to keep him from pulling away.

His eyes softened. "You're afraid you're going to be trapped as a wife again, like you were with the baron."

"I wasn't a wife," she somehow managed to force out despite her quivering lips that wanted to sob. "I was a matrimonial prisoner."

He laced his fingers through hers. "I would have saved you even then if I'd have known."

"I know," she breathed out, unable to speak any louder.

He dropped his gaze to her hand in his as if he were afraid to look at her when he admitted, "I loved Sarah, and I will always love her. But now it's you, Sydney, who is my future." He lifted her hand to his lips and kissed the backs of her fingers. "All I want is you. So I will sign whatever documents you want giving you complete control over all your property and money—over what little of mine there is as well." He arched a brow. "But you should be warned that it's mainly just my horse and a pair of old boots."

A short laugh broke through her gathering tears, and she pressed her free hand against her mouth.

His eyes met hers as he promised, "I will gladly give everything I possess to be with you."

Her fingers tightened in his as her chest filled with his strength and resolve. He was so warm and strong, so kind and...well, *not* gentle in every sense. And she loved him for it.

"I want a marriage of equals with you, Baroness, which is going to be difficult," he conceded with a sigh, "since you already outrank me in position, kindness, and goodness." He leaned over and placed a kiss to the back of her hand as it lay entwined with his on her knee. "I can't promise that our life together will be perfect, that there won't be problems and arguments." When he lifted his head to gaze up at her, he covered her hand with both of his. "What I *can* promise is that I will never intentionally hurt you, and I will never be cruel to you in any way."

Her throat knotted, and she didn't dare say anything for fear she'd surrender right then and beg him to marry her. But a tear slipped down her cheek.

He solemnly reached up and brushed it away with his thumb. "I can't offer you position or property. I can't give you anything but my love and protection." He shrugged. "And a nightshirt."

She laughed despite the tears. Only Nate could make her feel like laughing and crying at the same time. Dear God, how much she loved him! At that moment, she was both so incredibly happy and so very afraid that she shook. A new future was opening for her, if she only had the courage to seize it.

"If there is one thing that our pasts have taught us it's that life is precious and love is sacred, and I don't want to waste a moment of either."

Neither did she.

Emotion overwhelmed her. She sat forward to cup his face between her hands and kissed him. She drank him in like a woman dying of thirst. He was hers, now and forever, and she planned on never letting go.

"Yes," she whispered and buried her face against his neck. Her heart knew there was no other answer she wanted to give. "Yes, I will marry you."

"Well, it's about time."

Gaping, she pulled back and swatted at his shoulder. "Why, you arrogant, impossible—"

In one smooth movement, he stood and lifted her into his arms as he rose to his feet, then sat down in her chair and brought her onto his lap. He kissed her with love and happiness. His hand slid down her arm to rest possessively at the small of her back, and heat radiated out from his palm and through her like a warm summer rain.

She knew then that she'd made the right decision. Her future was bound to this man, and so was her heart. For always.

But in his kiss, she tasted something else… She pulled back to search his face. "What's wrong?"

He paused before answering quietly, "I told you who my father was, that I'm the illegitimate son of the late Earl of St James."

"Yes, and it makes no difference to me."

"It might." He curled his fingers around hers. "Because the Sinclairs want to recognize me."

Her breath caught. She couldn't have possibly heard… *"Recognize you?"*

"I want nothing from them. I've made my own way in the world, and I will continue to do so. Acknowledging who my father is won't change the past." He blew out a hard breath, and his shoulders sagged beneath the weight of it all. "But recognition might make things easier for you as my wife, especially now that Robbie will be with us." He brushed his knuckles across her cheek. "What do you think, Baroness? Could you tolerate having the Sinclairs as in-laws?"

In other words, would she let him sacrifice his pride in order to possibly make life a bit easier for her and Robbie? Her heart swelled, unable to fathom how selfless and heroic he was, even with something as personal as this.

"I think that would be lovely." She meant it. She couldn't imagine anything more wonderful than to have a large and loving family.

"Just remember you said that come Christmas," he grumbled, "when we're all crowded around the dining table in Harlow House, pretending that Lady Agnes didn't spike the punch."

She laughed, then reached up to affectionately brush a chestnut curl from his forehead. "You and St James do look alike."

"We're nothing alike," he growled irritably.

She resisted the urge to laugh again. Oh, they were *exactly* alike!

"You have the same cheekbones and jaw, the same hazel eyes..." She trailed her fingers along his jaw to the curve of his ear and felt him shiver. "How long have you known the truth?"

"A while." When she arched a prompting brow, he clarified, "Since I was a boy. I knew my mother once worked for St James at Pelham Park as a maid, but I never knew why she left or why there were no traces in our home of the man she said was my father, whom she claimed died when I was a baby." He leaned forward to place a kiss to the side of her neck. "When I was fifteen, I wrote to the local vicar in the village near Pelham. I learned that there was no record of death or marker in the churchyard for a George Reed, that he had never been a tenant farmer there, and that my mother had never been married at all."

"Oh, Nate...I'm so sorry."

"Don't be. I never had a father so there was no one to miss when I learned he'd never existed." A grim smile tugged at his lips. "A few years later, right after St James died, my mother received an inheritance from some distant relative we'd never met. It was exactly enough to pay for my commission into the army. That was Isabel Sinclair's first attempt at making amends."

"And offering recognition is another." Her eyes softened on him. "Be kind to her, Nate. She's not your mother, but she has a mother's heart. I know how that feels."

"Yes, you do." His gaze drifted to the stairs that spiraled up into the tower overhead. "How do you think Robbie will feel about being my best man at our wedding?"

She couldn't stop another tear from falling. "I think he'll love it."

"Let's find out." Grinning with happiness, Nate shouted toward the stairs, "Major Robert! Come here. We need you."

"Sir?" A few moments later, McTavish appeared on the wooden landing halfway up the tower, with Robbie's young face peering out from behind his legs.

Sydney slipped quickly off Nate's lap and fussed with her skirts. She turned away from her son's curious stare as her face heated.

"Robbie, the baroness and I want to marry, and I want you to be my best man," Nate announced as he climbed to his feet. "What do you think about that?"

"Deuces!" Robbie shouted.

"Deuces, indeed," Nate agreed with a wink at Sydney, which deepened her blush.

Robbie raced down the stairs. Nate scooped him up into his arms and brought their eyes level, man to man.

"Do I have your permission to marry your mother, Major?" he asked the boy.

"Aye, Captain!" Robbie gave an enthusiastic salute.

Nate tossed him into the air. The boy burst into giggles and laughed joyfully as Nate passed him off to a very befuddled-looking Sergeant McTavish, who had finally reached the bottom of the stairs.

"Off to bed with you." Sydney placed a tender kiss to the top of the boy's head. "We'll see you in the morning, and we'll discuss it more then."

McTavish led Robbie back upstairs, taking on the unenviable task of putting to bed the now overly excited boy. There was zero chance of Robbie sleeping a wink.

"So we're engaged." She wrapped her arms around Nate's neck and teased half-heartedly, with more truth than she'd admit, "But you're still leaving me at dawn, aren't you?"

"Can't be helped." He soothed that answer by nuzzling his cheek against hers. Then he growled rakishly with a possessive nip to her earlobe. "So it's a good thing that I have the rest of my life to make up for it. Starting right now."

He scooped her into his arms and carried her upstairs to her bedroom.

Twenty-Eight

SYDNEY'S EYES FLUTTERED OPEN AS SHE AWOKE. SHE took a moment to remember where she was and why the room was so dark except for the small slant of sunlight falling through a single narrow window.

Ah, the Armory…the old building that Nate had brought her and Robbie to yesterday evening. A medieval castle on the outside with its gates, portcullis, and crenellated central tower, but a luxurious gentlemen's club on the inside, complete with two well-appointed bedrooms off the main tower where they'd spent the night.

She couldn't prevent a smile as she stretched to shake off the last fog of sleep. She was scandalously naked, exhausted from making love all night, and thoroughly satiated. Most of all, she was unbelievably happy.

She laughed. Engaged! She was going to be married, and this time to a man who loved her unconditionally. Perhaps she was still dreaming.

She sat up and saw the note lying on the nightstand. Her smile faded.

No. Not a dream. Because in a dream, Nate would still be here with her. He wouldn't have left at dawn to put his life at risk again. *That* was the first thing she planned on changing once they wed.

> Baroness,
> *I'll be back by sunset with more news. Stay inside the Armory with McTavish.*

And then her smile came back with stunning force.

> *Be prepared to wed me within the sennight. I'm never letting go of you.*
>
> Nate

Soft laughter drifted into the room through the little window and stole her attention away. It was the only window she'd seen so far anywhere in the building, and it was less than half a foot wide, three feet tall, and starting at the height of her chin. It reminded her of those arrow slots medieval archers had used to rain terror down upon anyone who dared to attack a castle.

She crawled out of bed and stepped softly on bare feet to peer outside. This window would have given His Majesty's sharpshooters the same advantage in defending the Armory.

But it also gave *her* a grand view of the yard beneath and of Robbie and Sergeant McTavish as the two played at what looked suspiciously like a military drill, complete with a wooden stick against her son's shoulder that served as a rifle. The little boy eagerly tried to march to perfection, but his turns sometimes went the wrong way and sometimes he spun in a complete circle. But words of encouragement from the old sergeant lit his round face and had him bouncing through his steps.

"My baby boy…" Her heart swelled with love. All the pain she'd suffered in those years without him was nothing compared now with all the hope and joy she held for the future.

Humming to herself—oh, she was simply too happy not to!—she slipped into her shift, stays, and stockings and did up her hair as best she could in the small oval mirror over the gentleman's shaving stand and the dim light from the window. Then she reached for her dress, and the humming died in her throat.

Not her dress. Miss Jenner's.

Where was the governess now? Had General Elliott brought her all the way back to London, or was she being held in custody somewhere secret where even Scepter couldn't find her? Not that it mattered. Either from the work of Scepter or the Home Office, Sydney knew she'd never see the governess again.

As she put on the dress and tugged it into place, she couldn't wait to be able to return to her town house. Yes, she wanted to put the events of the past several weeks behind her, starting with changing into a dress that didn't belong to a cold-hearted murderer. But she also couldn't wait to show her house to Robbie, let him pick out his own bedroom, and fill it with all kinds of toys and things he loved. It would be his new city home. But their main home would be in the country, she'd already decided. Oakwood Manor had been Robbie's first true home, and now it would be her first true home, too. With Nate.

Fastening the last button, she returned to the window. She couldn't resist taking another look at Robbie as he played, but she couldn't see him or McTavish now.

Unease blossomed at how quiet the yard was in the mid-morning sunlight because she'd already learned that no child worried a mother as much as the one she couldn't hear.

Then a new worry pricked at the backs of her knees. If they weren't in the yard playing with a stick gun, were they inside the Armory playing with real weapons? After all, the Armory held what looked like all the swords and bayonets from the Peninsular campaigns. So many weapons filled the training room, in fact, that McTavish had warned Robbie not to go into the room at all without him. Nate had been bolder and threatened to take away his pony for an entire month if he dared to stick even the tip of a toe over the threshold. *That* certainly caught Robbie's attention.

Well, she would just go downstairs and check, and for an excuse, she'd say that she simply wanted to find out if Sergeant McTavish and Robbie had eaten breakfast yet. There was a kitchen in the basement where she would most likely find food, although she had no idea how to cook it once she'd found it. Or if the food would even be edible. Nate had told her that the former soldiers who used this place as their club, training salon, and sanctuary were considering hiring staff to oversee and run the place, including a butler and cook. But for now, the kitchen was left to the men to use as they wanted, and she could only imagine what that meant for cleanliness and food storage.

"Sergeant and Major," she called out as she hurried down the spiral staircase that snaked along the side of the tower. "Would you like to join me for breakfast?"

No answer.

She stopped at the bottom of the stairs, her unease growing. She couldn't see them anywhere, and the building was unusually silent for containing an exuberant boy who loved all things military.

"Sergeant?" The little hairs on her arms prickled at the silence. "Robert?"

A soft sound of scuffling came from the training room, and her shoulders relaxed. *Of course.* She rolled her eyes with a smile. Where else would the two of them be?

"Every army marches on its stomach," she declared as she stepped into the training room. "You won't be able to learn to fight unless you—"

The words choked in her throat, and she froze midstep. For one dreadful moment, her heart stopped.

"Hello, Sydney."

Charles Langley, Marquess of Hawking, stood in the center of the room with one hand holding Robbie by the scruff of his neck and the other clamped over the struggling boy's mouth to keep him silent. McTavish sat bound and gagged in the corner.

Her blood turned to ice, and she rasped out, "Let go of him."

"Imagine my surprise to find you here." He dragged Robbie forward. "But then, you always did enjoy the overdramatic."

"Don't hurt him." Desperation stung at her eyes. "Please, Charles...you know who he is and what he means to me."

She reached out toward Robbie, but when she took a step toward him, Hawking yanked the boy back.

She dropped her hand to her side and rasped out, "How did you get in here?"

"That's the secret about these old armories. For all their thick walls and defenses, they can still be breached by the doors." He took another step forward and stopped with Robbie directly in front of her. "Imagine my surprise to find the yard door left open and your son playing on the gravel."

"Please," she whispered and blinked hard. She twisted her hands in her skirt to keep from reaching for Robbie again. "He's a defenseless little boy."

"I won't hurt him."

Her shoulders slumped with overwhelming relief, yet terror still slithered down the length of her spine.

"If I wanted to hurt him, I would have been able to a hundred times over by now." Hawking's eyes gleamed icily. There was no trace in him of the man she'd once believed was a friend. "Did you really think I wouldn't have someone watching you the entire time, from the moment you first visited the Horse Guards dressed like a boy to your trip halfway across England and back?" He raked his gaze over her and sneered, "A baroness with a cavalry captain... *slumming*."

Her heart lodged in her throat.

"Don't worry, Sydney. I'm not here to hurt the boy."

To make his point, he released Robbie with a fierce shove that sent him tumbling backward onto the floor with a loud cry.

Sydney started forward to protect him. Hawking grabbed her by the arm and yanked her toward him.

His hot breath fanned across her cheek. "I'm here to kill *you*."

A knife blade flashed in the light from the gas lamps overhead as he pressed it against her throat.

"Noooooooo!" Robbie screamed.

He launched himself at Hawking, scratching with his fingers and kicking hard with his boots. He knocked the surprised marquess backward just far enough that Hawking loosened his hold on Sydney in order to shove the boy away.

She wrenched herself from Hawking's grip. She grabbed Robbie into her arms and raced with him to the edge of the room where swords and rapiers hung on the wall. With every step, she heard Hawking's pounding stride behind her. She tore a rapier free from its hooks and slashed wildly through the air in a wide arc to keep him away.

The marquess snarled and stepped back, just out of reach of the razor-sharp blade.

"*Don't*," she warned through clenched teeth. She tucked Robbie behind her to protect him. "If you take one step closer, I will run you through. You will *not* hurt my son!"

Hawking bellowed a fierce curse, and his eyes flashed like brimstone. His hand clenched the short knife so tightly that it shook. Sydney knew if she took her eyes away from him even for one heartbeat, he would pounce.

"Back," she ordered as she stepped slowly down the length of the wall, driving him through the central room and toward the narrow stone passageway that led to the front door. The blindingly bright sunlight slanting into the passageway told her that the metal barrier had been left open when he'd entered. That was the same way the bastard would leave.

Step by agonizing step, she forced Hawking to retreat at sword point, and always, she kept Robbie tight at her heels. The terrified boy had started to cry, but she didn't dare look down at him, didn't dare move her attention away from Hawking.

They crossed the Armory into the narrow entranceway one slash of the blade at a time. Her arm ached from the strain of holding the rapier at the ready, but she didn't dare lower it, although she had no idea what she would do once they reached the door.

When they crossed the stone threshold into the passageway that led outside, she called down to Robbie over her shoulder. "Run back into the training room and free Sergeant McTavish. Use one of the knives from the wall to cut his bindings. Quickly!"

Robbie didn't let go of her skirt. "No! I'm not leaving you."

"Go free McTavish," she bit out angrily.

She heard a sniveling catch of breath at the harshness of her words, and it broke her heart. But they desperately needed help, and none would be coming until Nate returned at sunset. They had to mount their own attack.

"That is *an order*!"

His fingers released her skirt, and she felt him slip away. The loss was nearly unbearable. Only when she heard the soft running of his footsteps across the stones toward the training room did she allow herself to feel any relief at all.

"Keep going," she commanded Hawking and slashed the blade again as she stepped forward. "You will go right out that door and *never* come—"

His hand shot out and clamped around the blade. The rapier cut into his palm with a sickening slice, but he gritted his teeth and gripped it so tightly that she couldn't move it to free it from his grasp, not even when bright red blood dripped down his arm.

With an animal growl, he wrenched the rapier from her grasp and threw it away. It clattered onto the stone floor, far out of her reach. His bloody hand clenched her throat and pushed her back. She tripped over the thick chain that ran along the edge of the passageway and held the heavy portcullis in place above, but Hawking's hand at her throat held her upright. Then he pinned her to the wall.

She struggled to free herself, but it was no use. His grip was too strong at her neck, and every time she tried to wiggle free, his fingers tightened on her throat until she could barely breathe. Black spots danced before her eyes, and the rush of blood through her ears with every pounding heartbeat was deafening. She was trapped between his heavy body and a tall wooden lever positioned against the stone wall.

"You're the only person who can link me to the assassination attempts," he snarled.

The knife blade gleamed in the slant of sunlight from the open door as he raised it toward her face and turned it back and forth so she could see it. The bastard wanted her to be afraid.

But as long as Robbie was safe, she would never be terrified at the hands of a man again.

"Revolutions always cost lives." He lowered the knife toward her belly. "Now, you'll sacrifice yours."

Summoning all her strength, she let out a fierce cry and shoved him as hard as she could. He stumbled back.

She grabbed the wooden lever at her side and yanked. The chain lock released. With a deafening clanking of metal sliding across metal, the chain blurred as its links sped across the floor, and overhead, the rattle of wood and metal against stone vibrated against the passageway walls. He jumped back as the spiked gate crashed down. The portcullis slammed to the floor between her and Hawking, sealing him outside.

"Bitch!" he bellowed furiously. From between the slats, he threw the knife at her. She ducked and dropped to the floor. The knife struck the wall just above her head.

A loud strike of metal against stone reverberated off the walls, and the second portcullis behind Hawking slammed down into place. He was trapped in the narrow passageway.

From the blinding sunlight behind him, a tall figure stepped forward into the shadows.

Nate.

He stood like a mountain in the doorway, with one of the battle-axes that framed the outside door resting across his shoulders, the same axe he'd used to drop the second portcullis. His eyes stared past Hawking as the man threw himself repeatedly against the thick gates in a futile attempt to break free, and his gaze landed on Sydney. The look in his eyes—a mix of love, regret, worry, and fury—stripped her breath away and drew the first sob from her lips.

"Mother!"

Robbie flung himself into her embrace. His little arms wrapped around her neck. He pressed himself against her as tightly as he could, while behind him McTavish hurried from the training room, a sword in each hand.

"You should have known better," Nate told Hawking as he lowered the axe to his side. "Never come between a child and his mother."

Robbie tightened his hold on her, and she cooed softly to him as she rocked him reassuringly in her arms, her mother's instinct strong and pure. There were no more doubts now that she would be a good mother, just as there were no doubts about her future with Nate.

"We're safe now." She raised her head to meet Nate's gaze, and her promise was as much for him as for Robbie. "No one will ever separate us again."

Twenty-Nine

NATE STOOD SHOULDER TO SHOULDER BETWEEN Clayton Elliott and St James. In front of them, Charles Langley—soon to be the former Marquess of Hawking—sat bound and gagged on one of the Armory's large leather chairs.

"What do we do with him?" St James muttered beneath his breath.

What Nate wanted to do was kill the bastard with his bare hands for threatening Sydney and Robbie.

His gaze slid across the room. The baroness and her son sat in the corner, where she did her best to distract Robbie from the scene playing out in front of them. But the boy was still too upset to be taken upstairs. With McTavish guarding the outer door, Robbie took comfort in having the three men there and in keeping both his mother and Hawking in his sight.

Nate certainly understood that. He wasn't taking any chances with Hawking himself. After all, the marquess had nearly escaped that morning when he and Clayton had gone after him to arrest him. He'd been under surveillance at his London town house by trusted men from the Armory, but he'd somehow managed to slip away without being seen. Thank God they'd been able to track him—directly toward the Armory. Nate had reached the old building just as Sydney dropped the first portcullis.

Nate had never been more proud of her. Or more terrified out of his mind that he might have lost her.

"We escort him under guard to Newgate," Clayton answered. "St James, would you call in the men of the Armory to help us? I'm not letting anyone from the Home Office or the Horse Guards anywhere near him." He glanced at Nate. "No offense."

"None taken." They'd finally caught Scepter's leader. They wouldn't risk Scepter having more men inside the ranks of the Home Office or the Guards who might make a play to free Hawking en route. Or kill him before he could be properly questioned.

"We know why he went after Lady Rowland and the boy," St James murmured. "But why did he lead Scepter?"

"Let's find out." Clayton stepped forward and unkindly ripped the cloth out of the marquess's mouth. "Your lordship."

Hawking spat onto the floor and flexed his mouth to loosen it from being gagged. "So you're going to interrogate me now, are you?"

Clayton grabbed one of the chairs from a nearby reading table and pulled it up in front of Hawking. He turned it around and straddled it backward, his arms folded across the chairback in a casual pose that belied the tension surrounding them. "I have questions that need answers."

"But I have no answers to give."

"Oh, I think you do." Clayton leveled a hard gaze on the

marquess. They all knew he would swing at the gallows, that his title and position in the government wouldn't save him. Bound and bloodied, Hawking looked nothing like the man he'd been only hours before…the third most powerful man in the British empire after the prince regent and the prime minister. Truthfully, even the king had held less power these days, but both men had seemingly gone mad. "Starting with your role in Scepter. We know you're its leader."

The three men *didn't* know for certain. They'd only speculated on his role with the group. But the way Hawking's face turned ghostly white proved their suspicions.

"I'm with Scepter," Hawking clarified. "But I'm not Scepter."

Clayton frowned at that cryptic answer. "What I want to know is why you became involved with them." When Hawking didn't reply, Clayton shrugged. "Might as well tell me. You're under arrest for the murder of a British general and the attempted murder of a baroness and her son. You'll be tried, found guilty, and hanged on the gallows. Nothing can stop what's going to happen to you."

He flashed a ghastly smile. "Short of a pardon by His Majesty."

On a cold day in hell… Nate would make certain of it by positioning men around the clock at St James's Palace, Carlton House, and Windsor Castle until Hawking swung dead by the neck. He might not be able to prevent a royal pardon from being issued, but he could sure as hell prevent it from arriving in time.

"You might find it comforting to confess. It can't add to

your guilt or your punishment." Clayton solemnly made eye contact with Hawking. "Why Scepter?"

The marquess's mouth twisted. "It's not enough for a man to want to start a revolution these days?"

"Not for you," St James interjected. "Not for an English marquess who regularly dines with the regent."

"Then how about simple revenge?" Hawking asked.

Clayton shook his head. "There are easier ways to gain vengeance. For the first few years, Scepter was more criminal than revolutionary, establishing illegal businesses and smuggling operations across England. That took too much time and effort for simple revenge."

"Because the brothels and smuggling operations Scepter ran gave us access to great amounts of cash and information." Hawking seemed to take a ghoulish pride in the way Scepter had destroyed lives. "We leveraged those resources to blackmail people in important positions or to buy others into doing our bidding. We placed people at every level of the military and government, even inside the royal household itself. All willing to do or say what we wanted, including calling for the abdication of the monarch, and all at our signal."

"A signal? Like the assassination of the prime minister and prince regent?" Nate muttered in disbelief. Good God, the man was mad. "Do you really think it could have been that easy, to depose a monarchy by mere outcry?"

Hawking focused his gaze past Clayton at Nate. "What do you think allows a monarch to rule or a president to lead? He doesn't retain power because he's ordained by God or elected to office." Hawking sneered at the idea. "He rules by *the will of the people*. If the people decide a monarch has no power, then he has no power. It *is* that simple." His eyes gleamed. "What would happen in the confusion after the assassination of the prince regent if politicians, peers, and military officers at all levels called out for a new form of government to rise from the ashes? If they all demanded a republic based on a new constitution? The monarchy would be powerless, the government useless. But I'd be there, waiting to step in and lead them all into the future."

Nate drawled, "A second Glorious Revolution?"

"Without a shot fired." Hawking smiled. "All that Scepter's army needs to be put into play is a signal, and they'll call out in unison for revolution."

"Impossible." St James shook his head. "What you were after would have taken the army, the militia, officials at all levels— They'd never refuse their orders and turn against the monarch."

"Wouldn't they? You were a soldier in the wars. Surely, there were orders you would have refused, orders you would have been morally *obligated* to refuse, even if generals—or the king himself—issued them." Hawking sized him up with a look. "Such as the slaughter of unarmed civilians."

The old men, women, and children his brother had helped to burn alive in America… Nate's blood turned to ice. "Is that what Scepter was about—revenge for what General Braxton and your brother did at Bois Saint-Louis?"

His eyes narrowed. "Jonas did nothing at Saint-Louis! When he realized what Braxton planned to do, he refused his orders. *That's* why Braxton was going to have him court-martialed, why he was sent into the fray only a few weeks later and killed. My brother did the honorable thing, and he was killed for it while that bastard Braxton emerged a hero."

"Your explanation doesn't answer everything," Clayton interjected quietly, drawing Hawking's attention away from Nate. "If you wanted revenge for your brother's death, you could have just killed Braxton and gotten it. You wouldn't have needed to overthrow the government."

"You think it was only Braxton who was responsible for my brother's death?" Hawking spat onto the floor again. "The king is mad, his whelps immoral disgraces...and the oldest, fattest whelp of all was responsible for getting us into war with the Americans in the first place." He jerked his head in the direction of Whitehall and the palaces. "I don't lay complete blame for my brother's death on Braxton's head. I put it on the regent for not keeping us out of war in the first place!"

Hawking leaned forward as far as the bindings allowed.

"How many other brothers, sons, and fathers have died because of that drunken, half-mad, gout-ridden, lecherous bastard, one who has the gall to wear a field marshal's uniform when he's too fat to even sit a horse? He's an affront to every man who has died for England, who has lost arms and legs and eyes in service of country and crown. *God's anointed.*" The last came with a sneer so fierce it was almost a snarl. "A damnable joke."

The mad depths of Scepter's plot swirled around Nate like a lifting fog, and he mumbled, "Revolution *is* your revenge."

"Prinny murdered my brother as surely as if his fat fingers were the ones that fired the musket." Hawking's voice quivered with rage. "*That's* why I want to overthrow the monarchy, to keep those royal bastards from ever sending another brother, son, or father to his death again. And for what? A treaty claiming status quo ante bellum...everything returned to how it was before the war, as if no fighting ever took place. Tell that to the weeping mothers and children, and ask what comfort that brings them."

Hawking leaned back in the chair. He repeatedly clenched and unclenched his tied hands, agitated by his fury and grief.

"Revolution isn't the answer," Clayton countered. "*Reform* is. The system is best changed from within, with clear purpose and cautious progression." Nate could tell from the tone of his old friend's voice that Clayton meant every word. "Revolution creates a power vacuum and leaves despots and dictators in charge, those who care only for their own wealth and power."

"Revolution brings change," Hawking argued. "And quickly."

"It also brings death and destruction," Nate interrupted. "To *everyone*. Not just to the guilty but the innocent as well. Not just those who want revolution but to all people."

God knew he'd witnessed that firsthand on the Peninsula during the wars. The flames of the French Revolution had consumed nearly all of Europe, and after all that death and destruction, the French were right back where they'd started, with a Bourbon king reigning over a pile of ashes and corpses.

"The innocent don't deserve to be caught up in your vengeance." Nate looked across the room and met Sydney's gaze.

The look of love for him in her eyes stripped his breath away. "*None* of us do."

Without another word, Nate turned on his heel and walked away, leaving Hawking to his half brother and Clayton. His mission was over.

He crossed the room to Sydney, swept Robbie into his arms, and leaned down to kiss her. In that kiss, he tasted the promise of a new life.

Together.

Epilogue

Oakwood Manor
Three Months Later

THE HORSE GUARD GALLOPED UP THE DRIVE, HIS RED uniform the same color as the setting sun sinking toward the horizon behind him. He reined his horse to a stop in front of the house.

"Sir." The guard saluted as Nate jogged down the stone steps to greet him, but he didn't dismount. He pulled a letter from beneath his jacket and leaned down to present it. "A message from London."

"Thank you." Nate took the sealed message and nodded toward the stables. "Put up your horse and spend the night. You can ride back in the morning. There's a roast that's still warm in the kitchen."

He nodded with gratitude. "Yes, sir!"

As the guard trotted toward the stables, Nate broke the plain red seal, opened the note, and scanned Clayton's scribbled message. One word—

Dead.

Charles Langley, former Marquess of Hawking and

Scepter's leader, had swung on the gallows, just as the men of the Armory had made certain he would.

Nate crumpled the paper in his fist, turned on his heel, and hurried back up the steps into the house. He paused in the front hall to stick the note into the flame of the oil lamp on the side table and watch it burn to ash. He pulled in a deep breath.

Finally, it was over.

He passed the drawing room on his way to the stairs. Inside the warm and inviting space, his mother played cards with the three Sinclair ladies. She lived here now, helping to make Oakwood a true home. As soon as the mission had ended, with Charles Langley within Newgate's walls and the reward money safely in Nate's bank account, he married Sydney, then rode to the Earl of Buckley's estate, resigned his mother's position, and moved her out of the rented cottage and into Oakwood, where she immediately embraced both Sydney and Robbie as her family. She loved Robbie like a grandson, and he doted on her in return as a grandmother.

Then there were the Sinclair ladies.

Isabel, Agnes, and Elizabeth had descended upon them only days after he'd brought Sydney and Robbie here to start their new life together. The ladies had arrived in a flurry of surprise without invitation or warning—perhaps exactly because they wanted to surprise—to welcome Sydney to the family, to meet Robbie, and to make whatever amends they could to Nate's mother.

For three years, he hadn't had a woman in his life, but

good Lord, now they were everywhere. Every last one of them was thrilled that he'd been recognized by the Sinclairs, even if Nate was less so. His acceptance of the situation would come with time and patience.

His brother and his new wife were absent. Alexander Sinclair and Olivia Everett surprised everyone by eloping to Scotland, and then they'd left immediately on a bridal tour, which gave time for the Sinclair ladies to pay an extended visit to Oakwood. Unfortunately, Alec and Olivia weren't expected back for at least six months, which left the Sinclair ladies with nothing to do except...

"We should hold a grand party!" Lady Agnes declared as she trumped Isabel's ace and won the hand.

...torture him.

"Or a ball," Isabel chimed in. "Those are always fashionable in the country this time of year."

He rolled his eyes.

"An entire house party!" Elizabeth practically bounced in her chair at the idea. "Oh, we simply must host one!"

Nate blew out a hard breath and headed up the stairs, but he couldn't keep his exasperation from blossoming into happiness. He now had the home he'd always wanted, surrounded by family and friends, and a bright future before him.

Most of all, though, he now had love.

He stopped in the doorway of the nursery and gazed tenderly inside at Sydney as she sat at Robbie's bedside. She glanced up as she stroked the sleeping boy's hair and smiled at Nate with an expression of such happiness that his heart melted. Again.

He crossed the room to her side, careful not to wake Robbie.

As if reading his mind, she whispered with a small shake of her head, "All those years, all that fear that I wouldn't be a good mother...all that time wasted."

He placed his hand on her shoulder. She covered his hand with hers and squeezed his fingers.

"I'll make mistakes, I know it," she added in the same soft whisper. "But they'll be mistakes made out of love, not selfishness as my parents did, and I think Robert will understand why I made them."

"I know he will." He kissed her temple. "You're a good mother, Sydney."

"And you're a good father." She turned back toward the sleeping boy. "I can't begin to tell you how much of a relief that is. Especially now."

Nate sat on the edge of the mattress as the boy nestled down in the bed with only a shock of his blond hair sticking out above the tangle of sheets and covers. He smiled absently and rubbed his hand over Robbie's small back. "Why now?"

"Because I've missed my last two courses."

His hand stilled. He didn't move. Not even to breathe.

"I'm not absolutely certain yet, of course," she clarified. When he finally met her gaze, stunned, she fought back a brilliant smile that threatened at her lips. "But I'm most likely enceinte."

"Baroness," he murmured, unable to believe it. But he could tell from the way she glowed in the lamplight that it was true, and his heart refused to believe otherwise.

He pulled on her hand and brought her out of her chair and onto the bed with him. With a happy laugh, they tumbled together down onto the mattress, and the movement woke Robbie. Nate grabbed both of them into his arms and held them against him as Robbie giggled at the fun and Sydney began to sniffle with tears.

Together, the three of them had finally found the loving family they'd each been searching for.

He nuzzled his mouth against her hair as he held Sydney and as she held Robbie in her arms. He would find a quiet time later tonight to tell her about Clayton's message. He was certain she would weep for the man who had once been a friend to her, despite everything, because her heart was simply that kind. But for now, all he wanted was this moment and the promise of their future.

The past could no longer hurt them.